BOUND IN BLUE

Book One of the Sword of Elements

Heather Hamilton-Senter

Two Paths Publishing

Two Paths Publishing
www.twopathspublishing.com

Book Layout © 2014 BookDesignTemplates.com
Cover Design © 2014 BookCoverArtistry.com

Bound In Blue/ Heather Hamilton-Senter. -- 1st ed.
ISBN 978-0-9938225-0-6

To my family, eternally.

A mermaid found a swimming lad,
Picked him for her own,
Pressed her body to his body,
Laughed; and plunging down
Forgot in cruel happiness
That even lovers drown.

—WILLIAM BUTLER YEATS

CHAPTER ONE

Fear is white and thickly veined with sea-blue.
I reached over the bed rail and touched Mom's cheek. The industrial clock on the wall ticked once, loudly. Jerking my hand back, I rubbed the tips of my fingers against my jeans.
She was cold.
I reminded myself that her skin was always cool. Except for her black hair, everything about Mom was cool and pale, even her eyes.
They were cloudy now and staring at the ceiling. I couldn't make myself close them the way people always do in movies. I couldn't touch her again.
Gripping the sides of the chair as the color of fear washed over me again, I felt ashamed. The only thing Mom was ever afraid of was a man with silver hair. I saw him once when I was little, across a busy street. We were driving, but Mom stopped the car and pulled me down to the floor. As she held me close, the sound of her heart was a wave crashing against rocks.
Rhiannon, listen to me. We cannot be seen. Hide in the shadows and be still and silent.

As I listened to her, I imagined a blue shadow covering me, protecting me from whatever it was that she was afraid of. My own fear broke apart like ice on a churning ocean and the colors of all my emotions erupted out of me for the first time, dashing themselves against the blue like they were trying to break free. I wrapped the shadow closer and my colors calmed and dissipated. I wasn't sure how much of that was a real memory, but the man didn't see us.

I'd been seeing colors ever since.

I once tried to tell Mom about the colors I felt, but she just smiled and looked away. I didn't try again. It would have been nice to talk with someone about it. I'm sure my colors would be a nice break for some psychiatrist bored with the usual budding Unabombers.

But fear is white and cold and veined in a wet and moldy blue that echoes the color of the hospital walls.

A sudden vibration made me jump and startled pink sparkled across my vision. Fumbling in my pocket, I nearly dropped my phone as I pulled it out. My fingers were as numb as if I'd pressed them against ice.

"How is she?"

It was Peter. I stared at the screen a moment before shoving the phone away. I couldn't answer him. If I did, it would make the nightmare true.

The chair made a vicious scraping noise against the floor as I stood and I froze, heart pounding, imagining the corpse popping up like they do in bad horror movies. Of course, it didn't move.

Mom didn't move.

I backed away to the door to look for someone to come and tell me what I was supposed to do. The nurse on duty had left to give me time to say goodbye, but there wasn't anything here to say goodbye to.

A woman walked past me into the room and strode up to the bed. She wasn't young, maybe mid-thirties, but she was the most stunning person I'd ever seen. With a mass of dreadlocked, white-blonde hair, and wearing a skirt that looked like a cascade of expensive rags, she was Goth Barbie's slutty older sister. Touching a black-lacquered finger to Mom's forehead, the woman whispered, "Viviane, you stupid fool."

"Hey!"

I couldn't think of anything to say after that. *Don't call my dead Mommy stupid?*

A strange impulse to laugh bubbled up inside me, but I shoved it back down and only a strangled squeak escaped.

Good thing. Laughing over the body of my dead mother might buy me a one way ticket to a psych eval.

The woman turned at the sound and seemed surprised to see me standing there. "You must be Rhiannon. We have never met, but my name is Morgan." I stared at her and she gestured to the bed. "Viviane was my sister."

I shook my head. "Mom didn't have a sister." The woman didn't respond and a flash of violet impatience made me blink. "If you're her sister, how come you didn't come when she got sick? Why didn't Mom even tell me about you?" Crackles of red across the violet surprised me—surprised me at how angry I was that I'd been forced to endure all this alone. A long-lost aunt would be a relief, but how could it be possible?

I glanced out the door to see if I could catch one of the nurses' attention, but they seemed to be busy with some emergency down the hall.

The woman was still staring at me. Despite the eccentric clothing, she held herself straight and rigid with her chin lifted slightly and her arms held a little away from her sides like a ballerina.

Just like Mom.

"Why didn't you come?" I whispered, hating the weakness in my voice.

The woman sighed and looked down at the bed. With a graceful motion, she brushed her fingers across Mom's arm. "Viviane made her own choices—choices I knew would be her undoing. I saw no reason to force my witness upon them. Still, for the sake of the common cause that once bound us, and for the love I bear her still, I would have come if she had asked it of me. She never did. Any emotion felt for my sister was always a one-sided thing, and she was ever of her own mind."

Morgan talked funny—strangely formal like Mom did— but this refugee from a heavy metal music video couldn't be my aunt.

Because that would mean Mom lied to me.

Anger was coming in red streaks now and I walked over to the bedside table and reached for the emergency call button. In one swift movement, the woman was in front of me, grasping my hands hard enough for me to know that she could stop me if she wanted to.

"Do not be afraid. I mean you no harm."

I pulled back and after a brief resistance, she let go. "I don't know you," I muttered.

Morgan raised an eyebrow and crossed her arms. "Viviane and I have walked different paths for so long that we could no longer meet in the space between them, but I felt her passing. I would have taken her to rest where she belonged, in the free air under the moon. She shouldn't have been here, hidden away from the sky."

There was an accusation in her voice and my cheeks went hot. As we stared at each other, I saw that her eyes were pale—so pale you might think you were looking at a blind woman. I'd never seen anyone with eyes like that before.

Except Mom.

I slumped down into the chair by the bed. I'd been up all night waiting for the end. I didn't have enough energy left to be suspicious.

After a few uneasy seconds of silence, the woman spoke and her voice was gentler. "What did they say was the cause?"

I shrugged. "Lupus. Maybe. The doctors weren't sure. Some auto-immune thing that made her organs shut down one by one. They didn't know how to stop it."

"The doctors of this world are fools."

I didn't disagree. I rubbed my eyes, but they were dry and gritty, as if all the tears in them had turned to sand.

Morgan stiffened and made a hissing sound between her teeth. "Be still. Others are coming." And then she walked up to me and poked me hard between the eyes.

"Hey!" I yelped. "What the hell?"

Morgan leaned in close. "Stay still. Be quiet. Do not move." Familiar commands I couldn't help but obey. Her fingernails dug into my shoulder as she pushed me down into the chair as if somehow she could make me sit more deeply and decidedly than I was already sitting.

Auntie Morgan is crazy.

And then the stream of truly crazy filed into the room.

A young woman sporting a red mohawk who shopped at the same stores Morgan did, but in the blisteringly neon department.

An older woman with a long braid of white hair wrapped around her waist like a belt.

A huge, dark-skinned man with a lip ring connected to a gold chain threaded through a piercing in his ear.

There were more, all as strange as the first three. A curious nurse peered into the room with wide eyes, but a glare from Morgan sent her away.

I was abandoned to the freak show.

Some of them touched Mom's forehead with gentle fingers. A few whispered soft words to Morgan. I just sat there as they ignored me—as good as invisible—while the numbness spread from my fingers up into my body and the white of my fear went black and dirty on the edges like snow on the side of the street.

"Hello, Morgana," an amused voice drawled. A good-looking guy leaned in the doorway and smiled at Morgan. Longish hair with a hint of ginger poked out from under a red baseball cap and he had the kind of five o'clock shadow that's grown on purpose.

She didn't smile back. "I prefer to be called Morgan now, as you well know, *Thomas Redcap*." She made his name an insult.

The man's smile widened. "Ah yes, you're all modern and casual now. I'd heard. Love the outfit by the way. Did you join a band?" He sounded Irish or something. Miming a tip of his cap, he sauntered into the room and leaned forward as if to kiss her on the cheek.

"Don't. You. Dare."

He gave her a mocking bow. "Well you can't blame a lad for trying, Morgana the Fair and Perilous." As he approached the bed and didn't even glance in my direction, orange irritation crackled along the edges of my vision. It faded to grey shame when he closed Mom's eyelids with gentle fingers.

"Poor Viviane," he murmured. When he looked back at Morgan, his face was serious. "Do I have your leave to continue?"

She grimaced. "Get on with it."

Redcap nodded and then quickly—so quickly I almost couldn't understand what I was seeing—his hand shot out and a sharp fingernail dragged down Mom's arm, peeling flesh from it in one long curl like the skin off an apple.

Horror cut through me like bright lightning and bile burned my throat. I tried to stand, but my legs were dead and the chair only moved a little across the floor. The man's head shot up and I stared straight into amber eyes edged in red. Caught in those impossible eyes, I couldn't breathe, until he frowned and his gaze wandered away as if he couldn't see me at all. With a small shrug, he relaxed.

And then Redcap put the long strip of my mother's skin into his mouth and ate it.

I tried to scream, but my voice had been ripped from my throat and the place on my forehead burned where Morgan had touched me. Wild, panicked colors surged through me as I imagined the skin on my face blackening and peeling away. I couldn't move. I was frozen and incinerated all at once.

Stay still. Be quiet. Do not move.

I was obeying every command. As I stopped struggling against my invisible bonds, the pain faded.

Morgan shuddered delicately as she flipped the blanket on the bed to cover my mother's arm. "I know your duty, Redcap, but I do not have to enjoy watching you perform it."

A faint flush appeared on the man's cheeks, but his face was sad. "Poor Viviane," he repeated. "Her essence is in me now, but there are too many things missing, things which should have been preserved."

Morgan looked at Mom with a strange expression on her face. "Viviane keeps her secrets then, even in death."

Redcap snorted. "Secrets Cernunnos would pay dearly to know."

She glided over to the man and though they were the same height, Morgan seemed to tower over him. "Will you search them out, Thomas Redcap?" she whispered, her mouth close to his, seductive and dangerous. "Will you sell what you find to the highest bidder?"

The man didn't move, but his back was to me and I could see his muscles straining the fabric of his shirt across his shoulders—he was holding himself very, very still. "No, Morgana the Fair and Perilous, not even to you."

She backed away, her eyes fixed on him like twin moons. "Then let us take our separate paths and be gone from this place."

"Hey Rhi . . ." Peter poked his head into the room and I stood so fast that the chair skittered away and hit the wall. Whatever it was that had held me captive was gone.

I began to babble as I rushed over to my best friend. "Call the police! You need to call the police! That man, what he did, I can't believe what he did . . ."

But I couldn't find the words for what Thomas Redcap had done.

"Slow down. What are you talking about? What man?"

"Him!" I whirled and pointed. The room was empty except for the silent body of my dead mother.

And then all color in the world was gone and there was only black.

CHAPTER TWO

The light of the sun stabbed me through my closed eyelids and I knew I couldn't hide in bed any longer. Bunching my thin quilt into a ball, I threw it across the room in the general vicinity of the laundry basket. It might have made it in too if the basket weren't already overflowing with dirty clothes.

Pushing myself up, I rubbed my aching temples. Two months had passed since the day Mom died—since the day I fainted and hit my head—and the headaches from the concussion were a daily event. I winced as my feet touched the floor; all my nerves felt exposed. Purple irritation rushed across my sight and then, without warning, I was blinded by a spinning kaleidoscope of color. All the strength left my limbs and I fell off the bed onto the floor.

Normally my colors only appeared when my feelings were intense. I suspected I didn't have much of an imagination either because they were predictable—pale blue for sadness, hot red for anger, and all the colors in between for the various shadings between those emotions. White was fear and black was despair, but usually everything was mixed up and confused without one color predominating. Over the years I'd become used to them slithering through my brain and streaking across my vision.

I wasn't so used to them hitting me in my gut.

When my colors faded and I could see again, I used the bed to stand up, but sharp pain pulsed through my head at the movement. As vomit rose into my throat, I breathed slowly through my nose until my stomach settled.

After tottering into the shower and scalding my body back into submission, I felt better. Good thing because I had a hell of a day waiting for me. Mom could be pretty vague most of the time, but on some things she was crystal, even when she went all Wicca on me. As she got sicker, she made me promise to scatter her ashes at the lake by sunset of the third day after the next blue moon. She was that specific. This was the third day. It was also the first day of my last year of school, so, double whammy.

Picking through every piece of clothing I owned, even the dirty ones, I decided on white jeans, a striped t-shirt, and a navy cardigan. I hoped I looked nautical in a cute way, not a Popeye kind of way.

As if anyone would ever notice.

I was dragging a brush through my hair when there was one knock at the door, a slam, and then the sound of my battered couch groaning under the weight of a six-foot teenage boy.

"Oh, by all means, let yourself in," I called as I gave up trying to force my hair into a sleek ponytail.

"Blah, blah . . . what was that? Couldn't hear you!" Peter already had the TV on and was channel surfing when I came out of the bedroom, something he would have never dared to do while Mom was alive.

"What could possibly be worth watching before eight in the morning?"

Peter grinned. "There's always sports on somewhere. Besides, I've been up for ages. I'm already bored out of my mind waiting for you to get ready."

"You've only been here three minutes, jerk." I tossed a pillow at his face, but he caught it and put it behind his head.

"Yeah, but when you have a high metabolism like mine, three minutes is actually like three hours."

"What stupid comic book did you learn that one from?"

"Hey, graphic novels are an art form."

"Sure they are. And the superbabes in skintight onesies have nothing *whatsoever* to do with your *art appreciation*." I put my hand up just in time to block the pillow that sailed back at me.

Laughing, I crossed to the tiny kitchen facing the living room and opened the door of my ancient, avocado green fridge. The bare bulb flickering at the back couldn't hide the fact that my only options were a can of diet soda, a carton of milk way past its expiration date, and a shriveled apple. Or maybe it was a plum.

I sighed. I'd have to rely on take-out again if I didn't want to starve. I was sure I'd picked up groceries on the weekend, but ever since the concussion, I sometimes got mixed up in my days. That seemed to bother the doctor at the clinic a lot more than my headaches did. I almost thought I could see the canary yellow of his concern.

I didn't go back. I didn't need to start seeing colors for other people too.

Slamming the door and giving up on breakfast, I pushed Peter's feet away as I plopped down on the other end of the couch. From the day we met when we were three years old, Peter and I were soul mates of the non-romantic variety. We did experiment with kissing once when we were twelve, but it was awful and we promised each other to never try it again. Luckily for Peter Larsen, being a handsome, blond, star athlete—with just enough nerd in him to be interesting—meant getting many more chances to find a compatible kissing partner.

For mostly invisible me, not so much.

I grabbed the remote so I could check the time on the channel guide. "We should go in five."

Peter grabbed it back and continued clicking through the channels. "Lots of time. How's your head today?"

Peter's constant concern was beginning to get on my nerves. My memory of the day Mom died was messed up. I could remember the awful moment when the rattling sound of her breathing stopped, but not much after that. I couldn't even remember Peter coming to the hospital. He tried to catch me when I passed out, but I hit my head on the bed rail and was unconscious for ten minutes. It took ten stitches to close the gash inside my hairline and I spent the night in the hospital for observation. Peter seemed to think it was somehow his fault I'd fainted like a tragic heroine in a Victorian novel. All summer he'd treated me like I might break apart into pieces at any moment.

"It's OK," I lied.

"So, today's the day, right?" Click, click, click.

I took the remote and turned the TV off. "Yup." We both stared at the blank screen.

The couch shook as Peter slapped his knees. "Right, let's do this then." Taking me by the hands, he hauled me to my feet so fast I nearly fell. "Are you ready for the best year of our lives?"

Amber flared on the edges of my vision. "I'm ready," I lied again.

Gathering my things, I followed Peter outside. I didn't bother locking the door—the giant weeds surrounding the yellow stucco and green roofed house were proof that nothing was worth stealing inside. I scuffed my shoe at a vine that was beginning to creep onto the bottom step. Windfield Farm's gardens were beautiful until Mom got sick.

I wondered if the Larsens would hire someone to replace her. The thought hurt. I doubted it though. Peter's great-grandfather had established the stud farm in the Twenties and many famous racehorses had been born and trained here, but its glory days were over. There were still a few horses on the property, but Peter's parents had begun selling the land off to developers and a new subdivision was growing behind the barns. I hated the thought, but I knew the city that had been creeping in for years would soon pounce and gobble the whole place up.

Mom had talked her way into living in a guesthouse in exchange for maintaining the gardens, but even then there were fewer and fewer visiting celebrities of the racing world to impress. I'd realized pretty young that our little house was basically charity from the Larsens. Now they were my guardians. I loved them a lot and had always spent most of my free time up at the main house with Peter, so nothing much had changed. I paid for my few expenses out of the little bit of money Mom had saved from her small salary.

I got into Peter's car and we drove past the main house and out the wrought iron gate that led to the city road. A few minutes later and we were pulling into the student lot at our school—Eastdale High, home of the Screaming Eagles.

"C'mon, c'mon," Peter muttered as he honked the horn at the car in front of us trying to navigate the broken concrete parking lot.

"What's with you?"

"I'm meeting some of the guys before class. We're working on how to get some intel on O'Neil's team before the first game."

Peter's excitement was proof that our high school experiences had been vastly different. He had a ton of friends and the never-ending football rivalry with O'Neil, the school across town. I associated school with the nervous mustard yellow crawling under my eyelids that matched our hideous school colors perfectly. Our team jerseys were bad enough, but our cheerleaders had the worst of it. In their teeny yellow and black striped skirts, they looked like cold bumblebees. That's how I thought of them even out of uniform.

We parked and Peter paused with his hand on the door handle. "You know, I could go with you. It's going to be hot and the Celica's AC doesn't work. Dad's truck would be better on the dirt road too."

"It's OK. I think it's something Mom would want me to do alone. Thanks though."

He nodded. "You'll feel better once it's over."

"Yeah." I got out of the car, and as we walked towards the school, I put my arm around his waist and gave him a quick hug. Some of the cheerleaders were lingering at the entrance, giving Peter flirtatious smiles. He was a big favorite with all the girls at school. He treated them like ladies, even the ones whose reps were more like ladies of the evening. I knew I was lucky to have such a great guy as my best friend and I hugged him again.

Go ahead, Bumblebees, stare.

But it was him they were looking at, not me.

Our lockers were on different floors and Peter ruffled my hair before bounding up the stairs. I felt a splash of crimson that almost immediately disappeared—I could never stay mad at him for long.

Hurrying into the nearest bathroom to check on the damage, I smoothed my hair down and then paused, surprised. Someone came in and brushed past me as they went over to the farthest sink and turned on the water, but I couldn't drag my eyes away from the girl in the mirror. Rhiannon Lynne was such a fancy name that I'd always felt more comfortable with Rhi—short and sweet—but the girl who gazed back at me could actually pass as a Rhiannon. Her hair was long and wild and forgotten trips to the grocery store had produced a face that was sharp and defined. Her eyes were smoky grey and mysterious.

A wave of dizziness passed over me and I grabbed the sink to keep from falling. Head swimming, I looked at the girl in the mirror again and had the strangest feeling that she was the real Rhiannon and I was some pale copy—an imposter. Her eyes darkened with fury and I knew I had to hide before she could find me and punish me for taking her place. White fear blossomed and I heard my mother's voice.

Rhiannon, listen to me. We cannot be seen. We must be small, so very small together. Hide, Rhiannon, hide. Hide in the shadows and be still and silent.

I closed my eyes and imagined a blue shadow covering me—a barrier between me and the fear. After a moment, the tension flowed out of me into the deep, soft blue and I was calm again.

"Hey, how'd you do that?"

A slap of yellow and I opened my eyes, blinking at the fluorescent lighting; I'd forgotten where I was.

"Sorry, I didn't mean to scare you, but that was fairly impressive." A petite girl in a black mini tutu and baby doll top was observing me with a crooked smile. Her black hair was punctuated by two white stripes caught up in ponytails above her ears and she stared at me with almond-shaped eyes thickly lined in black.

"What?" I asked stupidly.

"You know, how you were there and then, poof . . . ." She waved her fingers in the air. "And then you came back." She tilted her head and frowned. "Maybe not all the way though. What's the trick?"

I hadn't had a lot of practice responding to questions and I certainly didn't know how to answer this one. When I didn't respond, the girl shrugged and pulled an eyeliner pencil out of a battered leather bag. "Forget it." She began to darken the winged lines around her eyes.

I glanced at the mirror and was relieved to recognize the face looking back—not a Rhiannon, just a Rhi.

The mind plays tricks when it's been bashed up a bit.

I pushed open the door to leave, but when I glanced back, the black-haired girl was leaning on the sink smirking at me.

Warning yellow trailed between us like ribbons.

CHAPTER THREE

After the final bell rang, I trudged to my locker and dumped my books into it. The rest of the day had been just like every day—I was still Eastdale's own invisible girl.

I bet no one would notice me even if I walked naked into the cafeteria and started playing the ukulele. While tap dancing.

It was a running joke between Peter and me. I knew I wasn't literally invisible—I wasn't crazy—but being seen and being *seen* were two different things. When I was younger and very shy, it was a relief when someone's eyes would pass over me or go distant when I spoke.

Now it's just annoying.

I hadn't even managed to collect a dirty look from Lacey McInnis. It was almost disappointing. Head cheerleader, the top of our class, the lead in all the plays, and the most popular girl in school—Lacey was basically a walking, talking cliché. Dirty blonde and ten pounds heavier than was ideal on someone only five foot two, she still entranced everyone she met. They loved her and she loved them back.

Except me. She hated me.

Because our last names were so close in the alphabet, our lockers always ended up next to one another. Unlike the rest of the student body, Lacey was painfully aware of me, but today she was preoccupied. She and another Bumblebee were watching a knot of students at the end of the hall with Peter at the center.

Lacey adjusted her ponytail. "They're supposed to be brothers, but they don't look much alike so I'm not sure. And there's a new girl too. She's . . . interesting." I guessed she was talking about Bathroom Girl. As if conjured by Lacey's words, the girl came around the corner, her skirt hiked up to the very limits of public decency. She smirked at me as she passed and the yellow ribbons were back.

"Wow," Lacey mouthed.

Peter had detached someone from the group and was steering him our direction. Lacey straightened and looked up hopefully, but Peter was watching Bathroom Girl and walked past without noticing. Flushing, she glared at me and dragged the other Bumblebee down the hall.

Bingo. All's right with the world again.

"Hey Rhi, this is Daley. He's new. Daley, this is my best friend, Rhiannon Lynne."

"Ow!" I jumped away from the wall of metal lockers as static sparked across my arm. My cheeks went hot.

Great first impression, Rhi. He's going to think you have Tourette's. That's if he even remembers you at all.

Daley was tall and lean, and his sandy hair, dark blue eyes, and straight jaw all added up to movie star gorgeous. His face was hard though; he didn't look like he belonged in high school. Around his neck he wore a strangely feminine necklace—an aquamarine stone in silver filigree. As he stared at me, mauve unease gathered along the edges of my vision. I felt exposed.

I change my mind. I'm just fine being a naked, ukulele-playing tap dancer that no one notices.

I forced myself to speak. "Aren't you kind of old to be a senior?" It was the first thing that popped into my head. Hearing the stupid words out loud, I could have cheerfully kicked myself.

Finely arched brows pinched into a frown. "We move a lot because of our dad's work." He paused as if he was thinking over his answer carefully. "I need to pick up some classes before I can graduate."

I nodded. Daley stared at me. I stared back. It took me a moment to realize he was actually expecting me to respond. I normally followed along in whatever conversation Peter was involved in, nodding and interjecting occasionally. No one usually bothered responding so my contribution to the discussion ended there.

I'd heard the expression before, but never actually seen anyone's eyes glaze over with boredom before. Turning, Daley called down the hall, "Hey Ty, come here!" Relieved of the pressure of his gaze, I blinked and my colors disappeared.

The guy who approached us was big—almost scary big—but he had young face and dark hair a bit on the shaggy side.

Sexy shaggy, not shaggy dog shaggy. I give it a week before the Bumblebees abandon Peter and start stalking this guy.

"This is my brother Tynan. Ty, meet Peter Larsen and Rhiannon Lynne." Daley gave our full names the way adults do when they introduce people.

Daley's brother brushed the hair out of his eyes and smiled shyly. "Hi."

Peter grabbed his hand and began shaking it; the Larsens were big on proper etiquette. "Man, you're huge! Have you ever played football before? We could use someone like you."

Tynan shook his head. "We might not be in town long. Dad's work moves us around." He looked at me and smiled. "You have a pretty name. Do you know your genealogy?"

It took a moment for the startled pink starbursts to clear. "What?"

Tynan launched into a string of enthusiastic sentences. "Your family history. Where you come from. Rhiannon is Gaelic. I speak Gaelic—a little bit anyway. Your name means Great Queen so I thought maybe you might be Irish or Welsh. That's what we are. Welsh, I mean. That's how I know. Rhiannon's a figure in Celtic mythology and there's even a cool song about her. Lynne is Gaelic too. It means 'lake'. What are your parents called?"

Peter and I shared a look and I could tell he was trying not to laugh. Tynan had gone from zero to sixty in five seconds flat. Peter might find it amusing, but it was making my head ache.

I change my mind about this whole talking to people thing.

"My mom was Viviane Lynne," I said finally.

Tynan's eyes widened. "Really! That's the same name as the Lady of the Lake in Arthurian myth. Your mom's name literally means 'Viviane of the Lake'. Where was she born?"

He's so excited. It makes me feel bad that I want to punch him in the mouth to make him shut up.

"Rhi's mom died a couple of months ago," Peter said quietly when I didn't answer.

Tynan hunched his back as if he could somehow make himself smaller. "I'm sorry," he said very quietly as he stuck his hands in his pockets and bent his head so his hair shadowed his cheeks.

I shrugged. "It's OK."

"Your mother's name was Viviane Lynne?" Daley interrupted, staring at me with weird intensity. I almost gasped out loud when the light caught his eyes funny, almost as if something bright had streaked across them.

My mouth was dry and I had to swallow before I could answer. "Yes. Why?"

He blinked and turned away. "Nothing," he muttered. "We should go soon, Ty." Daley strode down the hall and out the back door.

Tynan didn't seem to realize his brother had left him there alone. "I'm really, really sorry, Rhiannon."

Bright red swirled with purple swamped my vision as his concern ignited equal parts anger and irritation. "It's OK!" I snapped. Tynan stiffened and Peter looked at me in surprise.

So this is why nobody ever talks to me—I'm a bitch.

"It's OK," I repeated in a softer tone and smiled to hide the lie. "But don't call me Rhiannon. It's just Rhi."

Tynan brushed his hair out of his eyes and smiled back shyly. "I think Rhiannon suits you."

I was grateful for the change of subject when Peter jerked his chin down the hall. "Hey, Ty, do you know that girl?"

Lacey and some of the Bumblebees had surrounded Bathroom Girl and seemed to be trying to engage her in conversation. Even from where we stood, it was obvious that Bathroom Girl couldn't care less.

Tynan's smile faded. "Yeah."

"Can you introduce us?"

When Tynan hesitated, I decided to help Peter out. "Me too. We met this morning, but I didn't get her name."

"Sure, c'mon," Tynan agreed and we followed him down the hall. Bathroom Girl raised her eyebrows but didn't comment when we approached.

Lacey looked grateful for a new and more appreciative audience. I doubted she was used to anyone being as obviously unimpressed with her as Bathroom Girl was. "You're Tynan, right? Where have you been hiding?" Lacey asked brightly, ignoring me and Peter.

"I was just getting to know Rhiannon."

Lacey blinked. "You mean Rhi."

"I mean Rhiannon." Tynan smiled as if we shared a secret.

Lacey tried to smile too, but her jaw was clenched so tight I almost felt sorry for her. She was the only person in the entire school who was even vaguely aware of me most of the time, probably because she was crazy about Peter and saw me as an obstacle to getting him. They'd been out a few times, but he just wasn't into her. To Lacey, that was unacceptable. In her mind, I was the real problem.

Tynan gestured to Bathroom Girl. "Miko, this is Rhiannon and Peter."

Before the girl could speak, Peter grabbed her hand and began shaking it up and down like he was pumping for water. "Hi!"

"Hi." She retrieved her hand and began twirling one of her ponytails.

"How was your first day?"

"Fine."

"How long have you been in town? I can show you around if you want. There's a few cool places."

Miko didn't look like the kind of girl who needed any help finding the cool places, but she surprised me. "OK," she said with a crooked smile.

"Yeah?"

"Sure."

Monosyllabic must be the new black.

Peter was grinning and I felt another unexpected flash of sympathy for Lacey as she wandered away with the Bumblebees. Peter never even noticed.

"We could go now, if you want. Unless there's somewhere else you have to be."

Instead of answering, Miko turned to me. "Are you coming?"

All the unexpected attention was beginning to wear on me and I was glad I had an excuse to bow out. "Sorry, I can't. I've got to be somewhere soon."

"Maybe we could all do something together this weekend," Tynan said.

It took a moment to process that someone was asking me to make weekend plans. "Sure, that'd be great."

Daley opened the door and reappeared. "C'mon, we've got to get going. Dad wants us home right away."

"We've got to go," Tynan parroted his brother as he walked around me to join him. They stood silhouetted in the doorway and it was true what Lacey said: they were nothing alike. Tynan was hot, but beside Daley, he seemed unfinished somehow. I rubbed my arms as they prickled with static electricity again.

"Are you coming?" Daley asked Miko, but she shook her head. A nod from him and a quick wave from Tynan and they were gone, the door slamming shut behind them.

Miko was watching me. "They're not real brothers," she said as if she could tell what I was thinking. "More like foster brothers. It's Taliesin's thing; he picks up strays. Me included, I guess."

"Who's Taliesin?" The name rolled off my tongue, strange but somehow familiar.

"Their father." She air quoted the word father.

Peter was as confused as I was. "So you're their foster sister?"

Miko snorted. "No."

"But you came here with them?"

The girl shrugged. "I stay with them, so when they move, I do too. We move around a lot."

So they all keep saying.

CHAPTER FOUR

Impatience was crimson, yellow, and grey all twisted together into one butt-ugly mix.

Stuck in the back with an enormous sports bag that reeked of an entire summer of forgotten gym clothes, I was forced to endure Peter's scenic route home. Oshawa was nice enough, but every minute spent driving past a local tourist trap to impress the new girl was a minute less I had to get to the lake before sunset.

When Peter finally pulled up in front of my little house, I didn't wait for them to pull away before rushing inside. Throwing everything I thought I might need into my purse, I retrieved the urn with Mom's ashes from the top shelf of the book case.

I'd expected the funeral director to give me something more like a vase—I had vague memories of seeing a movie where a rich man's ashes sat above the fireplace while his heirs fought over his money until they were killed off one by one—but this was a wood box with a gold latch. When Mom got sick, she made all the arrangements without telling me.

I put the urn in my purse and took it out to my car where I set it on the passenger seat and fastened the belt over it. With the air conditioning not working, a lifetime of nightmares awaited me if I somehow managed to lose my mother's ashes out the open window.

Two hours later, I parked at the top of the steep path that led down to the cottage Mom had rented every summer since I was eight. I'd picked up the key from the rental agency on the way, but when I tried the front door, it was unlocked. The place was so secluded that security wasn't a problem.

I stepped inside and put my purse down on the kitchen table, disturbing a thick layer of dust that made my nose itch. In the main room nothing had changed—two plaid couches, a coffee table with a couple of coasters propping up one leg, a small box of a TV that got one channel, and a bookcase made out of planks of wood and old bricks. There was a faint smell of mildew. Anemic light filtered through the curtains and an intermittent brushing sound could have been the scratching of mice in the walls or the fluttering of bats inside the crumbling fireplace. The door leading to one of the bedrooms was partly open.

I had the strongest feeling something was hiding behind it and watching me.

Citrine swept through me. Grabbing my things, I hurried back out into the sunshine. Skidding a little on the grassy path, I ran down the hill to the water's edge and then stopped and looked back. The cottage was the same as it had always been—a clapboard building with cracked windows and curtains with faded strawberries on them.

The stain of my emotion faded, but there was no way I was going back inside.

Slipping off my sandals, I stepped onto the long dock that jutted out from the shore. As I passed out of the shadow of the trees, I squinted at the gold glare of the early evening sun bouncing off the lake. The lake was small but deep, and only a few feet from shore you couldn't see the bottom, just fallen trees stretching into the wet darkness like an ancient shipwreck.

Pushing my purse into the center of the dock, I lay down at the edge with my stomach pressed against the warm wood and peered into the water. When I was little, I used to pretend the drowned trees were the entrance to an underwater kingdom. I would dive in and try to reach them, but always got spooked halfway and had to swim back up.

Mom loved the water. On warm nights, we would sit on the dock in silence, watching the reflection of the stars in the lake and the turning of the moon. Now all that was left of her was going to be mingled in the water and maybe even the very air. Mom never asked me what I wanted—if I wanted her to be buried rather than cremated. She didn't even tell me she was sick until almost the end. The tears in my eyes burned away in the rise of a red emotion.

It's not fair.

I batted at the water just to see it disturbed, but stopped when I noticed the reflection of something moving towards me. For a moment, I thought the color of my anger had taken shape. Fishing the object out of the lake as it drifted into reach, I held up a red baseball cap.

"Hello! I almost didn't see you there." A man in a canoe glided towards me. As he approached the dock, he back-paddled fast and bumped against it lightly. He held out his hand and it took me a moment to realize he was reaching for the hat. I handed it to him and he put it back on. Between the gold light bouncing off the water and the shadow of the brim of his cap, I couldn't get a good look at him.

The man placed his paddle across his knees and put his hand on the dock to keep the canoe from drifting. "Thanks. I burn something wicked without a hat."

I got to my feet and backed away as I pretended to brush off my clothes. I'd never seen the man before and there was only a handful of cottages on the lake. "How did you lose it?"

"Well, that's a wee bit embarrassing. I was getting hot, so I took it off for a minute and managed to knock it out of the canoe with the paddle. Every time I got close, the water whisked it away. I guess it prefers the company of pretty girls." He winked at me, and while it seemed like a friendly wink and not a pervy one, I hadn't been winked at enough to be sure. Or ever.

"Are you visiting?"

"Sorry?"

"You don't sound like you come from here originally. I thought maybe you were on vacation or something . . ." I trailed off lamely.

"Ah," he said, nodding in understanding. "I'm Scottish. Originally." He winked at me again and my cheeks went hot. "But I haven't been back for so long I'd probably sound out of place there too. I had a powerful urge to go somewhere green and quiet, so I found myself here." He sighed. "It reminds me of home."

The man in the canoe bobbed up and down as he gazed at the high hills stretching up from the lake. He was nice—and kind of hot for an older guy—but I was discovering that despite what I'd always wished, being noticed all the time was

exhausting. Hoping he would wander away and simply forget
he'd ever seen me like most people did, I looked out into the
water.

And saw something strange.

A large fish was slipping in and out of the drowned trees,
but I'd never seen anything bigger than a sunfish in the lake
before. The pale shape was difficult to track and I kept
squinting from the sun on the water and losing sight of it. I
edged closer. It was really too big to be a fish. Maybe it was a
piece of sail from a boat. I discarded that idea when the shape
changed direction and started coming towards me. It couldn't
be, but it looked like a person, and I realized the sparkling
yellow almost blinding me wasn't from the sun after all.

Holy crap, there's a naked girl in the lake.

She had light hair parted in the middle and pulled back
from an oval face, and while she was definitely moving, her
pale arms and legs hung limp. She was like a fish being reeled
up on a hook.

Even though yellow worry and white fear warned me not
to, I leaned out over the water to see. It wasn't until the girl
was a few inches below the surface that I realized I was
staring at the fixed expression, closed eyes, and slightly
smiling mouth of a corpse.

"Get back!" the man yelled just as waxy, wet arms surged
to life and grabbed me by the ankles.

I overbalanced and hit the lake in a painful belly flop. Cold
hands pulled me down deep and fast. Flailing in panic,
blinded by florescence, I broke loose. Pain exploded in my
knee as it connected with a jagged branch on one of the
drowned trees; I'd finally made it to my underwater kingdom.

Kicking hard, I reached for the surface, but when my fingertips touched air, I stopped. The girl—*the thing*—had my legs again. As I struggled against its grip, my foot hit something soft and yielding. Looking down, I saw that the water-filled skin on the creature's face was now dented and loose. Stomach heaving, I exhaled precious breath. I was going to be forced to breathe in water. Color faded as a voice in my head promised to take me down to the place that erased all light and hid all sorrows in the deep dark.

I opened my mouth.

There was a flurry of motion around me and my legs were suddenly free. Strong hands grabbed me under my arms and pushed me up out of the water. Clutching the edge of the dock, I pulled myself onto it, coughing and spewing. The man from the canoe hauled himself up beside me. "Are you all right?" he asked when he caught his breath.

"Did . . . did you see that?"

The man—who had somehow managed to keep his cap on—didn't answer as he got to his feet and looked out over the water. "L'Inconnue de la Seine, you are far from home and this place is too small for you. Go and find deeper channels and leave the children of the land alone!"

I noticed he kept back from the edge, even though his canoe was upside down and sinking. The sun dropped behind the hills and when the stranger turned back to me, I could see his face clearly for the first time.

His eyes were amber and rimmed in red.

"Thomas Redcap," I whispered and the name unlocked the gate to my memories. "Mom," I whispered again as I remembered everything. I'd been saved from that creature in the water by a monster.

The man stared at me and when he spoke, his accent was stronger. "Since I saved your life, I don't mind us being on a first name basis, but what do you know of a redcap?" He said it like it was a thing, not a name. "It's strange you should be attacked by L'Inconnue, a creature of the old world. Stranger still that I should feel compelled to come here at all. What are you, then? A little *bana-bhuidseach* meddling in powers too big for herself?" His shadow blocked the setting sun.

The sun!

Scrambling to my feet, I pulled the urn out of my purse and fumbled to unlatch the lid. It released with a soft click, but then I hesitated. What if that thing down there was waiting for me to throw the ashes, scattering them like fish food for her pale mouth to gobble up?

One glimpse of the sky told me I had to decide fast. Hoping I was doing the right thing, I opened the lid and heaved the urn into the air as high and as far as I could. The dying rays of the sun flashed off the metal latch as the box dropped into the lake and sank out of sight.

"Viviane!" Thomas Redcap cried.

Searing pain assaulted me and for the second stupid time in two stupid months, everything went completely black.

CHAPTER FIVE

It was cold. A tight band restrained me around the waist and my knee was sore and hitting against something hard.

"So we're awake now, are we?"

There was a flash of dazzling white terror, but then my eyes adjusted to the gloom and I was able to see and think again. I was cold because my clothes and hair were damp and the air-con of the Celica was pumping out frosty air into my face. I was wearing my seat belt and my knee was knocking against the door on the sore spot where it had connected with the tree in the lake. Moving my legs a bit, I could feel my purse and sandals on the floor at my feet.

There was still a faint glow on the horizon and I could see quite clearly that Thomas Redcap was driving my car.

I pushed myself up out of my slumped position. "What did you do to me?"

Redcap chuckled. "Sorry love, but don't blame me. You went down like a stone. It's lucky for both of us I caught you before you fell back in the lake. I bundled you up in here to take you home."

Anger mixed with fear was a surprising pale persimmon. "How do you know where I live? Have you been stalking me?"

"I checked your wallet for your address. You know, I'm getting a little offended at being treated like the villain here. After all, five minutes with you and I end up tussling with L'Inconnue de la Seine, and that's someone I'd rather stay clear of, thank you very much. And then you repay my gallantry by throwing Viviane's bloody ashes into the bloody lake! So what I want to know is who the hell are you and what do you want from me?" His hands were gripping the steering wheel so tight that his knuckles were white.

I remembered those hands. I remembered everything. "I saw what you did, you psycho! You . . . you . . . defiled my mother's body! You ate her skin!" Remembering it made my stomach heave and I forced myself to breathe slowly through my nose. How could I have forgotten what this man did to her?

"What are you talking about?" I was thrown hard against the passenger door as Redcap swerved off the road and skidded onto the soft shoulder.

"My mother!"

"Your mother? Are you talking about Viviane?"

"Of course I am! I'm Rhiannon Lynne. And quit changing the subject! I saw you! I was there when you did it, only . . . I didn't remember until now. . ."

Well that sounds lame.

Redcap took off his hat and tossed it on the dash. "Morgan put you up to this. She's trying to ferret out Viviane's secrets."

Morgan. Goth Barbie's slutty older sister.

"Morgan's my aunt," I said as I remembered that too.

A bark of hard laughter. "Sweet Auntie Morgan—do you expect me to buy that?"

"That's what she told me. She said she was Mom's sister."

"Viviane and Morgan are sisters all right, but that doesn't say anything about you. Maybe I should just turn you over to the police and let them sort it out. Was it some kind of prank? See if you could steal something valuable and dump it?"

"I was there. I saw you take Mom's skin and eat it!" I pressed on. "You called Morgan 'Morgana the Fair and Perilous', which ticked her off. You said some guy named *Kernoonos* wanted to know the things Mom had hidden. I was there!"

Redcap drew a long breath. "So the walls did have ears that day, though I would never have guessed it was you, *mo leanabh*. Morgan hid you well. Or perhaps you did it yourself, eh? I didn't see you at the lake until I was right on top of you."

"Maybe you were too busy doing something else like, I don't know, eating my dead mother's skin, you pervert!"

The man slammed the palm of his hand hard against the steering wheel. It reminded me I was trapped in a car on a lonely road with someone I was very sure was completely and totally dangerous.

And I mouthed off at him and called him a psycho. Haven't I watched enough movies to know you never, ever tell the villain you're on to him?

His voice was low and soft. "Don't make the mistake of comparing me to a common flesh-eater. I'm the last of my kind. I preserve the Great Ones of my race when they pass on.

I have within me something essential of Viviane herself. Because of what I did, she will never be lost to us."

I stared at him without responding while I calculated the odds of getting to the phone in my bag before he could stop me.

Redcap sighed and shook his head. "All right then, I don't know why I care, but I'll prove it to you." He scratched at the shadow of his beard. "About nine years ago, Viviane was careless. She'd been keeping a low profile, but thought she was finally safe. On a whim, she decided to go to the movies for the first time. She'd never had much interest before, but someone—a child— had been pestering her to go." He paused. "It was you. I can see you through her eyes. You look happy." He snorted. "Skinny too. And in need of a hairbrush. Anyway, not long after the movie started, Viviane had a strong feeling of danger."

I thought of the silver-haired man. I'd only seen him that one time, but I knew Mom was always watching for him.

Redcap whistled through his teeth. "She was afraid. I can see it in her face. I can feel the echo of it inside me. I would never have thought Viviane would be afraid of anything. She dragged you out." He paused and frowned. "She said something to you, something I can't quite capture." I remembered.

Rhiannon, listen to me. We cannot be seen. Hide in the shadows and be still and silent.

The man cocked his head and snorted as if he could see it all on the windshield in front of him. "The way you're glaring at her, well, let's just say that few in this world have ever dared to look at Viviane that way. The next morning, she went to a bakery and brought back something to leave on your nightstand for when you woke up . . . something small . . ."

"A french *macaron*," I whispered.

"Yes, that's it. She knew the confection was your favorite, but there was still so much she didn't understand—like why the movie with its sound and light and laughing children was even important to you. I can feel she wanted to make you happy—that she tried—but she didn't know how. You were a creature she never truly understood."

My eyes filled with tears. "How do you know all this? Did she tell you?"

"I hadn't seen or even heard of Viviane in an age of the world. She is in me now."

I rubbed my eyes. "Right, you ate her skin and now you know everything she ever did. Do you think I'm stupid?"

The corners of his mouth twitched. "Perhaps, since it seems you have no idea whatsoever who Viviane was. Maybe there's a land where the spirits of my kind dwell after death, but I keep some part of them here in this world, within myself."

"That's crazy!"

Redcap didn't respond. Shifting the car into gear with a jerk that rattled the windows, he drove back onto the road. Shivering, I switched off the AC with a snap. Had he fixed it? It was a reassuring thought that maybe he wasn't planning on raping and murdering me if he'd gone to the trouble of fixing my car.

Maybe he just really likes my car.

I contemplated the man. Except for his eyes, he seemed normal: handsome, well-dressed, older. How much older, it was difficult to tell. Not as much as I'd originally thought. I couldn't pin down anything exact about him at all.

And I have to admit if you ignore the whole eating my mom's skin thing, he's been a perfect gentleman.

"I guess I should thank you for saving me from that thing in the lake. And for driving me home too." A thought occurred to me. "How will you get your own car back?"

"I don't have a car."

That's weird.

"And you're welcome. For the air-conditioning too, I might add."

"You did fix it! Why?"

Redcap was silent for so long that I didn't think he was going to answer. "I don't like broken things," he said finally.

We drove for a while in silence and I began to relax a little. "So what was that thing at the lake? You called it a name—Connie something."

"L'Inconnue de la Seine," he corrected.

"Whatever. What was it?

He shrugged. "A story. A legend. In the 1880's, a girl's body was found in the river Seine in Paris. A common enough result of either murder or suicide, but this one was strange. She wasn't decayed and bloated as she should have been after her time in the water, and she'd drowned with a smile on her lips. Touched by her beauty, someone at the morgue made a plaster cast of her face." He chuckled. "More touched by the desire to make a buck or two, he began selling copies. In a few years the girl's death mask was a common decoration on the walls of the living rooms of Europe. Do you know CPR?"

"I had a demonstration during a baby-sitting course."

A waste of time since no one's ever called me up and asked me to baby-sit their kid.

"Then you've seen her before. The man who invented the CPR dummy used her face as his inspiration."

"That's creepy, but it doesn't explain anything."

"Doesn't it *mo leanabh*? There will always be foolish romantics ready to fall in love with beautiful dead things."

"But it was real!"

Redcap glanced at me before returning his attention to the road. "Of course it was real. Fools who worship objects never stop to think about the power they're giving them. But then, how could they know the body they dredged from the river was a goddess."

"A goddess," I squeaked.

"She was known by the Gauls and the Celts as Sequana, the goddess of the Seine, but when her worshippers abandoned her, she faded and died. This new generation bestowed adoration upon her image, wrote love poems to it, and gave it the kiss of life every day. That was enough to restore her, but it changed her too. Clawing her way out of whatever common grave her body had been dumped into, she was reborn as L'Inconnue de la Seine—the unknown one of the Seine. The image of her face has spread through the world and now she's no longer bound to her river."

I had to swallow before I could speak. "Why was she at the lake?"

He shrugged as if it didn't matter, but his face looked concerned. "She must have been drawn by Viviane's ashes as I was. They are alike in some ways after all."

"What do you mean?"

Redcap sighed as he took the red baseball cap off the dash and put it back on. "Don't you get it, lass? Just like the original Sequana, Viviane was a creature out of myth and legend."

"You're crazy. My mother is dead. Because of you and Morgan, I lost my memories for an entire summer. I want to know what's going on!"

When the man didn't answer, I sat back in frustrated silence. After a couple of minutes, we drove through Windfield's gate and I pointed the way to the smaller road leading up to my house. He pulled in front, turned off the engine, and handed me the keys. With the headlights off and clouds now covering the moon, I could barely see him, and when he spoke, his voice was low and angry.

"*Mo leanabh*—do you know what it means?" Redcap didn't wait for me to respond. "It means my child in Scottish Gaelic. My mum used to call me that when I was little. But are you just an innocent child? How could you claim kinship with Viviane and not know what she was? How can you be ignorant of the world as it really is, *mo leanabh*?" The impossible red circling his irises burned.

"I don't understand anything that's happening to me," I whispered.

Redcap cursed quietly and got out of the car. I hurried to follow him.

"Rhiannon," he said and his voice was now gentle, "I don't know who or what you are, but there's something I know for a truth—you are not Viviane's daughter."

"What do you mean? Wait!" I cried.

But he had turned and slipped away into the darkness.

CHAPTER SIX

I spent the next few days avoiding Peter, but since he had football practice and student council meetings to attend, he didn't seem to notice. It was a relief. I'd never kept a secret from him before, but I didn't know how to make any of what happened up at the lake sound real. He would tell his parents and I'd be back at the hospital with doctors dipping into my head again.

Viviane is not my mother.

Each morning I would wake up and think I could march into her room and demand some answers. On the third day, I made it all the way in before the sight of the empty bed reminded me she was gone.

Mom wasn't like other mothers. She wasn't like Peter's mom. Mom never hugged me or yelled at me. She never asked me how my day was. She didn't like it when I went to the movies with Peter or stayed after school to work on a project, but she never said why. We were usually quiet when we were together. Sometimes she would smile, but I had no memory of seeing her laugh. I couldn't remember her ever saying she loved me.

I had a recurring nightmare when I was little. When she heard me crying, Mom would come and I would tell her about it. She would put her cool hand on my forehead until I calmed down and went back to sleep. Standing there staring at the empty bed, it occurred to me Mom never once told me the nightmare wasn't real.

Red anger flared across my vision and I went back to my own room. Grabbing some clothes off the floor, I dressed and began searching the house.

Viviane is not my mother.

Why should I believe Thomas Redcap? I had no reason to trust him, except that he'd saved my life.

And fixed my car.

Maybe he meant I was adopted. It would explain how different Mom and I were. I pulled the house apart but couldn't find my birth certificate or anything else that might prove my theory. I even checked under her bed, but only found a family of lonely dust bunnies.

Discouraged, I fingered through the jewelry in the small ceramic dish on the nightstand. Static electricity bit the tips of my fingers as they brushed against a delicate silver charm bracelet and I lifted it up to the light. A single charm dangled from it—a stylized daisy, or maybe a wheel—and the chain threaded through one of the spaces between the spokes. It was simple but beautiful and I wanted to put it on, but Mom's things didn't feel like they belonged to me. As I put the bracelet back, I noticed the corner of something peeking out from under the dish.

It was a business card with R. Goodfellow & Associates printed on one side and a phone number written on the back. It sounded like a law firm. If I was adopted, her lawyer would know, but wasn't there attorney/client privilege or something? I went into the living room and popped the card in my purse just in case.

I sat down on the couch. It was quiet. Mom liked things to be quiet. When I would turn on the TV, the noise would drive her out into the garden. Peter and I would go to the movies instead or watch up at his house so we wouldn't bother her.

In a surge of defiance, I hit the button on the remote and jacked up the sound till it filled the house. Then I went back to her room and began rifling through her armoire. I was almost tall and pretty slim, but Mom was skeletal and all legs—most of her skirts would be too long. Instead I hauled out a bunch of filmy tops I thought would fit. Claiming ownership of everything Mom had left behind, I also took the silver charm bracelet. The wheel shape was simple, almost childish, but I wanted it. As I draped the chain over my wrist and fastened the clasp, another spark of electricity ran across my skin, but this time it didn't hurt.

It felt exciting.

CHAPTER SEVEN

The light was strange—grey and dim. The trees around me were cruelly twisted and their bare branches appeared to be claws reaching out to snatch me from the arms of the woman who carried me. I pressed my face against the soft, wheat-colored hair spilling over her shoulders and down her chest, but the rapid beating of the heart beneath was no comfort. We came to an abrupt stop and I was put down on unsteady legs onto the smooth path cutting through the trees. Another woman stepped out of a dazzling light to meet us. Her hair was black and her eyes were pale and cold—it was Mom. She took my hand and tried to lead me towards the light, but I began to cry and pull away. I reached for the beautiful woman who had abandoned me, but she was already leaving. As a dark shape slinked after her and the trees closed behind them like a gate, I tried to scream, but there was no sound.

I woke with my heart pounding and couldn't see through icy blue streaks until it slowed down. I hadn't had the nightmare in years; thinking about it must have resurrected it. The dull thud of my constant headache began again.

I never told Mom she was in my dream. I didn't even realize it was her at first. The woman in my dream was larger, brighter somehow. Now I knew it was undeniably her face, her thin hand that held mine, and her pale eyes that seemed to see nothing and everything at once.

I dressed for school in jeans and a peasant blouse I'd pilfered from Mom's wardrobe. I was still wearing the charm bracelet. The little wheel looked like some kind of good luck charm and I tucked it under my sleeve and decided to keep it on; I could use a little luck.

Peter wasn't the only one I'd been avoiding. After the novelty of the new kids' attention wore off, I felt strangely uncomfortable with it. Perversely, I was also afraid of the disappointment when they began ignoring me like everyone else did. When the lunch bell rang and Miko stepped out of a classroom into the hallway in front of me, I stopped and hoped she hadn't seen me.

As she walked away, I felt relieved, but also unkind; from what I'd observed during the week, no one was going out of their way to make friends with the girl. Gathering my courage, I ran after her, but instead of heading to the cafeteria, she went through the door that led to the dressing rooms on the side of the stage. It seemed kind of stalkerish to follow her, but so did lurking in the hall waiting for her to come out. I was just about to leave when I heard singing and what sounded like a harp. Curious, I opened the door and went down the corridor to the girls' dressing room. The door was open. Miko sat on the long counter running under the wall to wall mirror with a small harp in her hands. Looking up, she blinked in surprise.

"We've got to stop meeting like this," I joked.

Raising an eyebrow, she didn't respond as she stuffed the instrument back into her bag.

My heart sank as I realized she was now ignoring me like everyone else did. "That was pretty. You have a beautiful voice."

Miko went very still. "You heard that?"

"Yeah, sorry, I didn't mean to interrupt you. Is that a harp?" When she didn't answer, I plowed on with nervous chatter. "I thought they were bigger. I've never known anyone who could play the harp. You're really good."

The girl stared at me as if I'd grown another head. "You could hear the music?"

"Um, yeah, of course."

"I knew it!" Miko's smile was triumphant. Grabbing me by the arm, she propelled me out of the dressing room and through the door into the hall.

"What are you doing?" I protested.

"Proving a point."

For such a tiny person, her grip was iron as she dragged me into the cafeteria and over to the table Peter, Tynan, and Daley were sitting at. Depositing me into a chair, she plopped herself down on Peter's knee and her pink miniskirt hiked up to show even more leg than usual. Peter didn't seem to know where to put his hands and his neck was so red I was afraid something was going to pop.

"It's Friday," Miko announced. "Let's do something."

"Count me in," Peter said and was rewarded with a kiss on the cheek. The blush spread from his neck up into his face.

Tynan brushed the hair out of his eyes and flashed me a quick smile. "I'm in."

"Like what?" Daley looked up from the massive book he was reading just as I yelped from the prickle of static running through the metal chair into my thighs.

So much for making a good second impression.

"Oh, I don't know." Miko twirled a strand of hair around one finger and her eyes glittered. "Rhi likes music. Don't you Rhi?" She turned back to Daley before I could reply. "She likes my harp. She thought my singing was really pretty."

Daley closed his book with a thump and Tynan pushed his tray away and sat up straight. Everyone was staring at me.

Anxiety drifted like tangerine fog along the edges of my vision. "I don't know where any bands might be playing. Sometimes in the summer there are underage dances, but . . ."

Peter wasn't going to let me ruin what he'd probably been angling for all week. "But we could go to that restaurant I was telling you about and then catch a movie." I felt a twinge of jealousy; movies were our thing.

"Great!" Miko said, hopping off his knee and flashing more leg at the student body. "It's a plan. You can pick us all up at 6:00."

I sat there as Miko arranged my very first date for me. It wasn't until I was walking to my next class that I realized I wasn't sure which one of the brothers was supposed to be mine. Touching the wheel charm tucked inside the sleeve of my blouse for luck, I made a wish.

Let it be Daley, please.

CHAPTER EIGHT

The teacher droned on as if he somehow knew how desperate I was for the class to be over and wanted to torture me for it. I was excited at first, but the more I thought about going on a date—about socializing with anyone other than Peter and the Larsens—the more I felt like I was breaking apart. My head throbbed as colors streaked across my interior vision and my skin was tight and hot where the charm rested against it. When I lifted my sleeve and looked at my wrist, I was shocked to see a round mark, almost like a burn. I'd felt the charm's electricity a number of times, but hadn't realize it had actually raised a raw, red welt. The spot was painful, but I'd continued to wear the bracelet even though I must have known it was hurting me.

What's wrong with me?

It was suddenly all too much. No matter what I'd wished for before, I no longer wanted to be seen. I tried to remember Mom's voice, but it was thin and far away. Closing my eyes, I focused on the watery blue that usually calmed me, but I couldn't grasp it and it dissipated like mist on the surface of a lake.

Anger surged through me and a flash of light beneath my eyelids followed it. Startled, I opened my eyes and jumped to my feet, but the sparkles of pink I would have expected didn't appear. Everything was too bright and the glare made the world look like it was painted in black and white.

When Mr. Porter turned and crossed his arms, it took me a moment to realize he was waiting for me to apologize. Someone in the back laughed. My cheeks flamed and I wished everyone would stop staring at me.

Everyone is staring at me.

"Is there something you'd like to share with the class, Miss Lynne?" After three years, five days, four hours, and twenty-two minutes, one of Eastdale's teachers had decided to acknowledge my existence.

"No . . . uh, sorry," I stammered, "it's just . . . I thought I saw . . ." I searched for a plausible excuse for jumping out of my skin and standing there like a moron. "I saw a spider." More laughter. "I don't like spiders," I added unnecessarily.

Mr. Porter had small eyes made even smaller by thick, black-rimmed glasses. They seemed to contract now into dark dots. "And is it too much to ask for you to take your seat, Miss Lynne? Or would you like us to all drop everything and go searching for spiders so you'll feel more comfortable?"

"No. Thank you. I'm fine now."

"Well that's wonderful," he drawled before turning and continuing to scrawl on the board in his illegible handwriting.

Lacey McInnis leaned over from the seat behind and whispered, "Don't mind old man Porter. I bet everyone here wishes they could stand up and walk out. He's just mad you're the first one to try it."

It took me a moment to process that she was speaking to me. Civilly. "Wish I tried it years ago," I murmured and she laughed.

After class, Lacey hesitated by my desk and then seemed to decide something.

"Hey Rhi, I just wanted you to know, I understand. I bet it's hard watching Peter drool all over the new girl."

So that's it—the enemy of my enemy is my friend.

"I guess." There was no point telling Lacey I didn't care if Peter drooled all over every girl in town—she wouldn't believe me.

"If you ever want to talk . . ."

"OK. Thanks."

I was the recipient of my first ever Lacey McInnis smile before she waved and joined a couple of Bumblebees on their way to cheerleading practice.

The school day ended on such a weirdly pleasant note that I took courage and began to look forward to going out that night.

After a quick snack and a long shower, I rummaged through the contents of a laundry hamper that now contained the majority of my wardrobe and came up with a slightly wrinkled jean skirt and one of Mom's chiffon tops. Neither were dirty—I'd just thrown them at the hamper because I was too lazy to hang them back up. As I took the charm bracelet off and placed it on my night table, I was glad the long sleeves of the top covered the burn on my wrist.

I was slipping on a pair of sandals when Peter started honking outside. Stuffing my phone and some money in the back pocket of my skirt, I rushed out.

"Hurry up!" he yelled through the open window of his mom's mini-van. It wouldn't be stylish, but at least we would all fit. The automatic side door slid open. "In the back," he ordered.

"Why?"

"I want Miko to with me. Besides, don't you want to sit with Ty?" He pulled away so fast I was almost thrown out of my seat before I could get my belt on.

"I don't know, do I?"

"You should. He's been asking about you all week."

"Really?" I wasn't sure I believed Peter. If Tynan had wanted to talk to me, he could have found me any time.

"Really. He's like, obsessed with you. I hope Daley found a date or it'll be weird. He wanted to know about you too, but Ty was all over it." My heart dropped as I realized my wish had gone unanswered.

We went north on Simcoe Street, the same road Winfield was on, until we passed Port Perry. Following the directions on my phone, we turned off and headed towards Lake Simcoe. When we arrived at the address we'd been given, neither of us spoke for a moment. Mansion might sound like somewhere one of the villains in Peter's comic books would live, but it was the only word that fit the sprawling stone building at the end of a dirt lane, backed by forest. The other two and three acre lots around it were still bare and waiting to be bought and built on.

Peter pointed at the red sports car parked in front. "Do you know what that is? It's a Jag F-Type V8 S! They start at a hundred grand and go up."

The others were waiting for us on the massive stone porch and were in the van before Peter could get out and open the doors. "Nice ride," Tynan laughed as he buckled himself into the seat beside me.

Peter flushed. "Well at least we're not sitting on top of one another."

Miko ignored her seatbelt and slid across the front passenger seat to nestle into Peter. "Now *that* sounds like fun." His blush went nuclear.

Daley climbed into the back. "We need to stop somewhere first."

When Daley gave him the address, Peter caught my eye in the rearview mirror; we both knew it very well. Twenty minutes later, we were at Lacey McInnis' house. Tynan and I got a bright hello as she climbed into the van. Peter and Miko were ignored.

"Hey, Day," she said as she sat beside him.

I would have bet big money that Daley would hate the nickname, but all he said was, "You look nice." She did too. Lacey carried her extra ten pounds better in a t-shirt, sleek jacket, and ruffled skirt.

"Wow, that's beautiful."

"Don't touch it!" I turned in surprise to see Daley tucking the chain and its pendant under his collar. Lacey looked like she might cry.

"Sorry," he apologized after a moment. "It caught in my hair and you pulled it." I could hear the lie, but Lacey smiled in relief.

Miko snorted and made a face as she snuggled in closer to Peter. "We need to make another stop."

"Sure. Where?"

"Somewhere quiet."

He grinned. "I know just the place."

Uncomfortable, I shifted in my seat and gazed out the window.

We drove across town to Parkwood, a historic estate and one of the few tourist attractions in town worth checking out. The grounds were almost always open, but I'd heard it was easy sneaking in even after hours.

It's amazing what people will say around you when they don't notice you're there.

We parked and walked past the house and down a path to a sunken clearing with a stone pavilion at one end. During the day, the area was used for weddings. During the night, it was occasionally used for the type of activity that resulted in some of those weddings.

Peter draped his arm over Miko's shoulders and wandered away from the rest of us. Not to be outdone, Lacey glared at him and then put her arm through Daley's. Tynan and I stared at one another awkwardly. I wanted to say something witty or cute, but feared I'd probably end up making out with him just to avoid speaking to him.

"I'm sorry," he whispered.

"What?" The horrible thought occurred to me that he was sorry he didn't want to make out with me.

Tynan looked at his brother. Daley and Miko had both detached themselves from their partners and Daley nodded back at him. Tynan straightened into full and impressive height and pointed at the trees on the one side of the clearing. "*Ae veyll ooœk ee - œrree bee œgh!*" he yelled.

Dandelion yellow flashed across my eyes. As Tynan continued to shout gibberish into the shrubbery, I had the terrible feeling I was about to get punked the same way that poor girl Carrie did on the night of her prom.

Before I could move, the air became wet and I closed my eyes against a blast of icy wind. Colors swirled in my mind's eye and shaped themselves into something monstrous.

A white form licked by corpse blue flame. Silky hair slicked in dew. Glistening fangs. Dog shaped and yet as far from a dog as a nightmare is from a dream.

Three short howls echoed through the clearing. The vision in my mind wavered and I opened my eyes.

Peter had put himself between the direction of the sound and the rest of us. "Better stay back. It might be a coyote or a wild dog. Try not to make any sudden moves."

I shook my head. "That's not what it is."

"You can see it somehow, can't you," Miko whispered as she sidled up behind me, "even though it's not yet fully present in our world."

"What?"

"Don't play dumb."

I shook my head again. "I don't know what you're talking about."

Another howl and the bushes shook and swayed. Peter looked around wildly as he tried to locate the source of the sound. Lacey whimpered.

"What is it?"

"A member of the Wild Hunt, a hound of Avalon. Most supernatural beings have many names, but the Welsh would call it a Cŵn Annwn. The Hunt guards the Wall between our world and the world of magic. Tynan called this one from its pack."

I stared at her in shock. "Why?"

Miko's lopsided smile was full of mischief. "To win a bet."

I might have slapped it right off her pretty little face if hell hadn't suddenly erupted. A white creature burst into the clearing. It landed facing Peter, snarling and huffing. The beast matched what I'd seen in my mind except for the glowing red of the inside of its ears. It was beautiful.

And completely pee your pants terrifying.

Peter held his ground out of range of its claws. "Get back to the van! I'll hold it off somehow!"

"Protector," Miko murmured. "Check."

Lacey didn't need to be told twice. When the beast's gaze remained fixed on Peter, she raced up the stone steps and out of sight down the path.

"Useless," Miko sneered. "Check two."

I looked at Tynan, but he was staring at the ground and wouldn't meet my eyes. Daley stood with his arms crossed, watching us. "Do something!" I screamed. Neither of them moved.

Rhiannon, listen to me. We cannot be seen. Hide in the shadows and be still and silent.

Mom's voice rang through my mind like a bell in my skull. I had to obey and disappear. I waited for the color that always followed her words to pass over me, but could only find wisps that I could barely focus on. I blinked my eyes and then even they were gone.

The beast turned its head to look at me with eyes like moonstones.

"He sees you," Miko said. "I don't know how you've been hiding yourself from everyone, but you're all here now. What are you going to do?"

Even if I'd had an answer, there was no time. The creature moved so fast it seemed to fly. The air was knocked out of my lungs and when I could think again, I realized I was flat on my back with the Cŵn Annwn's cold paws on my chest. Claws like curved, bleached bones dug into my ribs, but the creature was strangely light. I gasped as its claws pierced the fabric of my top and it lowered its head to look at me intently. It wasn't attacking. Yet.

I should have been blank and white with terror, but its touch seemed to have changed something. Or maybe I'd hit my head when I went down and couldn't comprehend the reality of my danger. I tried to focus on the Cŵn Annwn, but it shifted between a dog-like beast with white hair and a creature made from the glowing blue-green of marsh gases and the silvery grey of windblown skies.

I couldn't help myself—I put my hand out to touch it. Peter hissed at me to stop. The Cŵn Annwn growled as my fingers sank into the slick, wet fur at its neck and I froze, expecting razor teeth to sink into my skin, but the creature shook its head as if confused.

Some instinct told me to close my eyes. The Cŵn Annwn was still there in my mind as an aura of pale flame. I felt it flicker up my arms and across my body. It called to me.

I let go of the beast's fur and reached for the tongues of flame flickering blue, then green, then silver and grey. In my mind, they leapt up in response. As they seeped into my skin, a pleasure spread through my gut that I'd never experienced before. I felt the beginnings of ecstasy, but it wasn't fast enough. Impatient to have it all—to feel it all—I imagined myself reaching out to grasp the Cŵn Annwn's colors and my palms burned with cold fire.

I opened my eyes when the creature whimpered and everything I thought I knew about myself and my synesthesia was blown to hell. I could still see the flames that danced across my hands and their connection to the beast.

I think I can see magic.

The weight on my chest increased and I knew the Cŵn Annwn was preparing to attack. Acting on instinct again, I tightened my grip on the beast's aura and yanked it away.

Sensation swept through me. I could smell the rich odor of wet earth, fallen leaves, and running streams. Wind slapped my cheeks and I exulted in the reckless joy of the hunt. I raced across misty moors and dove into salty seas. I tore through the skies and fell on my prey like a bolt of lightning. I felt a joy so pure I wanted to cry.

The weight disappeared and I was forced back into myself. The Cŵn Annwn was gone.

"Are you all right? Are you hurt?" Peter skidded to his knees beside me and I thought I saw a thread of brilliant green connecting us, but my head started throbbing and I lost it.

An oval face smiling a lopsided smile swam into view.

"Anomaly," Miko said. "Check three. I win!"

CHAPTER NINE

We sat on one side and they sat on the other—enemy camps separated by the no man's land of the table. Tynan appeared miserable and even Daley seemed uncomfortable. I could tell Peter was angry, but Lacey was harder to read.

The only one who was perfectly relaxed was Miko. She was wolfing down an apple crisp slathered in whipped cream. I considered the bowl of chocolate mousse in front of me and picked up a spoon to shovel a generous portion into my mouth.

Lacey broke. "How can the two of you sit there eating after what just happened?"

Miko didn't bother looking up. "Have some. You'll feel better."

"How is dessert going to make me feel better about being attacked by a monster?" Lacey cried, but it was a topic no one was ready to discuss.

One by one, the others began to eat what Miko had ordered for them. Even Lacey began to pick at her shortcake until she was finishing it with enthusiasm.

Fortified by chocolate, I was ready for answers. "How did you know?"

Miko didn't blink. "Know what?"

"That chocolate mousse is my favorite and pecan pie is Peter's?"

"Everyone likes to claim they're into wheat grass and steamed vegetables and whatever, but I can see past the illusion of the lie they tell themselves to uncover the truth." She grimaced. "People rarely appreciate being told what they really want."

Tynan nudged her gently with his shoulder. "We do, Meek."

I was sick of all the games. "So she is your sister then, and not just some chickie who works for your dad." Tynan ducked his head and his hair fell over his eyes. His refusal to look directly at anyone for long was starting to irritate me.

The noise Miko made was a cross between a laugh and a snort. "I told you, unlike these two losers, I have a family of my own—even if I'm not on speaking terms with any of them at the moment."

"So what did you win in this bet of yours then?"

Lacey dropped her spoon with a clatter against her plate. "What bet?"

"I think it was a bet we wouldn't get killed, at least, not too quickly."

Daley shook his head. "I would have stepped in if the Cŵn Annwn had attacked. Up until you did whatever it was you did, it was only curious. We search for Potentials. Miko can usually sense what category they fall into, but you three were difficult to sort out. It was her idea to try something a little bit unorthodox."

"Potential for what?" Peter asked. "And what was that thing?"

"Not potential," Tynan corrected from beneath the curtain of his hair, "a Potential. Someone with untapped abilities. Magic."

"Magic," Peter said, laughing.

"Magic," Lacey said with wonder in her voice.

I didn't say anything. I already knew that magic existed.

A waitress arrived with mugs of hot chocolate and we were silent as she passed them around. "The boys and I still need sugar," Miko explained after the woman left. "Using magic depletes the body's physical and mental resources."

"Tynan was the one who called the Cŵn Annwn."

"Tynan has that ability. At the moment." Tynan flushed and looked away. "Daley was maintaining a perimeter to contain the beast. I was holding a glamour over us to make sure no one witnessed our little experiment."

Peter laughed. "You're kidding, right?"

Daley sighed and ran his fingers through his hair. "I know it's a lot to take in, but Miko has a magic device—a harp—that gives us information on where a Potential might be."

"Oh come on!"

I put my hand on Peter's arm. "Just listen for a minute." His pale eyebrows shot up, but he nodded.

Daley flashed me a grateful look. "Sometimes the harp is as specific as a name and a place, but usually it's just a general area and we have to narrow it down ourselves. The harp sent us to Ontario, but we've been searching cities since the spring and it's been like chasing ghosts. Since most abilities show up in adolescence, we normally start in the schools and Eastdale was the first on the list here. Miko could sense something, but she wasn't sure what. Since there were three of you in one place—which is unprecedented—it was probably messing with her abilities."

Miko perked up. "I was being blocked!"

"Maybe," Daley conceded.

"But then there was the weird thing in the bathroom," Miko interrupted.

Lacey wrinkled her nose. "What weird thing?"

Miko ignored her and looked at me. "You were doing some kind of magic I'd never felt before."

"I have no idea what you're talking about."

Daley frowned. "You said you were Viviane Lynne's daughter. Our father has been looking for her, but she's been missing for years. Everyone thought she was dead." He paused when he saw the look on my face. "Sorry. We didn't realize it was true, or how recently it happened, until you told Tynan. Anyway, at the time, our father thought the name was maybe just a coincidence, but it was worth checking out. The three of you seemed connected so we watched you all, or at least, we tried to. You were always difficult to find. I'd track you down and then something would catch my attention and you'd be gone. You being able to hear the harp was another red flag. Miko had the idea of putting you in a stress situation to see what would happen and I agreed."

"And what's the harm of a few wagers on the side, right *Meek*?" I glared at the girl, but she was inspecting the polish on her nails and looking bored.

Daley made an impatient gesture. "If you want to be angry with someone, be angry with me."

"So what was the bet then, *Day*?"

A muscle jumped in Daley's cheek and his eyes narrowed. I was right—he didn't like the nickname. "Miko's bet was that within three minutes of facing a threat, she could confirm exactly what you were."

"What are we then?"

Miko answered with three black-tipped fingers raised as she ticked the points off. "A Protector, a Mongrel and an Anomaly." She smiled sweetly at Lacey. "You're the Mongrel, in case you were wondering." Lacey's mouth opened but no sound came out.

Miko pointed at Peter. "Protector. You've inherited the ability from a relative or an ancestor. We can check with Taliesin and see if we can find out who it was, but I wouldn't get your hopes up. Protector magic is one of the few abilities not diluted by breeding and you can never predict which generation it'll pop up in."

The finger turned to Lacey. "Mongrel. One of your ancestors mated with a lorelei or something. The hint of those abilities is what makes you more popular than you deserve. In ancient times, you might have had enough natural talent to become a witch, but now you'll probably become a weather girl on regional TV. National, if you're lucky." Cruel, but basically what I would have predicted for Lacey too.

The finger moved to me. "Anomaly. Do you even realize that sometimes you're almost invisible? That's a witches' trick, but I'm mostly immune to those. That day in the bathroom, I saw you fade before my eyes and then come back, though not as strong as before. It was like you were still out of focus."

Tynan pushed the hair out of his eyes. "We asked around and no one could remember what you looked like or if you were in any of their classes. Except Lacey. She definitely . . . knew you," he finished diplomatically. Lacey fidgeted beside me but remained silent. "She seems to be unaffected by whatever it is you do."

Miko thumped the table with a tiny fist. "The point is, I can smell the spells a witch casts from a mile away and I couldn't detect siren or lorelei on you either." She smirked at Lacey. "They both have a distinctly fishy scent, paranormally speaking." She pointed at me again. "You couldn't really be *the* Viviane Lynne's daughter—that was ridiculous—but you're not like any other Greylander we've encountered. Daley refused to even consider you might be an earth magician. . ."

"That's not true."

". . . but he was right, you're not. There isn't an earth magician on record who could do what you did to the Cŵn Annwn. We just wanted to see how you would react and then Ty would have sent the hound back. Somehow you pulled the Cŵn Annwn's power out and left something different behind. So, Anomaly!" she said as if that was proof of everything.

A faint vibration passed through the table and I glanced outside the window to see if a storm was coming. The sky was clear. When I looked back, Daley had placed his hands flat on the table and was staring at me with a frown. I had the strange impression that the vibration was coming from him. "The three of you could use some time to process this. Peter can take you home. I'll call for someone to pick us up. Come to the house at noon tomorrow and our father will explain everything." It was a command, not an invitation "Go on. I'll take care of the bill." We were dismissed. Peter slid out of the booth and Lacey and I followed him.

I stopped. Daley might be completely hot in an authoritarian sort of way, but I had to ignore that because there was something I needed to know. "Since you seem to have all the answers, who was my mother? Who was Viviane Lynne?"

He considered me with stormy eyes that didn't trust me at all. "She was the Lady of the Lake. Viviane was a goddess."

Lightning streaked across the cloudless sky.

CHAPTER TEN

I woke early the next morning feeling agitated and restless. My night had been filled with dreams of being chased by the Cŵn Annwn through twisted trees while lightning hit the ground around me.

I decided to go for a quick run across the property to clear my head. Even though it was early, the farm hand everyone called Old Tom had already let the horses out. Two of them were munching on the grass near the fence in the back paddock. Doll and Galileo were chestnut-colored siblings and direct descendants of the farm's most famous horse, Northern Dancer. As I approached the fence, Doll cantered over to see if I'd brought a treat.

"Sorry, girl." I kept my distance. The horses sensed my fear and reacted to it with their teeth. Every attempt to learn to ride had ended one of two ways: on my backside in the dirt or begging Peter to get me down.

My nose twitched as I caught the scent of something funny underneath the usual horse and hay smell. I'd never been to the ocean, but it was what I imagined it smelled like: salty, sharp, and wet. Doll shook her head and backed away in a funny sideways movement. Galileo trotted towards us, snorting and huffing through his nostrils. They both seemed to be staring at something over my head.

I turned around. Windfield was set up on a grid with tree-lined laneways branching off from the main road that led to the front gate. My house was about twenty feet down the second of those laneways. The two closest guesthouses were on the third and not too far from where I stood. The buildings were neglected and sinister; the perfect place for an intruder to hide. Northern Dancer's bloodline was valuable property and even though the barns were locked down at night with a state of the art security system, Old Tom was always on the lookout for anyone trying to break in and get at one of the horses.

Mauve shot with grey prickled on the edges of my vision as it occurred to me that security systems might not be too useful against someone—or something—with magic.

I glanced back at the horses. Doll's eyes had widened until the whites showed. Peter had taught me the signs; Galileo was anxious, but Doll was afraid. Maybe they'd been spooked by a rabbit and were acting up to get attention.

Yeah, cuz thoroughbred racehorses are just neurotic that way.

I jogged over to the first house and tried the doorknob, but it was locked. The place was in pretty bad shape. These two guesthouses had always been hardly better than shacks and were used as accommodation for temporary workers back when things were thriving. The houses closer in quality to mine were on the far side of the property and had already been torn down to make way for the new subdivision.

Flaking paint dug into my palms as I leaned on the window sill to get a better look inside. A kitchenette ran along one wall and a table with one missing leg leaned against the other. There was no other furniture. Two closed doors led to a bedroom and a bathroom. The house was as deserted as it should be.

I decided to check on the second one, just in case. From the outside, it was identical to the first except for a triangle-shaped window set in the door a little above my eye level. Rising on my toes to look through, I leaned on the doorknob to prop myself up. When the knob twisted unexpectedly, I fell forward through the doorway and onto the wet carpet. Scrambling up, I started to gag at the smell, and then froze— all thoughts of mildew and mold and rotting things forgotten. Cold white veined in dank blue the color of a thrashing sea passed over my eyes.

Beside the imprints of my hands in the soggy carpet, and all around the room, were the distinct marks of paw prints.

The smell of the carpet didn't seem to bother Peter at all. Years of mucking out the horse stalls had probably burned off the first layer of cells in his nose.

"Why'd you come in here anyway?" he called through the open door.

"I told you, the horses were acting weird."

Peter came out onto the porch and looked down the path to where Doll and Galileo were again happily munching grass. He snorted, but didn't comment.

"There was a weird smell too," I added. He cocked an eyebrow at me and I amended the statement. "Weirder than that."

Peter crossed his arms and ran the thumbnail of his right hand up and down the groove between his bottom middle teeth, something he did when he was thinking and a habit both his mother and his dentist hated. Coming to a decision, he walked back into the house and kneeled down in the muck to measure one of the prints against his hand.

I stayed on the porch. "Should we tell your Dad or Old Tom?"

Peter shook his head as he stood and wiped his hands off on his jeans. "I don't want to pull them into this."

"What do you mean?"

"It might be something like that thing you killed, the Coowinanoon."

"Cŵn Annwn," I corrected, "and I'm not sure I killed it."

"Well it isn't a coyote or a stray dog; the prints are too big." He pointed to some smaller marks. "And it has six claws on each paw."

Breathing through my mouth to keep out the smell, I took a step inside. "That's weird, right?"

"Yup." Peter walked over to the kitchenette and opened a bottom cupboard, then quickly slammed it shut.

"What is it?"

"I think I found its lunch."

"What?"

"Raccoon."

"Recent?"

"From the amount of maggots in it, yeah. But something was chewing on it first."

We both turned and looked at the first closed door. Mrs. Larsen was a huge X-Files fan and used to say Peter and I were proof ESP really existed, but we just knew each other so well that sometimes saying things out loud wasn't necessary.

Peter stepped lightly across the soggy carpet and I squished after him. Twisting the doorknob carefully, he opened the door to a bedroom. It was empty. I caught the smell again—a whiff of salt air—and pointed to the bathroom door. Peter nodded and padded over to push it open. He stood there, staring.

"What? What is it?" As I approached, I tried to ignore the disgusting slip and slide of my running shoes on the carpet; it was like walking through sewage.

When I was ten, I went through a major Little Mermaid period—the original story, not the sappy cartoon. I collected all the storybook versions I could find and one of my favorites had an illustration of the Little Mermaid diving through waving kelp with her hair streaming out behind her. So I knew what I was looking at. Peter reached into the tub and pulled out something wet and slimy.

A long strand of rotting seaweed.

CHAPTER ELEVEN

Peter was pre-occupied and tense as we drove to the mansion. Except for a puzzled question about my now working air-conditioning which I dodged, we were silent. I didn't mind. It had taken over half an hour to shower off the stink of mildew and seaweed and my head hurt.

When we pulled into the driveway and parked, Lacey was waiting for us beside a rusty old hatchback. Her cheeks went bright pink when Peter gave her a quick hug.

Peter knocked on the front door and a middle-aged man opened it.

"Yes?"

"Mr. Taliesin?"

The man laughed, his tanned skin wrinkling into deep lines. "Heaven forbid, no. But I'll get him for you."

"We're actually here for Ty and Daley."

"Oh I see, the new recruits. C'mon in." The man disappeared down a hallway as we stepped inside.

Lacey frowned. "What did he mean by 'recruits'?"

I shrugged and looked around. The foyer was two stories high and the staircase in front of us swept up to the top floor at the back of the house. Muted paintings hung on the walls and niches displayed tasteful decorative items.

Lacey pointed up at a crystal and iron monstrosity. "Look at that chandelier! It must have cost thousands. This place is amazing."

I decided to refuse to be impressed. "It's boring if you ask me."

"It's a rental," a voice with a lilting accent agreed. A trim man with close-cut salt and pepper hair and a neat beard entered from a side hallway. "It was more the location than the house that attracted me."

Lacey gave the man her brightest smile. "The house is beautiful, Mr. Taliesin."

"Please, it is simply Taliesin. Daley apprised me of the details of your misadventure yesterday and I agreed that I should meet with you to explain as much as I can. I have some business to attend to first, but I have asked Rowan to escort you to the dining room where lunch is waiting." He gestured to the man who had greeted us at the door and now returned to the foyer. With a nod, Taliesin exited the same way he arrived.

"C'mon kids." Rowan waved us over with a friendly smile. "This way."

We followed him down the hall into a grand room where a table that could easily seat twenty stretched from the window to the entry. Tynan, Daley and Miko sat at the far end.

"Ah, here the miscreants are," Rowan announced genially. He gestured to a sideboard with serving dishes on it. "Fill up and take a seat."

We helped ourselves as Rowan led a discussion on everything from whether any of the movies out were worth the price of admission to if there was a chance the new Bachelorette would find love. We all relaxed except Daley. I could feel him watching me. I expected a flare of yellow or orange in response—or even the more complicated mix of scarlet and rose I was starting to feel whenever he was around—but there was nothing.

"If you are finished, I would ask that you accompany me to the study." Taliesin's quiet appearance at the doorway was unnerving; the man moved like a ghost. Rowan thanked us for our company and as he left, all the ease and warmth left with him.

We filed after Taliesin into another tasteful cream on cream room. He sat down behind a massive mahogany desk and we settled into the couch and chairs around the room. I chose an overstuffed armchair and regretted it as I sank into the cushions. Daley leaned against the wall with his arms folded.

I examined Taliesin. The man wore dark jeans and a white cotton shirt, but his clothing was so crisp and tailored that it whispered, not shouted, designer. I knew I was anxious—a strong enough emotion to usually inspire some color—but all I could sense along the edges of my sight was a deep indigo. Pain suddenly swelled in my temples and I wanted to run and hide from this quiet, terrifying man.

Rhiannon, listen to me! We cannot be seen! Hide in the shadows and be still and silent!

Mom's voice seemed to scream at me and I imagined myself grasping at wisps of misty blue until I finally managed to drag a few scraps around myself.

Miko pointed. "She's doing it again."

Taliesin frowned as his eyes flicked around the room. A haze passed over my eyes and the world went dim, but I couldn't hold onto it. Mom's color slipped away, and indigo—an oilier, denser blue—replaced it.

"And now she's back. See?" Miko's voice was triumphant.

Taliesin nodded. "Yes, I do now."

"Daley didn't believe me."

Daley made an impatient gesture. "I didn't say that."

"You did!"

Their voices hurt my head. "I'm right here. What exactly do you think I'm doing?"

Taliesin raised his hand and the room went quiet. "Yes, you are definitely here with us now, Miss Lynne, but I could not see you in the room even though I had been warned about your peculiar ability." He leaned forward and rested his chin on steepled fingers. "No spell? No incantation?"

I thought of Mom's voice and the words I heard her speaking in my head but decided not to mention it. "How would I even know how to do something like that?"

His shrug was the barest of movements. "There is a great deal of dangerous information to be had if you know where to search. The internet has changed everything, even that. You had no idea that you were essentially rendering yourself invisible?"

Something about the man put my back up and I didn't like admitting what I'd already guessed. "Maybe everyone needs to get their eyes checked."

Taliesin leaned back in his chair and regarded the others. "Well?"

Tynan brushed his hair away from his face and flashed me a shy smile. "I thought you might still be in the dining room."

Miko sat with her legs crossed on a small ottoman. "I couldn't see her—which should be impossible since I'm the glamour girl here—but I've been working on keeping track of her just in case."

Great, now I have a tiny harajuku stalker.

"Mr. Larsen?" Taliesin prompted.

Peter snorted. "I think I would have noticed if Rhi had a habit of turning invisible."

"Typical Protector," Miko said, smirking. "What about you, Lacey?"

Lacey hesitated before answering. "I could see her."

"So could I," Daley volunteered.

Taliesin nodded thoughtfully. "Interesting. Given their close relationship, Mr. Larsen is likely Rhiannon's bonded Protector and would be able to sense her presence whenever she was near. He might not notice that he was not actually seeing her with his eyes. Miss McInnis' lorelei blood must protect her from this particular glamour as well. But why you, my son? None of your abilities should protect you from such a spell and I thought you said that you had trouble finding her at the school."

Something in my stomach jumped as my eyes met Daley's, but then he shrugged and looked away. "I don't know."

Miko fidgeted and twisted one of her ponytails around her finger. "Let's not forget that Rhi can also see and hear the harp even without me wishing it."

Taliesin tapped his fingers once on the desk before responding. "Yes, 'curiouser and curiouser' as Alice in Wonderland would say. But perhaps I should first explain to our new friends what happened yesterday and what it meant."

Lacey stood and balled her fists on her hips. "I know what happened. It was just some dog attracted to the garbage at the park. Miko saw how freaked out we were and thought she'd have a little fun. I don't appreciate being messed with like that." The two girls glared at one another.

Taliesin gestured for Lacey to sit. "Miss McInnis, please." His tone was firm and she obeyed. "I wish I could let you remain in ignorance, but the fact that we have taken an interest in you will not have gone unnoticed by the spies who make it their business to trade in this kind of information. Knowledge is needed now for you to protect yourself from those who would seek to make a trophy out of one of even your very limited ability.

The expression on Lacey's face shifted to outrage as she realized she'd just been told she was basically a magical non-entity.

Peter wasn't convinced. "Right, so I'm some sort of a magical security guard, Lacey's popular because great-grandpa knocked up a mermaid, and everyone thinks Rhi can float away and disappear. Oh, and yeah, the woman who planted the friggin' tulips in our friggin' garden was the Lady of the Lake!" It was as close to swearing as I'd ever heard my best friend get and was proof of how upset he was.

It was my fault; I should have prepared him for magic. Taking a deep breath, I came clean. "There's some stuff I haven't told anyone yet. The day Mom died, I met a woman named Morgan who said she was Mom's sister. Then a guy called Thomas Redcap ate some of Mom's skin—but that's a normal thing for him," I hastened to add when I saw Peter's shocked expression. "When I fell and hit my head, I lost my memory of what happened for a while. But when I went to the lake to scatter Mom's ashes, a river goddess tried to kill me and Redcap saved me. He told me Mom wasn't my birth mother."

I turned to address Taliesin because I couldn't bear the look on Peter's face. Except for the silver-haired man and my colors, I'd never kept anything from him before. It was time to fess up about at least one of those.

"I see colors in my mind when I feel things, but I always thought it was a weird kind of synesthesia. When I saw the Cŵn Annwn's magic, I knew I was wrong, or at least, not all right. I took its power somehow—I'm not sure how. Peter and I found paw prints and a bathtub full of seaweed on his property, but I don't know if it has anything to do with the Cŵn Annwn." Sinking back down into the chair, I fingered the wheel charm on the bracelet under my sleeve as I stared at a spot on the floor.

"I thought I would be the one providing illumination today." Taliesin's voice sounded amused, but when I glanced up, his face was stern. "You and I will talk on this further, but for now I will be as succinct as you have been." He considered each one of us until he was sure he had our attention. "Parallel to our world, there exists a place of magic—the Grey Lands of Avalon. The lord of that land was called Cernunnos the horned god by the Celts, though both he and his land are known by different names in all the cultures of the world. His three sisters reigned with him: Morgana, Morgause, and Viviane."

Shocked pink striated with orange alarm ran across my sight.

Taliesin raised his hand before I could speak. "I know you have many questions. Let me finish and perhaps some will be answered. The abilities of Greylanders are heightened in this world of light and dark so different from their twilight home. They found their way here and became the creatures of our myths and legends. Morgause and Viviane were goddesses in many lands. Morgause was a seer. Cassandra of Troy was one incarnation; Andraste of the Celts was the last before her current one as the Seer of New York. Viviane chose the moon and water as her symbols—Diana, Hecate, Tethys—she was all of these and more." His face was sympathetic. "It was fitting for she was known to be cold and barren. When she appeared among the Celts—my people—she named herself the Lady of the Lake."

"The ancient tales of gods falling in love with mortals were based on truth. The mating of Greylanders and humans sometimes produced children of unprecedented skill. Our abilities may vary, but we call ourselves earth magicians for we are loyal to it. But one was born who was gifted by the earth with pure magic sprung directly from it—the Earth King—and his power rivaled that of the Lord of the Grey Lands. Cernunnos sent Morgana, his most beloved sister, to destroy the King."

Morgana. Morgan.

Taliesin sighed. "It is a sad story of all too human betrayal and suffering. Despite the Earth King being already married, he and Morgana fell in love at first meeting. They planned to conquer this world and the Grey Lands and rule both together. They almost succeeded. In the final battle, Cernunnos brought down the Earth King through treachery—not to death, but to an ageless sleep. The chaos that ensued led to the time we call the Dark Ages. Cernunnos created the Wall between our worlds to protect himself should the Earth King ever rise again."

The lilting tones of the man's voice sent a shiver down my spine. "I lead the earth magicians and those Greylanders stranded behind the Wall who have sworn loyalty to me. Together, we fight the ones who have no love for the world and have chosen to become monsters. We stand ready for the day the Earth King awakens, for he is a tyrant who cares nothing for the lives of those who follow him. And we stand ready to fight on a last front against Cernunnos, who will not be content to remain behind his Wall forever."

Only Peter was brave enough to break the silence that followed. "Rowan called us 'recruits'. If you expect us to fight against this 'Earth King', I think we deserve to know his name.'

Taliesin's voice was soft but his eyes were hard.

"King Arthur of Camelot."

CHAPTER TWELVE

A lot of shouting followed the announcement that the great enemy of the world was King Arthur. Peter had a hard time accepting that the character he'd identified with in movies and novels was a world-conquering dictator.

"Enough!" Taliesin's shout brought immediate silence.

Wow. He could do Broadway with that thing.

"I understand this is difficult for you to believe. The legend of the great King Arthur and his noble knights of the round table is a powerful one. Indeed, much of it is true." He turned away to gaze out the window. "Whatever the blindness of his vision, Arthur was a true believer. He saw Morgana and those of her kind as victims of an evil overlord who oppressed his people and kept them in twilight. He was not entirely wrong. Arthur believed his power was a sign from God that he was to be the liberator of both Avalon and this world, whether the people in it wanted his liberation or not. I have set my life in opposition to his quest. I was a bard—a singer of songs and writer of poetry—and I was a warrior too, but I never expected to be anything but human. Yet the earth magic claimed me and so I must continue in life until it frees me."

Taliesin bowed his head. "We were friends once, brothers. I would have followed him to the steps of hell. I suppose I did. I was with him and his army when he attempted to invade the Grey Lands. Only eight of us returned. I saw then that the lives of men, especially those of no magic, meant little to Arthur. I chose a different path after that day."

"Sir, are you saying you're a couple of thousand years old?" Lacey's voice was respectful but disbelieving.

An unreadable expression flickered over Taliesin's face. "Most accounts of my birth give it as 534 B.C., but I was born a couple of hundred years before. I changed my name when it became clear I would not age and die naturally with the rest of my kin. Taliesin is the name under which I gained the notoriety I bear now, but last August the third was the two thousand, five hundred and twenty-second birthday of a Welsh baby named Gwion Bach."

"As to what you believe, Miss McInnis, after today it will be none of my concern. I am gathering an army. The hint of magic in your blood will be useful to you in all your pursuits. You are not, however, useful to me. Rowan will give you something we call a fith-fath which will allow you to mask your supernatural side if you feel threatened. There are also herbs and charms you can place around your home as a protection. We will give you the instructions, and as long as you are vigilant, you will be as safe as anyone else is in this world and I will have discharged my duty towards you."

"That's it?" she squeaked. "You expect me to go home, scatter a few herbs around, and just forget about everything?" Peter and I looked at each other. We knew Lacey wouldn't accept being so low on the food chain easily.

Taliesin sat back down behind the desk. "What would you have from me? Your abilities are slight and I need warriors not schoolgirls."

Lacey folded her arms across her chest. "Miko said I could become a witch."

Miko rolled her eyes. "I thought you didn't believe any of this?"

"Of course I do." Lacey looked around the room. "OK, do you honestly think I'm so stupid that I can't see what's right in front of my face?"

I shook my head. "You ran away before the Cŵn Annwn showed itself."

"I came back. Not all the way, but I could still see what happened. Just like I can always see you. I figured out a long time ago there was something weird about how no one except me ever seemed to notice you. I didn't know it was magic, but I knew it was something. It was another good reason to try to keep you away from . . ." she broke off and flushed as she glanced at Peter.

Taliesin's voice hardened. "I am sorry, Miss McInnis, but I have nothing else to offer you. I have enough blood on my hands. I will not add yours."

"What about me and Rhi?" Peter asked.

It was Daley who answered. "Being a Protector makes you a born warrior which is why you've always been so good at sports. If you join us, we can train you to access physical and mental abilities you can't even imagine now."

For a moment, Peter looked interested, but then he frowned. "What about college? My parents? I can't just leave them and take off."

Daley glanced at his father and they shared a moment of silent communication before he continued. "We can work around that for now. Taliesin is the hub, but the spokes of his army spread out over the entire earth. You will need to spend some time training with us, but then you can go home. All we ask is that if Arthur is awakened, you'll join us when we call."

I felt a chill as Peter crossed his arms and ran his thumbnail up and down the groove between his teeth. He was considering it. The comic book loving, wannabe superhero inside him could never turn down such an opportunity.

"And me?" I asked.

"You are a mystery that we must get to the bottom of," Taliesin replied. "Mr. Larsen and Miss McInnis may return to their homes, but for the moment, you will stay here with us."

I stood in alarm, but no colors answered my call. "What do you mean 'stay here'?"

"You will be our guest until I can determine the nature of your abilities and if you are a threat to our cause."

Peter was on his feet now too. "That's ridiculous! How could Rhi possibly be any kind of a threat?"

"Really?" Miko drawled. "And I suppose she didn't suck the power out of a supernatural watchdog? She's a mystery and mysteries are *always* dangerous."

"You can't keep me here against my will," I said.

Tynan spoke up. "Untrained abilities are dangerous. Our father can help you. When he found me, I had no memories of my past and my abilities were erratic."

"*Are* erratic," Miko muttered under her breath.

My breath caught at the hostile expression that flickered over his features. "I knew I needed to earn his trust. Dad is the only one standing between the world and scarier things than the Cŵn Annwn."

Daley's eyes seemed to flash with light. "Not to mention you were raised by the high priestess of our enemy. Viviane was as cold-hearted as her moon and either she was lying, or you're lying about being her daughter. That's enough reason for us to be careful."

"Enough." Taliesin's tone was mild, but Daley looked down and was silent. Taliesin's power was in the beautiful tones of his voice and the way everyone listened and obeyed. I could feel it when he turned his attention back to me.

"Viviane's purposes were always unfathomable. She gave Excalibur to Arthur. Later, she took it from him and aided his betrayer, yet she never returned to her place by her brother's side. Whatever her true aim, by abandoning Arthur and his people, she lost the worship which her power had become tied to and at last died a mortal death, as you were witness to. I admit that I neither liked nor trusted Viviane. There seemed to be no love in her for either humankind or Greylanders so why would she take you in, a human child?"

I couldn't answer that, but I didn't want to stay here. I wondered if I could see Taliesin's power and maybe do something about it. I closed my eyes and tried, but oily indigo lapped at the edges of my mind like waves at the shore.

It's some kind of spell.

I opened my eyes in shock. "What have you done to me?" Peter jumped to my side, but I pushed past him to confront Taliesin. "You've done something to me! I can see it!"

Tynan stood and moved towards me, but Peter stepped between us with his fists raised. Daley edged closer to his father in case Peter decided to strike in that direction.

"Careful," Miko murmured. "Protector, remember?"

"I'm not going to hurt Rhiannon," Daley said. "None of us are."

I was shaking. "What are you doing to me right now then?"

When Taliesin spoke, his voice was soothing and I could see the muscles in Peter's shoulders relax a little. "This is one of my abilities: to bind power temporarily. I am holding yours, whatever their true nature, just out of your reach. No lasting harm will come of it."

"All I can see is indigo blue trying to cover me."

He raised an eyebrow. "How interesting. Just as with the Cŵn Annwn, you are seeing the manifestation of my power as color." Taliesin sat back with a sigh. "Give me a show of good faith. Help me to trust you and you will be free to leave and never return if you so wish."

"And if I don't co-operate?"

His smile was wintry. "Then I may be forced to conclude that you are not to be trusted."

CHAPTER THIRTEEN

Taliesin's message was clear: stay and submit or else.

I shared a look with Peter and he stepped back and was in control of himself again. "OK, I'll do it, but I'm going to need some stuff if you want me to stay here tonight."

"Great," Tynan said eagerly. "I'll go with Peter to your place. He can get what you need."

"Thanks, but I need some personal items in my purse now, actually. It's in my car." Tynan blushed as I gave him the keys from my jeans pocket. Even barely alluding to feminine products was enough to psych out a teenage boy. I knew Daley was watching so I kept my face blank and innocent.

"It is settled then," Taliesin declared. "Miss McInnis will wait in the dining room for the fith-fath to be prepared for her and Daley will give Mr. Larsen a greater introduction to our history and methods. Rowan will escort Miss Lynne to her room." He turned to contemplate the view out the window. It was our cue to go.

Rowan had appeared at the doorway as if summoned by silent command. He gave me a rueful smile. "OK there, kiddo?"

"Just peachy," I said under my breath as I followed him out of the room and down the hall. Daley gave me a look that promised he would find out all my secrets as he ushered Lacey and Peter back into the dining room.

"It's going to be all right," Rowan assured me. He'd known all along how this was going to play out and I hated him a little for making me like him so much at lunch.

I paused on the first step of the staircase. "What's 'all right' about being kept here against my will?"

The man grimaced. "Don't think of it like that. Taliesin needs to be careful, that's all. He carries the weight and responsibility of protecting countless lives."

"Sure, I get it. The leader of a magical army that's supposed to protect us from King Arthur is afraid of a seventeen year old girl." Rowan was saved from replying by Tynan bounding up to us and delivering my purse.

"Thanks." I took a quick look inside to make sure he hadn't gone through it, but the contents were intact.

Tynan grabbed my hand and pulled me up the stairs. "Rhi's a guest, not a prisoner. I'll take her to her room." I followed Tynan as Rowan watched us from the foyer.

"Here," Tynan said, pushing open the door to the first room down the hall off the landing, "this is one of the nicest." It was a bedroom. A bit of relief somewhere in all the cream on cream would have been nice, but a large window showed the forest behind the house and the king-sized bed looked soft enough to accidentally suffocate in.

"I'll just be a minute." I brandished my purse and Tynan blushed again.

The bathroom was luxurious. Dropping my purse on the marble vanity, I pulled out my phone and the card from Mom's room.

Bingo.

Tynan was sitting on the bed waiting for me when I came out. "Isn't the bathroom great? It's almost as big as the one in Dad's room. We've had to camp out and use outhouses and latrines before, so this place is great. And the beds are . . ."

"Great?" I interrupted, but I smiled to take the sting out of it.

Tynan laughed. "Yeah." He threw himself back onto the bed. "C'mon, try it." I'd almost forgotten how handsome he was behind those shaggy bangs.

Playing along, I climbed into the space beside him and sank deep into the soft covers. It really did feel . . . great.

Tynan propped himself up on one elbow. "Listen, I'll talk to Dad. He's not usually so cautious. We lost someone recently and he blames himself. We'll sort it out and then you can go home, I promise." I noticed how his voice had changed, how much older he sounded, and how the almost pathological shyness he'd exhibited was gone.

I was suddenly aware of how close we were. I could see the faint line of gold around the brown of his eyes and he smelled like sugar and light sweat. His eyes widened and without warning, he leaned down to kiss me.

Whoa! Down boy!

Pushing myself away with my heels, I banged into the headboard as Tynan fumbled awkwardly to keep from falling on me. As I grabbed at the pillows to prop myself upright, a strange expression crossed his face, dark and ugly.

"I hope I'm not interrupting anything." Miko stood in the doorway, her leather bag under her arm and a grin on her face. Tynan got off the bed while I sat up quickly.

"Relax." She closed the door and then bounced onto the bed in front of me. "Rowan didn't like the idea of you two in here alone so I volunteered to act as chaperone, but don't let me stop you. If Taliesin's going to go all prison warden on you, you might as well have some fun."

Watching him from the corner of my eye, I could see that Tynan now looked as embarrassed as I felt. He'd gone back to hanging his head and letting his hair hide his eyes, but his cheeks were red. The best thing to do was to not make a big deal out of it. I pointed at the bag I'd seen Miko carrying around school. "What's that?"

She pulled out the harp. "I thought it was time you two were properly introduced. Rhi, meet the harp of Binnorie." The instrument had twisted knots carved all over the sound box and was painted in gold.

Tynan sat back down beside me. "Did Dad say you could do this?"

Miko's eyes narrowed. "I'm Binnorie's keeper, not Taliesin. Here." She pushed the harp into my hands.

Startled, I nearly dropped it; it was heavier than I expected.

"Close your eyes," Miko said. Triggered by those familiar words, I obeyed.

Thunder shook the ground and my eyes flashed open, but the world around me had changed. I should have been frightened, but I felt calm and distant, as if I were half asleep. I was standing on the banks of a wide river surrounded by misty hills. I heard a sound and turned. Beside me, two girls in long, richly embroidered gowns were arguing. They were both beautiful; one with dark curls bouncing on her shoulders and the other with a cascade of bright hair falling to her waist. In a sudden violent movement, the dark haired girl pushed the other one into the river. She thrashed and struggled to stay afloat, but the weight of her gown and hair kept pulling her under. Sister, the drowning girl cried as she slipped under one last time and was gone.

Another clap of thunder. The river had become a shallow stream and the girl's body had washed up on the shore. White bones showed through white flesh and I was grateful her tattered gown and golden hair hid most of what was left of her from sight. A man on horseback passed by on the road and when he saw the lovely ruin by the water, he dismounted and wept over it. Retrieving a knife from his saddlebag, he went to work on the body, severing bones and shearing hair.

I was reminded of L'Inconnue de la Seine and the worship of beautiful dead things in the water.

The thunder came again and I was now in a crowded hall where a young couple sat at the head table, whispering to one another and stealing quick kisses. It was a wedding celebration. Beside me was the man who had found the body of the girl and in his hands he held a golden harp.

I walked with him as he approached the bride and groom. The harper placed the harp on the table and sweet music sprang from it entwined with a voice which pierced my soul. It sang of two sisters who loved the same man, but he loved the younger one and her golden hair. It sang of how they walked by the river and how the jealous sister pushed the other one in. It sang of the harper who wept over the body of the drowned girl and then used her bones and hair to make a golden harp.

And then the harp accused the young bride in the hall of murdering her sister Binnorie and marrying Binnorie's beloved.

No clap of thunder, just a slow fade of the scene as I closed my eyes in the past and opened them in the present.

I took an unsteady breath. "What *was* that?"

Miko took the harp from my nerveless fingers and put it back in her bag. "You saw?" I nodded. "The harper carved the frame of the harp from Binnorie's breastbone and made the tuning pegs from her fingers and the strings from her hair. The harp sang the truth of how Binnorie died and Binnorie's sister was burned at the stake by the same husband she stole. I think after that the harp became obsessed with justice and uncovering hidden truths. I think it helps us find people with talent because they're hidden too, but it's not all-knowing and it does send us down some completely useless roads sometimes. Because of the sister's betrayal, it took me a while to earn the harp's trust, but it doesn't trust men at all. It hasn't forgotten that Binnorie's beloved transferred his affections to her sister after Binnorie's death."

"Is her spirit in the harp?" I was horrified at the thought.

Miko shrugged. "Don't know, but Binnorie must have had powerful earth magic for her bones and hair to still be alive with it even after her death. Too bad she didn't discover that before her sister murdered her."

I shivered. "Where did you find it?"

"It called to me. It led me to one of those old castles in England that's open to the public. The harp was sitting on a bookshelf, right out in the open, but no one seemed to see it. I don't know why it chose me, but I became its keeper."

I crossed my arms. "And now you use it to kidnap people."

Miko laughed. "Nope, you're the first."

Tynan wasn't amused. "Stop it, Miko. No one's being kidnapped."

"Really, Ty? Taliesin's paranoid and you know it. I mean, I agree we need to get to the bottom of things, but we could try asking the harp instead of locking Rhi up in a tower like Rapunzel. Now that we've introduced them, we could do it right now."

Tynan sat back down on the bed. "No. Not unless Dad says we can."

I wasn't sure I wanted to get any better acquainted with Binnorie, but I asked anyway, "If the harp is so good at finding truth, why would he say no?"

Miko grimaced. "He doesn't trust it. Or me."

"Why not?"

Miko lay back on the bed and pretended to inspect the black polish on her nails.

"It's the whole fairy thing," Tynan explained when Miko didn't respond.

I laughed and then stopped when I saw he was serious.

Time for a little payback.

"You're a fairy? Don't fairies have wings and put their hair up in ballet buns and need little children to clap for them or they die?"

With a sigh, Miko pushed herself up on her elbows and glared at me. "OK, listen up, cuz I'm not repeating it. Mom was a fairy—or a *sidhe* as you better call them whenever über Celt Taliesin is around—and Dad was human. He owned a ritzy department store in Kyoto—still does—and she was the model-slash-girlfriend of a well-known British lingerie designer. Did you know half the models in the world are at least part sidhe? Fairies can retract their wings into their bodies, and who else could look as good in thongs and pushup bras? Anyway, Dad was rich and kind of hot stuff so they hooked up. Mom got pregnant and I ended up with some fairy powers but no wings—genetics are a bitch. As soon as I was born, she dumped me on Dad and took off. Fairies are beautiful, *obviously*, but also lazy, cruel, and generally stupid. Dad spent a lot of time beating that out of me—literally—so when the harp called, I left and never looked back. Fairy powers are all about glamour and deceit and that makes me good at knowing the truth from a lie and not so good at getting people to trust me."

Tynan put his arm around the girl's shoulders. "I trust you, Meek."

Miko shook him off and rolled her eyes again. "Because you're an idiot who can't even remember the first fifteen years of his life. If you did, maybe you'd know better."

"Wait," I interrupted, "you were serious about that?' When Tynan flushed, I regretted asking.

"When Taliesin found him in New York, he was living on the street like an animal. He didn't even know his own name and his abilities were all over the place."

Tynan's face had gone bright red, but Miko was about as sensitive as a wooden spoon. "What about Daley?" I asked to change the subject. I didn't expect Miko to fall back on the bed laughing in response.

"Don't," Tynan warned. "He'll kill you if he finds out you told her."

"Oh, who cares!" She flipped over and looked at me with a wicked smile. "It's too funny to not share. Daley's been with Taliesin the longest and he's definitely teacher's pet. I've never seen anyone take Daley down, not even in practice, and he would have more control over the magic side of his abilities if he just tried harder to master it. But back then, nobody would tell me anything about him and even the harp was silent."

"The harp doesn't like Daley," Tynan added.

"The harp is flammable, idiot. Can you blame it? Anyway, like I said, Daley was a mystery so I kept my eye on him."

"He says you stalked him."

"Whatever. I was following him one day when the weather turned bad and then it happened . . ."

"What?" I asked, intrigued.

"Daley was hit by lightning."

"Was he hurt?"

"Nope."

"I don't get it."

Miko paused for dramatic effect. "He caught it." She frowned. "So technically, I guess he wasn't actually hit by the lightning." She was on her knees now and bouncing on the bed. "C'mon, it's no fun unless you guess. I'll give you some clues: lightning, big hammer, imagine Daley with long hair and a beard . . ."

"You can't be serious."

"Daley is 'The Mighty Thor'!" Miko fell back on the bed as she exploded into a fit of giggles.

"He's not Thor," Tynan said and then frowned and shook his bangs out of his eyes. "Except, in a way, he kind of is."

I shook my head. "What?"

"Daley is descended from the Greylander who came here and used his power over the weather to make himself the god of thunder. The people in the North called him Thor, but he had names in other places—Summanus, Tlaloc, Thunderbird—it was all the same guy. The old gods did that all the time. To the Celts he was Taranis."

Miko snorted. "And because Taliesin is like a billion years old and still thinks Britain is the center of the universe, we all use the Celtic names even though half of those are the Roman versions that got written down. But don't try telling Tal that. Practically all of the earth magicians alive follow him, so it's become a 'thing'." She air quoted.

Tynan shrugged. "It would be too confusing to use all the different names. Most of the old gods are gone anyway."

"They died?" I asked. "Isn't immortality the definition of a god?"

"They lost their powers. None of them were probably truly immortal, except maybe Cernunnos, but thousands of years can feel like it. Without their powers, most died sooner rather than later. A few still hold on. Becoming a god is tricky. When people worship you, it enhances and increases your power. But when the people who worshipped you stop or die off . . ."

"The power dies too?" I jumped to the logical conclusion.

"And not just the new power, but the amount you were born with too. It all gets mixed up together. That's what happened to Viviane, I mean, your mom."

I thought of how quickly the sickness came on and how her organs shut down one by one. "No one's been worshipping her for a long time. Why did it happen now?"

He shrugged and brushed his hair back. "Viviane was once incredibly powerful, but to you she seemed like an ordinary person. The Lady of the Lake was never seen again after

Arthur was defeated. She'd probably been dying for years and it finally caught up with her."

I felt sick as Tynan plowed on. "I don't know if Taranis is dead or not, but Daley's the first person in three thousand years to inherit the same abilities. Daley's parents adopted him, so no one knows which one of his ancestors Taranis hooked up with. He's a Protector too."

Miko grabbed the blanket at the end of the bed and wrapped it around her shoulders, striking a pose. "Well I'm going to keep calling him Thor. I bought him a cape last Christmas but he never wears it. Maybe I should get him a helmet this year."

Tynan tossed a pillow at her head which she ducked. "Maybe you should stop teasing him about it." It made me think of Peter.

"So Daley's like Peter?" I asked.

"Sort of. He's your bonded Protector. You don't know what that means yet, but he'd die to protect you."

"I'd do the same for him. He's my best friend."

Tynan shook his head. "It's not the same. You can *choose* to do it, but Peter *has* to do it. He'll protect you even if it means letting someone else he loves get hurt. Daley's different. Taranis wasn't just the god of thunder. There are ancient references to his powers that no one understands. His symbol was a chariot wheel with eight spokes."

My breath caught. The little charm tucked under my sleeve also had eight spokes. I pushed the bracelet a little farther up my wrist. For some reason, I didn't want anyone to see it.

"The wheel is a symbol of fate. Dad thinks part of Daley's inheritance is the responsibility to be a judge over the gods, to decide their fate. I don't know what that means, but we all get

pretty big guilt trips from him whenever one of us screws up."
Tynan laughed but there was an edge to it.

Miko was watching him. "Daley's a bully sometimes, but even I know he loves you, Ty." She paused and bit her lip. "More than anyone else alive on earth."

Tynan looked up and Miko shrugged and gave him a funny smile.

I think I'm missing something.

She glanced at me. "Daley's completely full of it sometimes, but he's as hard on himself as he is on everyone else. Taliesin plans for him to fill the void when Arthur is defeated once and for all. "

"Don't ever say that. There's only one Earth King." Tynan's voice was harsh.

Miko frowned. "Maybe. And maybe not. I do know Daley doesn't want to be the judge of the gods."

I didn't understand. "But you said the gods are all dead or powerless now."

Miko slipped off the bed and readjusted her ponytails in the mirror over the dresser. "That's the old gods. There are still gods on earth. Gods who can speak to harps, command armies, take power from a Cŵn Annwn . . ."

Tynan's eyes were sad. "We're the gods Dad believes Daley is destined to judge."

CHAPTER FOURTEEN

"Us?"

"Yup." Miko pulled out some eyeliner from her bag and began thickening and winging the black lines around her eyes. "But what happens when the gods go to war and judging one magic user means betraying another, or protecting a human means ignoring one of his own kind? Rowan started a bet that *Lord Thor's* mind won't be able to handle it and he'll go berserk and kill us all." She smirked. "I may have let that slip one day when Daley was being particularly annoying."

Tynan brushed my hand with his. I tried not to pull away.

"Daley's always searching through old books and checking out ancient sites where Taranis was worshipped to see if he can find out anything about what he's supposed to do with his power."

Miko threw her eyeliner down on the dresser. "And maybe Daley should decide for himself. Just because some moldy old book or a scratching on a pillar in a field tells him something, it doesn't mean he has to do it."

Tynan looked down so his hair fell over his cheeks and I couldn't see his eyes. "Fate is fate. You can't escape it.

Maybe it's better to know who you're supposed to be, even if you don't like it."

I thought about that for a moment. "I don't believe in fate," I decided.

Miko bounced back on the bed. "Me neither. I say, if all Daley wants to do with his power is roast hotdogs with it, then why not?"

All this talk about Daley conjured images in my mind—powerful images that stirred something inside me more deeply than Tynan's quick kiss had.

The front door slammed. There were voices and then one rose above them all.

"You can produce the girl now or my men will go and search for her, and they don't play so nice with things like Italian leather furniture and fancy ceramic doodads. Or doors. You'll lose your security deposit for sure, Taliesin." This was said in an English accent so broad it was almost comical and followed by a booming laugh I could somehow feel as well as hear.

That's my cue.

"Sorry guys. You should try to remember to get rid of any cell phones the next time you kidnap someone." I grabbed my purse and walked out the door.

"Ah, this must be Miss Lynne." The man at the bottom of the stairs was an impressive sight. Tall and broad shouldered, he wore a dark green suit accented by the triangle of a handkerchief in a brighter green in the breast pocket. His beard was full and bushy, and the tawny red hair spilling onto his shoulders was as masculine as the mane of a lion. The man stood in the center of a tableau that included Peter, Lacey, and two other bearded men on one side, and Rowan, Daley, and Taliesin on the other.

"Mr. Goodfellow?" I asked as I came down the stairs. Miko and Tynan had caught up, but I ignored Tynan's hand brushing my arm as if to stop me.

Up close, I could see that the man's eyes were also bright green, and it was a sprig of holly in his pocket. Drops of moisture like dew clung to his hair and beard, but the day was dry and sunny.

"Of course, my dear, I came as soon as I received your message. Viviane told me you might be in touch." His face became serious. "The world is darker with her passing."

"Thank you."

Pulling out a card from the inside pocket of his jacket, Goodfellow offered it to Taliesin but the bard waved it away with a tight smile. "Do not mock me, Silvanus. I know who you are, though I have only had dealings with your cousins."

"Yes, you and your kind make quite free use of my kin. But call me Robin Goodfellow, Bard. The name Silvanus died with the Romans."

"And I thought the Lord of the Forest no longer ventured onto the Paths to visit the human world."

Goodfellow shrugged. "True. You and your earth magicians have bound my kin to ferry your asses to and fro 'round the world, but I've eluded being pulled into this little *jihad* you and Morgan are working your way up to. That doesn't mean I've given up all care for what happens in the wider world outside the Greenwood."

Daley and Rowan had been watching the exchange with confused looks on their faces, but Rowan seemed to suddenly understand something and stepped forward. "Lord Forest," he said, bowing from the waist.

"It's just a Path guide, Rowan . . . ," Daley said and then his eyes widened. "Are you saying this is *the* Green Man?"

"The Green Man, Silvanus, Jack in the Green, the Green Knight, Robin Goodfellow, even Robin Hood—they are all his names," Rowan replied reverently. "He is the Lord of the Forest and the Keeper of the Paths." One glance at Peter and I could see he was almost overcome by the thought he was standing in the same room as Robin Hood. I wasn't so enthusiastic.

Couldn't Mom have a nice, normal, human friend I could rely on instead of another addition to the freak show?

Robin Goodfellow scratched at his beard, but he looked pleased. "It's nice to be recognized. As for my younger kin, you may call them 'guides' if you wish." He glared at Daley. "But remember they serve at my discretion and allowance."

"Take care, Lord Forest." Taliesin's voice was quiet, but I could hear the warning in it. Goodfellow seemed to shrink a little.

I'm glad I'm not the only one who thinks Taliesin's one scary dude.

The so-called Green Man gestured towards me. "Viviane asked me to come if ever Miss Lynne needed me. Miss Lynne called, so she's leaving with me, end of argument."

Daley was unimpressed. "Do you think you can take her if we don't want you to?" Either my colors were coming back or there were actual sparks of static electricity dancing in Daley's hair. Goodfellow flinched.

Wood doesn't like fire.

Taliesin put his hand on Daley's shoulder. "Easy, son. There is no need for us to be at odds. Miss Lynne has formed the impression she is being held here against her will and I apologize for that unfortunate misunderstanding. I am merely concerned for both her safety and the safety of others until she has greater knowledge and control concerning her abilities."

I'd had enough. "I've been around for nearly eighteen years and haven't managed to kill anyone yet, you know."

"For nearly eighteen years you were hidden in the dark of the moon," Taliesin replied. He meant Mom and whatever she'd done to me with that misty blue.

Taliesin crossed the floor to stand in front of me. He wasn't tall and we were almost eye to eye. "If you are no enemy to us, then I am no enemy to you. I will help you understand who and what you are and you will be free to choose your own path and destiny as long as it does not threaten mine."

"I want to go home," I insisted stubbornly.

"Will you at least return so we may investigate this ability of yours? Will you give us a chance to prove that we, at least, mean no harm?"

I gave in. "I could come with Peter after school on Monday."

Peter cleared his throat. "Sorry Rhi, but I'm staying for a few days."

"What? Why?"

"There are other Protectors here. They're out on patrol right now, but I'll meet them when they get back. This might be my one chance to learn about what I am." His eyes pleaded with me to understand.

I knew if I insisted, I could probably get Peter to come home with me, but would that be abusing the bond between us? Would I be yanking on his Protector chain or the friend one?

"What are you going to tell your mom and dad?"

"Early morning practices, crashing with one of the guys—it'll be easy."

I nodded and the relief on his face confirmed my suspicion that I could have made it difficult for him to go against me.

"I'll cover for you with your parents, but what about school?"

Lacey had been uncharacteristically quiet till now. "I've got it," she said. "If I take in a note to the office saying Peter has mono or something, they'll never question the signature." She was right. The staff loved Lacey and would just be happy the most popular boy and the most popular girl were back together. Peter thanked her, but for once, Lacey didn't respond to his attention.

Maybe it bums her out to know people only love her because she has lorelei blood in her veins.

Goodfellow clapped his hands together. "Then it's settled. I will escort Miss Lynne to her car. If she wants to come back of her own free will later then that's her business."

"Will you return then?" Taliesin asked.

I tried not to hesitate. "I'll come on Monday after school."

Taliesin nodded once to me and once to Goodfellow before turning and walking away. His footsteps made no sound.

"The bard preserves his skills I see," The Green Man commented. "Many a time he once padded through my forests, as silent as the wind." He glared at Daley and his electrified hair. "Now he contents himself with using my kin like pack mules to deliver himself through the Paths of the world."

Rowan cleared his throat. "Lord Forest, you know that's not strictly true. They are not your Paths to control."

Goodfellow grunted and lifted one shaggy eyebrow. "Are they not? Without me and mine, you'd be lost if you tried to walk them. The Paths are the ghosts of the forests of the world, and only those of my kind are truly welcomed by them. Remember that, Druid, the next time you order yourself up a Guide."

"Yes, my lord," Rowan murmured, bowing from the waist.

I gasped and turned to Rowan in panic. "Wait! Get Taliesin back! He left that indigo inside me."

"It's OK, kiddo. I'm the one who's been maintaining it. A binding dissipates quickly. To slow it down, I channeled it into the wood frame of the house. I'll remove it now."

Goodfellow chuckled. "You can take the druid out of the forest, but it seems you can't take the forest completely out of the druid."

Rowan made a complicated gesture with his right hand. Indigo cleared from my vision like a fog lifting, but a confusing mash-up of colors replaced it and blinded me for a moment. When I looked at Goodfellow, I thought I saw colors surrounding him: emerald, moss, and sage.

He motioned to the door and we all followed him outside. His men walked away into the trees on the one side of the property, but before I could ask where they were going, I had to jump out of the way as Lacey got in her car and sped off in a squeal of tires.

Peter pulled me aside. "Are you going to be OK?"

I forced myself to smile. "Of course I will. Go on. Go play with your new friends." He ruffled my hair before walking back to the house. The door was still open and I could see Miko sitting on the stairs playing with her hair. Daley stood on the porch looking, well, thunderous was the best way to put it. Tynan joined him and gave a small wave, but I turned away without responding. I would have to sort out how I felt about what happened when I didn't feel like I was going to hurl.

Following Goodfellow to my car, I nearly ran straight into his broad back when he stopped abruptly. He sniffed the air and then I smelled it too: the briny odor of seaweed. In all the drama, I'd forgotten about what Peter and I had discovered.

"Take care, Miss Lynne." Goodfellow shook his head and sniffed again. "Something may be hunting you." After that horrifying statement, he smiled and plucked the holly out of his pocket. The red berries gleamed against the greenish tint of his skin. "Place this over your door. Holly is a symbol of life, but its sign was a spear; it will keep most unwanted things from entering. Once upon a time, maidens would put it under their pillows in the hopes of dreaming of the man they would marry, but the holly may also bring dreams of another kind and it's wise to pay attention."

I took it, careful to not catch my fingers on the prickly tips of the leaves. "Thank you for helping me out."

He raised a shaggy eyebrow. "I've watched Gwion Bach since he was a child. *Taliesin* he calls himself now. He has power and even one such as myself should be careful not to anger him, but still, he's a pompous ass, isn't he?"

I nearly choked on my own spit as I laughed, even though a pounding whirl of colors was the price and I had to lean against the car to steady myself.

Goodfellow handed me another one of his cards with an address scribbled on the back. "Come and see me tomorrow around noon. I have something for you from Viviane." When I looked at him in surprise, he shook his head and didn't elaborate. In an old-fashioned gesture, he held my hand to help me into my car and then closed the door behind me. Then he walked into the trees and disappeared from sight. I tried to see where he went, but the forest had swallowed him whole.

I placed the card and the holly on the passenger seat and gunned it out of the driveway without waiting to see if anyone was still watching from the house. If I thought too hard about colors and magic and things hunting me, I would never have the courage to go home, but I'd made too much of a fuss about leaving to just turn around and admit I was afraid to go.

As I drove, my returning colors grew bolder. I'd always been able to see them and still see the world normally, but they were more tangible now, as if they hung in the air in front of me. My head hurt. Somehow I made it home and got to the bathroom before I vomited violently. Falling onto my bed, I collapsed into sleep, but color followed me even there.

CHAPTER FIFTEEN

Maybe it was because of the holly, but the nightmare was subtly different. I looked up from the warm embrace of the woman who carried me and saw a young man following us, though the light was too dim to make out his features clearly. The woman stopped and turned to speak to him, but I couldn't hear the words; the dream had always been silent except for the sound of her heart and my own breathing. She began walking with increased urgency and so did the young man though he kept his distance. With a familiar gesture, he brushed long hair out of his eyes.

I woke with a start.

It's just a dream. People see crazy things in dreams.

I could hear the drizzle of rain falling on the roof and the light filtering through the blinds was grim. Reaching for the glass of water and bottle of acetaminophen on my bedside table, I swallowed a couple of pills and closed my eyes until my headache receded.

After I showered and dressed, I decided to go to the bakery. It was a little bit of a drive, but it was the only place local that sold French *macarons*. When Peter and his parents went to church—they were heavily involved in their local congregation—Mom would never let me go with them. She would go to the bakery and get a box of *macarons*—jewel colored meringues shaped like UFOs with jam or cream in the center. I thought it was our special ritual, but maybe she was just pawning me off with a treat to keep me from wanting to go with them.

I suppose it's reasonable that a god might not want her kid to spend her Sundays learning about a rival one.

As I left the house, I checked the sprig of holly to make sure it was still wedged into the loose piece of siding above the door. Even after a chilly night, it was fresh and green.

The bakery was quieter than usual because of the rain and only one of the tables was occupied. I breathed in the sweet smell of sugar. Ordering a dozen *macarons* in raspberry, pistachio, and salted caramel, I promised myself I would save some for later, but knew I'd end up eating them all before lunch.

As I waited for my order to be boxed, I realized the group sitting at the table was watching me. I wasn't used to people paying attention to me yet and mauve discomfort filled me. When the waitress handed me my change, I rushed out of the café, fumbling in my pocket for my keys.

"What's your hurry?"

Startled, I dropped the keys on the pavement as a woman walked around me. She bent down to pick them up and held them in front of my face. I snatched them back and shoved them in my pocket.

We stared at each other. The woman's skin was pale and drops of moisture clung to the fiery red strands that had escaped from the elaborate braid draped over her shoulder.

Around her neck she wore a thick gold choker open at the center and engraved with strange symbols. I blinked first; the rain had turned to a fine mist that coated my lashes.

The rest of the group wandered out to join her, two men and another woman. They all wore black though the styles varied. The woman in front of me wore a leather jacket belted at the waist, leggings, and low-heeled boots.

Looks like someone rented the Matrix.

I made a move to walk past her and she countered to block me. "So you're the Anomaly." She almost spat it. There were some sniggers from the others. This was a gang—a very stylish one—but still a gang.

I was surprised. No one had ever noticed me enough to bully me. "Yup, that's me, the big old anomaly. Who the hell are you?"

The woman smirked. She knew who I was so she had to be one of Taliesin's Protectors. He may have backed down, but there was a real threat here, I was sure of it.

I tried to remember what I'd done by instinct when I faced the Cŵn Annwn. Closing my eyes, I tried to use my interior vision to see the power inside this woman—because she had power, I was sure of it. There was more laughter, but I forced myself to concentrate. The Cŵn Annwn was pure and simple, but as the outline of her form appeared in my mind, it was filled with an elusive and shifting landscape of color. A couple of hues dominated—gold and red—but tainting them all was a black that charred the others wherever it touched them.

I reached out my hand and heard her intake of breath when I brushed her arm. I shuddered. I could feel the blackness emanating from inside and eddying around her. The woman pushed me away but not before I managed to grasp some of it. There was shouting, but I ignored it. In my mind, I looked at the strand of blackness held in the mental image of my hand. It felt like despair. It felt like power fed by strong emotion. Power used to hurt.

Hurt just for the sick satisfaction of it.

The dark power seemed to acknowledge my recognition; it twisted in my hand and changed its shape into a whip. When I imagined snapping it at the ground, I heard the crack. Pain shot through me and I opened my eyes.

So much for synesthesia.

I held a length of some black substance in my hand and by the shocked look on the woman's face, I knew she could see it too. Pulling the trailing end across the wrist of the hand still holding the pastry box, I could feel its slithering weight on my arm. I snapped it at the ground between us and the woman jumped back while the others gathered in a frightened knot behind her.

A whip was the right shape for it. I wasn't sure how I knew, but this power was used to torment, even torture. I wondered if the woman knew. I wondered if she'd ever used it on anyone.

Shaking the black rope off, I grabbed the woman by the arm. Before she could resist, I closed my eyes to see the aura of color surrounding her and then hooked my fingers into it. She shoved me away, but I held on and pulled with mental, physical, and maybe even spiritual effort. After a brief resistance, black power flowed out of her and rushed towards me. I fell onto my back on the wet pavement as it surrounded me. It poked and prodded at me, trying to find a way in, but I held my breath and kept my eyes shut tight. I couldn't let it in the way I did with the Cŵn Annwn's power. I didn't want to know what this dark magic felt like.

The pressure disappeared. I opened my eyes and saw black smoke pluming into the air to be shredded and washed away by the rain.

I pushed myself up into a crouch. The pastry box was still in my left hand and I had to use my right to steady myself as I got to my feet. The woman stared at me, panting, before turning and walking away. She gestured and the others followed.

Nausea hit me as the pounding in my head doubled. I got the keys out of my pocket, but they slipped from my fingers and it took me two tries before I could pick them up. Stumbling to the car, I slid in and tossed the pasty box on the passenger seat, but a terrible smell cut through the pain and I pried open the lid. The *macarons* were ash that steamed and stank.

I threw the box out the window.

CHAPTER SIXTEEN

I parked in front of a building on a side street downtown and checked the back of Goodfellow's card to make sure I was at the right address. The place was abandoned and there were no other cars in the small parking lot. I expected it to be locked, but the front door opened into a dingy vestibule with an old elevator on one side and a roped off stairway on the other. I made my choice and pushed the cracked and yellowed elevator button. When the door jerked open and I stepped in, I tried not to imagine rusty cables breaking and sending me hurtling down to the ground in a heap of twisted steel.

The ancient contraption creaked its way to the next floor, and after a jolt, the door opened again and I stepped into a spacious foyer of white marble and walls covered in elegant grass cloth. The air was cool and damp.

"Hello?"

"Miss Lynne? Is that you?" Goodfellow emerged from around a corner wiping his hands on a frilly tea towel. He was dressed in head to toe green again. "I wasn't expecting you for another hour. Is everything all right?"

After the incident with the woman, I hadn't wanted to be alone and had come straight over, but all I said was, "I didn't mean to be early. I'm sorry if I'm interrupting anything."

He waved my apology away and tossed the towel back into what must be the kitchen. "Not a problem, my dear. Come into the living room and we'll have a little chat."

I followed him into a large room decorated in green and white and then almost immediately sank weak-kneed into the closest chair. Outside the floor to ceiling windows, trees stretched for miles and faded into distant, foggy mountains.

You're not in Kansas anymore, Dorothy.

"Where are we?"

Goodfellow held out his arms as if he could embrace the view. "One of my favorite places in all the world—Gwydyr Forest in the heart of Snowdonia. Wilder than Sherwood, more open than the Black Forest—pine and spruce and a view of great Snowdon peak itself."

I had to swallow before I could speak again. "Snowdon?"

"The highest mountain in Wales."

I stood and walked to the window to touch the tips of my fingers to the cold glass. It was real. We were in a house perched on the edge of a small, rocky lake. Trees swept away from it on all sides.

"How did I get here?"

I heard Goodfellow sigh. "I can't believe Viviane left you so ignorant. Why would she do such a thing?"

I had no answer.

Goodfellow folded his arms across his massive chest. "How did you get here? How did I get you away from Taliesin and his people? It's because of the Paths. I might not be able to defy the bard completely, but he knows I could tell my kin to make themselves scarce, if you know what I mean. I could make it quite difficult for him to traipse back and forth across the world with his army."

"I don't understand."

"You know about the Wall?" I nodded. "Before the Wall, the Paths were used to travel through the world or to Avalon when the way was still open. The Paths were once part of the ancient forests covering the earth when the magic of creation still flickered among the trees. Those first forests were sentient and allowed creatures to pass through them, or not, at their pleasure. Thus, the Paths were born and I found them."

His voice twisted. "Eventually I found Cernunnos at the end of one of them. But all things must pass away and new forests were born which had no thought and did not grieve or rage when they were paved over for strip malls and condos. But the ghosts of those original forests remember and their Paths remain. Except for me and my kin, few can find them. Of all the earth magicians, Arthur had the best sense of them, except for . . ." The Green Man shook his head and walked away, leaving the sentence unfinished.

I followed him. "Except for who?"

He shook his head again. "It doesn't matter. Someone who is lost and gone."

I was hungry for answers. "Who are your kin then?"

Goodfellow sat down on one of the white leather couches in the center of the room. "I am the Green Man and can walk any Path, but there are lesser beings who can also find them. I call them my kin and the earth magicians call them Guides. They are creatures of the forest—wood sprites, dryads, tree fairies—a network created to transport the earth magicians through the world. To their credit, the magicians are usually fair in their payment, but some have the power to force the Guides if they chose to."

"But not you."

"No. I am old, Miss Lynne, very old. In a way that I can't explain to you, I'm a part of those first forests. I feel them still."

I glanced back at the elevator door at the end of the hall. "I didn't exactly come here through a leafy trail."

Goodfellow laughed. "I can make a Path look like anything I want, even an elevator in an abandoned office building."

Sitting down on the matching couch across from Goodfellow, I noticed the long wooden box and thick folder on the glass table between us. "I really appreciate your help yesterday, but why did you want to see me?" As an answer, he handed me the folder and I opened it and dumped out the contents on the table. There were several bank books, bank cards, and a document which turned out to be a birth certificate with my name on it.

"It's a fake, but a good one. Viviane had several made up over the years when she needed to. She destroyed them after she used them."

"Why?" I asked in surprise.

"Names have power, even names on paper. It wasn't my place to ask what she was protecting you from. Perhaps she was just being cautious."

I took a closer look at the paper in my hand. It looked authentic to me. "You did this?"

The Green Man's laughter shook the windows. "I've kept up with the times, but not to the point of becoming a master counterfeiter. There's a banshee in Dublin who's the best in the business. Banshees know when someone is about to die. This one started out in identity theft and then diversified. The money is real though. I made all the deposits myself. You have ample funds in several institutions and currencies around the world."

I flipped open one of the bank books and gasped. "Where did all this come from?"

Goodfellow shrugged. "As a goddess, Viviane had received tribute from her worshippers, but most of it was gone by the time she asked me to take care of her affairs. The Seer of New York gave me a heads up back in the Seventies that a certain company with, shall we say, a very common fruit as its logo would be worth following." He winked at me. "Even a god is well served by a few good investments. I didn't do too badly myself."

"Why didn't she give this to me herself? How could she even know I would find your card and contact you?"

Goodfellow's smile slipped away. "She didn't."

"What do you mean?"

"Viviane was explicit in her instructions. I was to deliver these items to you and provide any assistance you might need, but only if you contacted me. A test of fate, she called it. All she said was that events had not transpired as she had once planned and she would not force their shape going forward. She had left things in place for you, but that greater gods than she would need to guide you to them, or away as fate decreed. I didn't understand it, but then, you know how she was." He seemed embarrassed, but I didn't know if was for himself or for Mom. "Miss Lynne, can I get you something to drink? I was just making some tea when you came in."

"No, I'm fine. What's in the box?" I asked bluntly. He was trying to distract me from the last item on the table.

"Smart girl," the Green Man murmured. Clasping his hands and leaning forward, he considered me intently. "I'll be straight with you. When Viviane told me what she wanted me to retrieve and keep for you, I was shocked. I tried to argue with her, but she wouldn't listen. 'Only if Rhiannon comes to you,' she said, 'only if she asks.' Since I figured it was highly unlikely, I agreed. I went to the location Viviane gave me and recovered this box, but I don't have to give it to you unless you ask. And believe me, Miss Lynne, you don't want to ask. Some things are better left hidden."

I wanted the answers Mom offered me in death that she'd denied me in life. "I'm sorry. You've been good to me, but I have to ask. Will you please give me what my mother left me?'

Goodfellow sighed as he slid the long box across the table toward me. It scraped across the glass; whatever was in it was heavy. Flipping open the silver clasp on the side, I lifted the hinged lid to reveal a long shaft of distorted grey and yellow metal. Something had been melted and left to harden into an ugly mess, but I couldn't tell what. Goodfellow made a soft noise and I looked up to see tears running down his cheek and into his beard.

"What is it?" I asked.

"Excalibur," he whispered.

CHAPTER SEVENTEEN

I spent most of the night too excited to sleep. *The Excalibur*—sword of legend and magic—was wrapped in a t-shirt in my underwear drawer.

How cool is that?

I was up and ready for school too early, but there was less chance of running into Peter's parents if I left at an unexpected time. I parked in the half empty lot and was dropping my books off in my locker when a dry voice said, "How wonderful it is to see a student arrive on time these days."

My heart jumped and pink sparkles danced across my vision. An older woman with short grey hair stood in the classroom doorway across from my locker.

"Oh, hi, Mrs . . ." The teacher seemed familiar, but I couldn't think of her name.

The woman cocked her head at me like a bird. "Come." She motioned for me to enter the classroom. "I would like to discuss something with you."

"OK." I followed her and sat down at a desk in the front row. She remained standing.

"I am Cailleach," she introduced herself. "I am taking over Senior English for the rest of the term." I fidgeted in my seat as she fell silent and stared at me with round, strangely opaque eyes. There was a strange flapping sound. Out of the corner of my eye I caught the impression of white wings beating against one of the windows, but when I turned to look, there was nothing there.

"Calm yourself, Miss Lynne," she murmured. "There is much we need to discuss."

The woman tucked a strand of hair behind her ear and I realized I did know her. "You were there!" I said in surprise.

The woman frowned, but before either of us could speak, Miko poked her head in through the open doorway.

"I thought I saw you come in here. We need to . . ." Miko faltered. Rushing forward and grabbing me by the wrist, she pulled me out of the classroom. "I need Rhi right away!"

"Sorry," I muttered as I passed the woman. "I need to go."

Ms. Cailleach never spoke a word, but I imagined I felt her watching us all the way down the hall until we turned a corner. We were inside the nearest bathroom before Miko slowed down.

"What were you doing with her?" she demanded.

I pulled away and rubbed at my wrist—the fairy's black-tipped nails had left crescent-shaped marks on my skin. "She said her name was Ms. Cailleach. She's the new English teacher."

"No, no, no!" Miko had her hair pulled into a high ponytail and it was shaking back and forth furiously. "Not *Ms*. Cailleach, just Cailleach." She stressed the pronunciation of the name—*kaliex*. "That was the Ancient Owl, the White Woman, the Great Hag!"

"What are you talking about?"

Miko looked like she wanted to strangle me. "Don't you know anything? Think of the eternal archetypes: Maiden, Mother, Crone. Every culture in the world fears the Crone."

I leaned back against the side of one of the stalls. "A Crone or *the* Crone?"

More exaggerated shrugging and eye rolling. "How should I know? The Celts called her Cailleach, but she has other names in other places. Maybe there's one. Maybe there's a whole bunch. Who cares? She's Beira, the Queen of Winter, and she rises at Samhain to bring death to the world!"

Great.

I went to the sink and splashed some water on my face. "I've seen her before."

"What?"

I watched Miko through the mirror. "She came to the hospital the day my mother died. I didn't recognize her at first because her hair was in a long braid that she had wrapped around her waist."

Miko was pacing now. "Cailleach cut her hair? That *has* to mean something."

I grabbed some paper towel and patted my face dry. "Like what?"

She stopped and frowned. "I don't know. Cutting hair can be a way to show grief or begin a new phase of life. Sometimes hair holds power—think of Samson or Rapunzel." Miko snorted. "I finally caught that cartoon on DVD, by the way. All the parents who took their kiddies to see it would wet themselves if they knew Rapunzel was actually a serial killer who used her hair to open locks from the inside."

I scrunched the paper towel into a ball. "Please don't ever, *ever* tell me anything that horrible *ever* again." I shuddered. "So Cailleach is going to kill us all in our sleep? Or should I be more worried about Cinderella showing up to take us out with Uzis?"

"You really don't know anything, do you." It wasn't a question. "Cailleach isn't evil. She just *is* the same way winter *is*—and just as dangerous. Let the witch do her thing and don't get in her way." Miko smirked at me. "And I don't know about Cinderella, but Snow White was a *baobhan sith* who used her fingernails to slit her victim's throats."

She dodged the paper ball I threw at her face.

I opened the door a crack and peeked out, but the hallway was empty. "C'mon."

Miko followed me into the hall. "Taliesin did say that once word started to spread about you, others would come."

"But how would she even know?"

"She knew Viviane. And most high-level Greylanders have their ways. Are there owls in the barns at your place?"

I thought of the beating of wings at the window. "Yeah."

"Owls are sacred to Cailleach. Maybe that's how she found out."

Owl spies—it gets better and better.

"Let's get out of here."

Miko had somehow scored Taliesin's Jag so we left my car in the lot. Miko drove too fast and had a tendency to grind through the gears. I hoped she was casting some sort of glamour over us because she would get her license taken away if we passed a cop.

"Where are we going?" I asked.

She grinned. "I think we need to eat breakfast and then drop a whole lot of money on crap we'll never wear."

I grinned back. "Agreed."

A few minutes later, we were sitting in the only restaurant at the Center open for breakfast. The rest of the complex was empty except for senior citizens doing a walking class and a few women with babies in strollers waiting for the stores to open. I'd ordered waffles and Miko was devouring an obscene mound of bacon, sausage, and egg.

Maybe Peter's right about the superhero metabolism.

"So this Cailleach, have you ever met her before?"

Miko shook her head and mumbled something around a mouthful of sausage.

I laughed. "What?"

She gulped down some juice and swallowed. "Sorry. I told you magic makes you hungry."

"You were doing magic?"

She arched her eyebrow at me. "Interesting that you couldn't tell. To use sci-fi parlance, I was cloaking us from the moment we left Cailleach until we sat down here. We were a couple of football jocks at the school and then two senior citizens doing the speed limit in a Jetta."

It felt like ants were walking across my back. "So Cailleach is big time dangerous as opposed to run of the mill, every day dangerous then?"

Miko snorted. "Who *isn't* in our world? The question is whether she's dangerous to you. She came to see Viviane when she died, so that's a plus. Maybe she cut her hair in mourning. Your mother was a real big deal once upon a time."

"I know what Taliesin said but what could she want with me?"

"Are you kidding? The Lady of the Lake called you her child. You have a mysterious, unknown power. The great Taliesin is frightened of you. Even Morgan-le-friggin-fay accepts you! Everyone is going to try to use you to their advantage."

I dropped my fork as the waffles heaved in my stomach.

"Whoa," Miko said in alarm, "are you OK?"

I nodded but didn't trust myself to speak.

Miko shook her head. "Sorry, but Viviane was cruel to not tell you about any of this. She must have known how dangerous it would be for you once she was gone."

I didn't answer until I was sure the waffles weren't going to make a reappearance. "A test of fate," I murmured.

"Huh?"

"Something Goodfellow said to me. Maybe Mom wasn't sure what to do and she decided to leave it to fate."

Miko gnawed on a piece of bacon. "Maybe." Shaking her head and dropping the bacon, the fairy pushed her plate away. "Let's talk about something else. Me first. Is Peter as much of a boy scout as he seems?"

"More."

"Too bad. Though I suppose it would be a step up from my last two boyfriends."

"Why? What were they like?"

Miko held up two black-nailed fingers as she counted. "Boyfriend number one—psychopath. Boyfriend number two—vampire."

Vampire and psychopath aren't mutually inclusive?

"Vampires are real?"

"Unfortunately. There are a lot of different blood-loving creatures—like our friend Snow White—but true vampires are rare and most of them keep a low profile. All those books and movies mean even the stupidest human knows how to pick one out and kill it."

I couldn't help myself. "So what are they like?"

Miko rolled her eyes. "Forget all the crap in all the teen paranormal romance books you've *ever* read. I wish they would. Vamps have bought into their own press in the last few years; they all think they're tortured and misunderstood. The truth is they just like to drink blood. They don't even need to. They could get by just fine on cheeseburgers and pizza if they wanted. The one I dated even had acne."

I sputtered and tried not to lose the mouthful of cranberry juice I'd just sipped. "So why did you date him then?"

Miko looked embarrassed. "I hate to admit it, but I bought into the whole tortured soul routine too. It was before I left home. Business was bad. Dad wasn't taking it well. Dad was taking it out on me with his fists. The guy with the really white teeth who played bass in a punk band seemed like a good idea at the time."

"What happened?"

She grinned. "Well, you know the story. Boy meets girl. Boy turns out to be a vampire. Boy tries to eat girl. Girl kicks boy in the nuts."

I knew I was opening myself up to all kinds of ridicule, but I couldn't help it. "And werewolves?" I asked eagerly.

"Dirty. Hairy. Smelly. More interested in camping than killing anyone. They usually end up on the west coast and become snowboarders. And forget the turning at every full moon thing. They can't control it, but most of them only turn once a year or so when there's a supermoon."

"Is that even a real thing?"

"Of course, dummy. Even though I had to lurk around your crummy school to flush you guys out, I graduated early and even have a few college credits." She straightened in her seat and pointed her finger at me. "A supermoon—or 'perigee moon' as we Astronomy 101 grads call it—is the moon when it is closest in its orbit to the Earth."

"And what about the psychopath?"

Miko's smile faded away. "Nothing much to say. Psycho liked his knives. Cut me up outside of a nightclub we were partying at—said I was flirting with the bartender and he was going to teach me a lesson."

Shock was like losing all my colors at once. "What happened?"

Miko's eyes glittered. "I survived and made sure he'd never get close enough to anyone to ever do that again. A little fairy glamour makes him look like he's covered in scars and boils to any girl he shows an interest in." She hesitated and then passed a hand over her face. The jagged scar sweeping from the corner of her mouth to her ear was angry red against the pale gold of her skin. "He gave me the idea."

I swallowed hard. "I'm so sorry."

Another pass of her hand and the scar was hidden under glamour. "Don't be. He paid for what he did. I call it poetic justice."

After a few minutes of silence, we settled the bill and went into the mall. As we wandered in and out of the stores, our good moods began to return. We shopped and laughed as if we weren't a wingless fairy and a dangerous anomaly.

For one precious day, we pretended moms didn't lie and boys didn't hurt.

CHAPTER EIGHTEEN

I didn't follow Miko to the mansion when she dropped me off at my car, even though I'd said I would. A day at the mall had made me feel normal again and I wasn't sure I wanted to re-enter Taliesin's world. The thought of what Miko did to the guy who scarred her was proof that it was strange and dangerous.

A week went by and each morning it took more pills to make the pain in my head go away. I missed Peter. I stayed away from the empty guesthouses even though Old Tom had locked them up again. He'd shaken his head at the sight of the rotting seaweed in the bathtub, but hadn't commented. I wasn't even sure he'd told the Larsens. As far as he was concerned, his horses weren't bothered so there was no problem. Peter texted that he'd reminded Taliesin about it too, but the bard hadn't come up with any answers.

But it was the dream that kept me from returning to Taliesin. Maybe it was just superstition, but the holly above my door seemed to have made a difference and each night the details became clearer. I was convinced at least some of it was an actual memory. Not Tynan, of course, but the other elements seemed so real. In the dream I was about three years old—the same age as when we came to live at Windfield. Maybe my childish brain had somehow interpreted the day I was given to Viviane into a vivid dream.

Which means the woman in my dream might be my birth mother.

I was almost grateful to have school to distract me. Cailleach turned out to be an excellent teacher and didn't seek me out again. The rest of my teachers continued to call on me to answer questions and give my opinion. They weren't the only ones to embrace the new and more visible me; kids who'd never spoken to me before were suddenly acting like my friends. I even turned down a couple of guys who wanted to "hang out" on the weekend. I didn't feel ready for that much attention.

Miko, Daley, and Tynan no longer bothered showing up at Eastdale—they'd all been homeschooled by Rowan and had graduated ages ago. Miko kept me up to date via text. Taliesin was disappointed I hadn't returned. The harp was silent on any new recruits. Peter was training with Daley and the other Protectors. He'd told his parents he had football practice before and after school and was crashing with one of his buddies who lived closer. Reading between the lines, Peter and Miko were spending a lot of time together.

By lunch on Friday, the strain of all the attention was wearing me out and I longed to be invisible again.

Not all the time, but I could use a break.

I paused with my hand on the cafeteria doors. Lunch was in full swing; it sounded like a pack of wild animals consuming their prey. I'd somehow disappeared for most of my life so I could probably manage it again for one lunch hour. I closed my eyes and tried to find Mom's voice, but fluorescent yellow panic filled me when I couldn't remember what she sounded like. Grasping for a memory, I saw her pale, frightened eyes as she hid us from the silver-haired man.

Rhiannon, listen to me. We cannot be seen. We must be small, so very small together. Hide, Rhiannon, hide. Hide in the shadows and be still and silent.

The words were the spell and a veil of blue mist closed around me. Opening my eyes, I pushed on the doors.

Not a single head turned. A guy who'd asked me out just that morning bumped into me as he walked out. Mumbling an apology, his eyes slid over me as if he'd already forgotten I was there.

Lacey entered the cafeteria from behind me. "Hey," she said and then stopped and stared at me. "You're doing it again. Fading or whatever." She was still immune to it.

"I wanted to see if I could control it, but it's getting harder. It's strange, but I think it was something my mom did to me and now it's beginning to disappear."

"Makes sense. C'mon, there's an empty table over there."

"I haven't got a lunch yet."

"You can have mine; I'm not hungry. My mom makes great manicotti."

Homemade manicotti sounded good. I followed her to the table and wondered where the rest of the Bumblebees were.

Lacey seemed to read my mind. "The girls are working on a routine. I didn't feel up to it." She passed me a Hello Kitty lunch bag and I suppressed a smirk because I really wanted that manicotti. Stuffed in a thermos, the pasta was squashed but tasty. I polished it off and refused to be embarrassed that Lacey was watching me while I ate.

I leaned back with satisfaction. "Thanks. I can't believe how hungry I was."

"Doing magic makes you hungry, remember?"

I glanced around at the students who were now oblivious to my presence and shrugged. I was pretty sure I was hungry because I was still relying on fast food places for dinner and skipping most of the other meals. "It doesn't feel like magic. I would have thought magic would feel more, I don't know, sparkly or something."

Lacey smiled. "You felt something when you fought the Cŵn Annwn, didn't you?"

"I felt powerful."

She stopped smiling. Something was different about her. In just one week, she was thinner, but it didn't suit her after all. I noticed a black tattoo peeking out from under the cuff of her denim shirt.

"You got a tattoo? Isn't that against the cheerleader code or something?"

Lacey tugged the cuff back over the swirly mark on her wrist. "I can cover it with makeup when I'm in uniform."

I looked closer. Lacey's hair was pulled back into a messy ponytail and her face was pale. Her eyes had dark shadows under them.

And to be honest, she smells a little.

"Did you get the fith-fath thing from Rowan?" I felt funny saying it; it rhymed with hee-haw. Miko had explained the rules of Gaelic and Welsh to me, but I just didn't understand how something spelled *sidhe* could be pronounced *shee*, or how *sith* could be pronounced the exact same way. *Baobhan sith* became *baavan shee*, *Cailleach* was *kaliex*, and my favorite name— which was pronounced shevon—was actually Siobhan. It was maddening.

Lacey shrugged. "I don't need it."

"But Taliesin said you could be in danger."

She shrugged again.

"What's going on, Lacey?" I was pretty sure I knew the answer. Lacey McInnis would never accept not being the best at something. Maybe she'd started investigating magic on her own. Taliesin had let it slip there was a lot of information about it on the internet.

Lacey rested her forehead against a clenched fist. "Nothing," she sighed.

Before I could press it, she sat up straight and stared at the door. I turned around and saw Cailleach walking towards us. Her white hair was straight the way only a flat iron can make it and she had a slim figure anyone would envy. I closed my eyes for a moment and could just barely sense the cold silver surrounding her.

The woman stopped at our table and crossed her arms. The sleeve of her blouse pushed away from her wrist and up her arm and I saw that black tattoos in curving and knotted designs covered every inch of her exposed skin. Ice crept down my spine.

Who needs the internet when you have the Crone slumming at your school?

"Miss McInnis, you were supposed to meet me in the library to discuss your independent study unit. I don't appreciate being kept waiting."

Lacey shuffled to her feet. "I'm sorry. It won't happen again."

"See that it doesn't. Follow me. There is still time in the lunch period to make some progress." Without waiting for a response, Cailleach turned and walked away, high heels clicking on the linoleum floor.

Gathering the lunch bag and stuffing it in her purse, Lacey gave me a listless wave as she left. I wanted to say something to stop her, but then I remembered how much Mom had kept from me. What right did I have to keep Lacey away from something she clearly wanted to do?

Cailleach stood waiting for her at the cafeteria doors. Lacey paused and looked back with a strange expression on her face—almost as if she expected me to do something—and then they were both gone.

I stayed invisible for the rest of the day so I could think in peace. Lacey could see through glamour based magic, so she must have known the truth of what Cailleach was right away. Taliesin knew the Crone was teaching at the school, but Miko said he wasn't concerned—even magical beings sometimes need jobs. I decided that Lacey had a right to make her own decisions and it was none of my business.

It haunted me later that maybe she wanted me to stop her.

CHAPTER NINETEEN

When I drove home, Peter's mom was sitting on the porch of the main house and motioned for me to park. Rising to greet me as I climbed the wide stairs, she gave me a warm hug. Even though I'd known her just about all my life, I still called her Mrs. Larsen. The Larsens were formal people and older than most other parents of kids our age. Peter sometimes called them Sir and Ma'am.

"C'mon in, Rhi. There's something I need to talk to you about."

I nodded and followed her into the house. I was surprised when she went into the formal living room and sat down on the sofa. It was going to be one of *those* kind of talks. She must have found out Peter was lying to her. I sat down beside her and braced myself to cover for him.

"I got a call from the school. They said you missed classes on Monday."

It took me a moment to remember the Larsens were listed as my guardians and of course the school would call them. I came up with the first excuse I could think of. "I'm so sorry. I didn't even think to tell you. I didn't feel well and I went home. I should have let you know."

Mrs. Larsen shook her head. "I'm not worried about that. But you see, it reminded me that I've been putting off something I need to do." She stood and walked over to the fireplace to pick up an envelope sitting on the mantle. "It's no secret I never agreed much with your mother's style of parenting—you were so little when you came to us and so starved for affection." She turned suddenly. "I don't mean to say she didn't love you. I'm sure she did." Her voice hardened. "She just never seemed to show it. I never once saw that woman hold your hand or kiss your cheek."

There was nothing I could say to that. I had no memory of Viviane—Mom—doing those things either.

Mrs. Larsen tapped the envelope against her palm and then crossed the room and sat back down beside me. "I'm sorry, honey, I shouldn't have said that. It just used to make me so mad. When you and Peter became close, I thought maybe I could give you some of the affection you were missing."

Tears sprang to my eyes. "And you did. I love you and Mr. Larsen."

"We love you too, sweetheart. You know that, right?" I nodded and she handed me the envelope. Typed across the top left corner was *R. Goodfellow and Associates*. "Your mother and I had an argument a few days before she collapsed." Mrs. Larsen grimaced. "Well, I had an argument anyway."

"What about?"

"You. Your mother told me she knew she was dying. Informed me just like that as if there were nothing else that needed discussing except for who would take over caring for the gardens—as if that was the only thing I would be concerned about. She actually seemed surprised when I asked if we could become your guardians. She said no. I wouldn't have argued if she had someone else in mind, but she seemed to think her death wouldn't make much difference to you at all."

"But she did make you my guardians."

"After I threatened to contact Children's Aid! The next day she presented me with this." She motioned to the envelope.

I pulled a sheet of paper out; it was another birth certificate. According to this one, I'd turned eighteen on my last birthday.

Mrs. Larsen shook her head. "I don't know why she lied about your age. Maybe it was a mistake she never bothered to correct. She gave me permission to take care of you for a little while, but you're legally in charge of your own life. I'm sorry it took me so long to give this to you, but I guess I wasn't ready to let go." She grasped my hands and gave them a little shake. "It doesn't change anything. We're family and no piece of paper can take that away."

After twenty minutes of reassurance accompanied by chocolate chip cookies, I went home. Sitting on the couch with the two nearly identical documents on the table in front of me, I searched my memory of the years and could only come up with seventeen of them. Goodfellow did say Mom had a few copies made up. This one had been created to free me from the Larsens' watchful eyes, but why? They'd never tried to enforce any authority over me after she died, but maybe only because they believed I was already legally an adult.

Viviane Lynne was listed as my mother, but no father. I looked at my name printed out in duplicate and a wave of pain passed between my temples. The words on the papers in front of me seemed to writhe and crawl. The longer I looked at my name—Rhiannon Lynne—the less it seemed to have any meaning and the more exposed I felt. Acting on impulse, I picked up the certificate Goodfellow gave me and ripped it right through my name. The pressure immediately eased.

I was just about to do the same to the other one when a thought occurred to me: even if it was a lie, the new certificate would come in handy. I didn't have to answer to anyone if they thought I was eighteen. I was free.

How can I be free when I don't even know who I really am?

After I put the remaining certificate safely between the pages of a gardening book in the book case, I felt better. Making a decision, I pulled out my phone to text Peter that I was coming and was ready to get some answers.

As if in response, three howls echoed through the fields behind the house.

CHAPTER TWENTY

Hunting for anything that howls is a bad idea, but I ran out of the house and circled it. Nothing. I even walked over to the guesthouses, but they were locked and quiet. Convincing myself it must have been Old Tom's collie, I put it out of my mind and went home to get ready.

Changing into jeans and a long-sleeved shirt, I tucked the charm bracelet under my cuff. I'd been wearing it almost every day even though red irritation ringed my wrist like a burn. I also decided not to show Excalibur to Taliesin. I didn't know why, but I wanted to keep both the charm and the sword a secret.

Just between me and Mom.

When I arrived at the mansion, Rowan was working in the garden and waved me over. "Did you do all this?" I asked as I admired the neat beds of shrubs and flowers.

Rowan brushed the dirt from his hands. "I thought I would make myself useful and leave things better than we found them. It's too late in the season to do much, but it's still an improvement."

I knelt down beside him and pointed to the clump of pink, ruffled flowers he'd been clearing the weeds away from. "They're pretty. What are they?"

"Anemone. I've been helping them along." Rowan ran his hands over them, murmuring words I didn't recognize in a humming drone. The plants swelled and stretched to meet his palms the way a cat arches its back to be stroked.

I gasped. "How'd you do that?"

The tanned skin around his eyes crinkled into deep lines when he smiled. "In another life I was a druid, a priest in the religion of the Celts." He touched a small Celtic cross on a chain around his neck. "In many ways, I still am. The earth blessed me with the power to nurture life. I may have wandered from the religion of my youth, but the abilities I developed have never left me." Following my gaze, he lifted the cross to show me. "You're wondering why I wear this symbol of faith."

"I guess I thought magic made religion irrelevant."

Rowan chuckled. "There are no more definitive answers to be found in magic than there are in anything else. Magic is just an ability; one as valid as a talent for singing, or painting, or fixing cars. There are Christian, Muslim, Buddhist, and Jewish magic users. There are some who cling still to the gods of the old world. There's even a small contingent of Rastafarians among the Greylanders beyond the Wall."

I stared at him for a second. "You're joking."

He laughed. "Yes, but I wouldn't be surprised. All beliefs are found among us, and for all our powers, not one of us knows for sure what lies beyond the veil of death, especially those of us who have cheated it for so long. We have merely been given more time to ponder the question. Despite what some might believe, we are not gods. I have faith there is something out there greater than myself, otherwise, why endure at all if everything we know and love will disappear into nothingness?" A shadow passed over his face, but then he smiled and it was gone. "I hear you met my wife."

I was thrown by the sudden change of topic. "Your wife?"

Rowan stood and offered a hand to pull me up. "Boudica. Or Bo as we call her. Tall, red hair, plenty of attitude. I think you ran into her at some bakery around town. Sound familiar?"

I brushed the grass off my knees. "You're married to *her*?"

He laughed again. "I see she made quite an impression. She usually does. I love my wife, but diplomacy is not one of her strengths. She caught it from Tal when one of the other Protectors tattled on her about your little encounter. Tal figured that's why you hadn't been by."

I nodded. My encounter with Rowan's wife had nothing to do with me not coming, but it seemed smarter to let them think that.

Rowan put a gentle hand on my shoulder. "Before we met, my wife suffered a great tragedy. She has a suspicious nature, but she'll come around. Try to give her a second chance, if you can."

I nodded and it seemed to satisfy him. As the druid escorted me inside, he called out—"Tynan, she's here!"— before winking and leaving me standing alone in the foyer.

Tynan bounded down the stairs "You're here!"

"I'm here," I repeated.

"Hello, Rhi." Dressed in a black leather jacket and jeans, Daley emerged from the dining room and my heart jumped in my chest as if I'd been shocked. Considering him with fresh eyes, I wondered how any of us had ever believed he was a high school student. Miko must have helped that along with a little fairy glamour. "You shouldn't have let Boudica put you off from coming."

"Yeah, well, it didn't exactly inspire me with confidence."

"If you'd heard Taliesin rake her over the coals about it, you might have been reassured—but then, you weren't here, were you." It was an accusation, not a question.

Tynan had edged closer to me and the way he hunched to hide his height made me feel like he was bending over me, cornering me. "It was bad. Dad stripped her of her command. Rowan thinks she'll get it back, but I don't know. Once Dad makes a decision, he usually sticks with it."

Daley's voice was cold. "She shouldn't. Boudica was under strict instructions to leave Rhi alone. She's never been good at taking orders and that makes her a liability."

Tynan looked away. "You don't understand her pain."

"It doesn't make it OK."

Great. Five minutes and I'm already in the middle of a sibling spat.

I cleared my throat to get their attention. "So Daley, how old are you anyway? Cuz you sound positively ancient. You're not Ty's Dad, you know."

"I'm old enough to know better."

"Better than who? Me? Or someone who buys her outfits at Bondage R Us and got her butt kicked by a girl carrying a box of pastries."

"From what I heard, nobody got their butt kicked, as you so politely put it. Boudica recognized she was facing someone reckless and untrained and made the smart decision to back down. The only smart thing she did, I agree, but still a lot better than throwing magic around in front of a bunch of civilians. She chose to walk away from a confrontation that might have hurt someone."

"She didn't walk. She ran."

That might be a little bit of an exaggeration.

Daley looked disgusted. "Is that something to be proud of? If you knew anything at all about what you're doing then you'd know how wrong that is. It isn't fear to stay clear of a rabid dog."

"Am I the dog in this scenario?"

"Don't be stupid. You know what I mean."

"No, I don't think I do. And Boudica didn't back off because she was smart. She was scared. I think she knew she couldn't take me. But if you don't believe me, maybe you'd like to give it a try and see how far you get."

"Are you challenging me?"

Strange emotions colored hot pink and candy apple red seemed to fill the air. "Not a challenge—a promise."

And could I be any more clichéd?

"Stop it!" Tynan stepped between us. With shame, I realized I'd forgotten he was even there. Glancing back at Daley, I saw sparks glistening in his hair and a hot light glowing in his eyes. Looking like that, I could believe he was the god of thunder.

"Ah, I thought I heard voices." Taliesin appeared in the foyer and I wondered how much he'd heard. "Tynan, please tell Miko to bring the harp to the study." Tynan nodded and went up the stairs.

"You two, come with me." The bard's tone was icy.

I guess he heard enough.

"I'm sorry. And it's twenty-one," Daley murmured as we followed Taliesin.

"What?"

"I turned twenty-one last April, so not so old after all."

My heart jumped again. I had no name for the colors I was seeing/feeling.

CHAPTER TWENTY ONE

Taliesin led us to the study. I pretended to examine the books in the bookcase and endured the awkward silence until Miko burst in carrying her leather bag over one shoulder.

"Finally! Now we can get some answers." She stopped and frowned. "What's wrong?"

Tynan pushed past her. "Rhi and Daley were fighting."

Peter's arrival spared me from responding. "Hey, Rhi. Did you see Mom and Dad?"

I punched him in the arm hard enough to make him wince. "I saw your mom. Don't ever make me hide anything from her again. They bought your story. That's not what we talked about though. I'll tell you about it later."

Peter looked curious but didn't press it. We turned together to face Taliesin who was sitting at the desk with his fingers steepled—his favorite pose. I held his gaze to make sure he read the message of our solidarity. Peter might be drinking the Kool-Aid here, but he was still my best friend.

Taliesin's lips twitched. Satisfied, I sat on the couch and Peter plopped down beside me.

"I am pleased Rhiannon has returned. I have used the time during her,"—the bard paused, eyes glittering—"*delay* to consult with an earth magician who has devoted his life to the cataloguing of the various types of magic currently present in this world. He agreed that Rhiannon's connection between magic and color—both in her own perception, and in its manifestation to others—may be unique. I have also spoken with Morgana to try to determine Rhiannon's true parentage. She confirmed that Viviane had never had a child of her own. She had thought her sister had simply taken in a foundling for her own inscrutable purposes."

I was surprised. I'd thought Morgan Le Fay—or Morgana as he called her—was Taliesin's enemy, and yet apparently he could pick up the phone and give her a ring any time he wanted to chat.

"What does it even matter? Whoever my real parents were, they obviously didn't want me."

Taliesin shook his head. "It matters a great deal. No Greylander or earth magician would give up their child willingly. Children of magic are precious."

"So what happened then?"

"I do not know, but it is a great and worrisome mystery that you should end up being cared for by Viviane. She was known to have long ago put aside any real interest in the human world. You are the second child I have encountered with unknown magic parentage." He gestured at Tynan who looked down so the sweep of his hair hid his face. "I do not believe in coincidences."

The mauve swirling through me was speckled with other, darker colors, but I shrugged. "I don't understand why any of this is important."

It was Daley who answered and his voice was angry again. "You don't understand because there are things no one here has told you yet." Surprisingly, it wasn't me he was mad at; he was glaring at his father. Taliesin nodded for him to continue. "About time," Daley muttered before turning back to me. "You might have destroyed that Cŵn Annwn. At the very least, you changed it. I could feel the power leave it like an electric charge in the atmosphere before it dissipated. You shouldn't have been able to do that to a hound of Avalon." Sparks of static electricity were flying from Daley's hair. Since no one else seemed worried he might set the house on fire, I wondered if they could see the manifestation of his power the way I did. "The Cŵn Annwn were created from mortal dogs to serve Cernunnos. If one falls, his power revives it; their power is his power." He paused for a moment to let that sink in. "There's no precedent for what you did except in the tales of the very darkest of creatures."

I swallowed hard. "What creatures?"

It was Taliesin who answered. "I have never encountered one outside of myth, but the Leannan Sidhe were said to have the ability to steal the life force out of a man, leaving only an empty shell behind. What you did could be described in a similar way. I think you can understand why this might give us cause for concern."

My head began to pound. "What do you want me to do?"

"Can you show me how your ability manifests itself?"

"I don't know. I've always seen my colors when my emotions were strong. I thought that's all it was—some kind of weird synesthesia. Maybe since my colors tell me something about myself, they can also tell me things about other people, like their abilities. I don't know how I made a color actually appear."

"Perhaps your power is strong enough to create a reality out of your perception. Or perhaps your special ability is the power to make corporeal some essential nature of magic we have not understood till now. You will never know unless you try, Rhiannon."

"OK." I stood and closed my eyes. Faint traces of the indigo binding still lingering in the house distracted me—it was like looking through glasses smeared with oil. I opened my eyes in frustration. "I can't."

Daley had crossed the room to stand beside me. "Boudica said you grabbed her and I saw you touch the Cŵn Annwn." I nodded and he took my hand. "Try again, Rhiannon."

His use of my full name did strange things to my insides and when I closed my eyes again, I saw streaks of hot pink shooting through the indigo. The outline of his form appeared in my mind, lined in blades of cyan and orange lightning. I jumped as electricity passed between our entwined fingers.

"What do you see?" he asked.

"I see you."

A pause. "What do I look like?"

I answered without hesitation. "Lightning. Cyan light and orange flame so bright it's almost colorless. And a stormy sky—charcoal and blue lined with silver."

After a moment of silence, Taliesin spoke. "Can you touch what you see?"

I heard the hiss of Daley's indrawn breath and white fear shivered across my vision of him. "What if I hurt Daley?"

The bard's voice was cold. "You did not hurt Boudica." Either Boudica didn't know what I'd done to her, or hadn't admitted to it.

"You can do it." Peter's voice was closer; he stood beside me now and I could see the bright green thread connecting us. Trust and confidence seemed to flow through it.

"I'll try." I tightened my grip on Daley's hand and lifted it in front of my closed eyes. In my mind, lightning danced over our fingers and around a small ring of light on my wrist.

The wheel charm.

The light flared and my interior vision was blinded as my wrist seemed to catch fire. I tore my hand out of Daley's, but I could feel some of his power come with it. There was a moment of resistance and a strange aqua iridescence swirled around me, but then Daley's power was mine. Opening my eyes, I gasped for breath and then froze.

A ball of lightning lay in my palm.

The wheel charm no longer burned where it was hidden beneath my sleeve, but the lightning I held was almost too hot to endure.

Taliesin frowned. "An illusion?"

Daley leaned down to touch the power in my hand with a cautious finger and then straightened and backed away. "It's real," he gasped. "She took a part of me."

I stepped towards him and held out my hand. "Take it! Take it back!"

He recoiled from me. "What did you do?"

Taliesin stood and put a hand on Daley's shoulder. "What did it feel like, my son?"

"Like she was clutching at my soul!"

"Be calm. How much did she take? Will you be all right?"

Daley took a shuddering breath and then seemed to get himself under control. "Not much. I'll be fine." There was no expression in his voice.

I had to say something. "Daley, I'm so sorry."

Taliesin interrupted, "No need to apologize, Miss Lynne." He returned his attention to Daley. "Could you have stopped Rhiannon if she had tried to take more?"

Daley's face was now a calm mask. "Maybe. I'm not sure."

"Take it back," I begged again.

"I don't know how." Daley turned away.

Crimson rage smeared across my vision. Putting all the force I could find behind it, I threw the ball of lightning at the ground. There was a crack of thunder, and then the acrid smell of wool burning. We all stared silently at the black hole in the Persian carpet. Peter stepped on a small tongue of flame to extinguish it.

Miko cleared her throat. "Well, not to say that wasn't interesting, but I think we should try the harp before jumping to any conclusions. The leanan sidhe left gifts of creativity for what they took, but I don't see Daley rushing off to write a poem." The fairy pulled the harp out of the bag. "Binnorie's been difficult lately, but she agreed to let all of you see and hear her. Just let me talk to her for a second." I didn't like how she called the harp by the drowned girl's name.

The minutes stretched on as Miko whispered to the harp. I was getting restless by the time she stopped in frustration.

"She's not listening to me . . ."

CHILD OF BLOOD!

An awful screeching filled the room and Rowan and Boudica rushed in through the door to see what was going on. Pain shot through me as if something had been pulled tight until it broke. The harp continued to wail.

Have mercy on us Child of Blood, Eater of Bones and Life!
Have pity on us Destroyer of Worlds and Scouring Wind!
He has waited long and you cannot evade.
You will rise to meet him or choose to fall.
On this hangs death on the right or the left.

The voice quieted and took on a singsong quality.

One will go forward alone.
One will return to the beginning.
Choose rightly and blood will run like a river.
Choose wrongly and it will pour out like the sea.
But do not say you were not warned by me.

The harp fell silent.

Boudica crossed her arms over her chest and looked at me with raised eyebrows. "Well *that* was reassuring."

CHAPTER TWENTY TWO

The harp was silent, but everyone else had a lot to say.

Boudica was yelling. "It's a prophesy! Are you telling me you know every prophesy ever made?" That was directed at Taliesin on a rising pitch that sent pain shooting through my head.

Rowan motioned at his wife to stop but his face was worried. "You have to admit it sounds like it could be a prophesy."

Taliesin ignored them both. "Miko, Binnorie is your charge. Was it a prophesy or has she finally gone mad after all these years?"

Miko hugged the harp to her chest. "She's not mad. Not yet. It has to be a true prophesy."

Daley snorted. "Since when has any prophesy ever been 'true'? You know as well as I do that prophesies are as slippery as nixies."

Boudica shrugged off her husband's arm and strode over to me, but I had trouble seeing her past the streaks of acid orange flashing in front of my eyes. "It's a prophesy and we know who its target is." Vicious crimson burst into my head. "I say we stop worrying about what the prophesy was about and just get rid of the who."

"Bo . . ." Rowan admonished.

Pain was coming in waves now, crashing against me so fast I could barely catch my breath. Everything was color; everything inside me and around me. Emotion, power, thought—I could see it all now and it was blinding. A part of me yearned to take the essence of what I perceived into myself. A part of me knew it would burn me from the inside out until my mind was just like the smoldering, stinking hole in the carpet.

"The first Rhiannon rode a pale horse," Tynan murmured. "Some say she was the goddess of death."

Daley frowned. "That's not helpful, Ty."

"Has anyone noticed how many horses there are where she lives?" Boudica spat.

Peter jumped to his feet. "That's my home you're talking about and what have horses got to do with anything anyway?"

Rhiannon, listen to me, we cannot be seen. Hide in the shadows and be still and silent.

The angry voices faded away and I could hear only her. Not Mom—Viviane. My mother was dead. It was a goddess that had left the remnants of her voice in my mind. The tattered mist of her spell slipped away and rage filled me— rage at what she'd done to me, rage at all the things she'd kept from me. Crimson swept through the other colors and overwhelmed them. Drowning in it, I grasped at a thread of bright green winking through the maelstrom.

Peter!

He turned to look at me. Everyone else went silent.

Taliesin took my hand and felt for the pulse in my wrist. "Rowan, call 911."

Miko stared at me with round eyes. "Where did all the blood come from?"

"What blood?" I asked. At least I tried to before I choked on the viscous mass in my mouth. I was covered in blood. With trembling hands I felt my ears, eyes, and nose; it was everywhere.

"It pours out like the sea." Boudica murmured.

"Enough!" Taliesin roared and the agony in my head jumped in response. "Rhiannon, can you hear me?"

Of course I can. You could pop an eardrum with that thing. I nodded.

"Are you in pain?"

I nodded yes again, but it wasn't the point. I lifted my hands to show him. "It's not blood," I said as clearly as I could. "Something inside me broke."

Taliesin stepped back in surprise. "Hang up the phone," he barked. The druid muttered some excuse into the receiver and put it down.

Peter took my hand. "I heard you calling me in my mind. What can I do?"

I couldn't speak. Color was coming faster; streaming out of my mouth and dribbling out of my nose, eyes and ears. Peter grabbed my shoulders as I thrashed backwards in a desperate struggle to breathe.

"RHIANNON!"

The power of the bard's voice made the color rushing through me tremble and falter. I managed to take a deep breath.

"Can you regain control?"

I shook my head violently.

"Tal," Rowan said, "if she can't stop it, it'll kill her as surely as losing that much blood would."

Taliesin's eyes widened, but his voice was calming. "I will have to try to stop it for you. Do you understand what that means?" I nodded again. He never moved, but a blanket of indigo dropped over me. Color dissipated like smoke and I coughed the rest out of my lungs. Miko handed me a tissue and I dabbed at my face—real blood had added itself to the flow.

"Thank you," I whispered.

With a hiss, Boudica stomped out and Rowan followed her with a murmured apology. Peter let me go, but his hands were trembling.

When Taliesin stood and stumbled, both Tynan and Daley rushed to help, but he waved them away. He leaned against the desk and passed a hand over his face. "I am fine, but it is taking all my strength to bind whatever that was."

"Should I get Rowan back?" Tynan asked.

The bard sighed wearily. "Later." He glanced at the bloody tissue in my hand. "Do you know what happened?"

I struggled to find the worlds. "I'm not sure. When the harp screamed, it felt like something inside me broke. I could see everything as color—my thoughts, my feelings, all of you—it was overwhelming."

"And what you perceive, you are somehow able to manifest in reality."

"I guess. But there was so much of it. I'm not sure where it was all coming from."

Taliesin sighed again. "With Rowan's help, I can contain this for a day, maybe two. You must gain control within that time. You cannot risk another deluge; that was real blood mingled with it." He shook his head. "I have never experienced magic as a physical entity. It is both fascinating and terrifying."

The knuckles on Miko's hands were white as she gripped the harp. "But if it was all just a manifestation of Rhiannon's power, where did it go?"

Taliesin looked at me. "Did the binding contain it?"

I couldn't sense anything. "It's gone, I think."

Daley's voice was quiet. "I took care of it."

Taliesin relaxed and smiled. "Well done, but you had better keep an eye on the sky tonight. Until all the energy disperses, the weather is bound to be unstable. Maybe I will come with you. It might be dangerous, but it is also likely to be spectacular. Rhiannon, I suggest you stay the night. I know who to call to help you and I promise I will release the binding once you are in control." I hesitated and then nodded. "Good. Tynan can get you something to eat and then you should rest."

A door slammed followed by the sound of voices. Daley was immediately alert. "That's Boudica's patrol returning. I sent them out while you were making your decision about her. What should I tell them?"

Taliesin's face was grim. "Tell them she is out of the command structure indefinitely."

"They won't like it."

"Then send them home. They may join your patrol or they may go their own way and see if Morgana will take them, but I will not tolerate insubordination—not from Boudica and not from them. Take Peter with you. He has made friends among her group and his presence might have a calming effect on the situation."

Peter looked at me with concern. "Are you OK now?'

Define OK.

But I nodded and Peter ruffled my hair before following Daley out.

The bard gestured to Tynan. "Take Miss Lynne upstairs and keep her away from the others. I do not think any of us want to deal with more drama tonight."

I gathered my purse and took the hand Tynan offered to help me up; my legs were still shaking.

Miko put the harp back in its bag. "What do you want me to do?"

Taliesin sat down in his chair and closed his eyes. "Stay with me while I make a call." She perched on the desk and he swiveled to face the window—Tynan and I were dismissed.

We slipped out the door and down the hallway stretching away from the foyer and Boudica's patrol. I couldn't see anyone from my angle behind the central staircase, but I could hear angry voices and Daley's cool response—they weren't taking the news of Boudica's demotion well.

"What will they do?" I whispered

"If they're smart, they'll fall in line and join Daley's group back home. That's Las Vegas, by the way. Dad wasn't kidding; he'll cut them loose."

"Isn't he afraid they'll go join Morgan?" We climbed the second staircase at the back of the house.

"If Dad can't trust his patrols to follow orders then they're no use to him. Besides, they'll do about as much good with Morgan as with us."

"I thought she was the enemy."

He glanced over his shoulder at me. "Only if she wakes Arthur. Until then, we basically do the same thing; we keep the monsters in line."

I bet Daley thinks I'm one of those monsters.

The thought hurt.

We entered the second floor from the opposite end and Tynan took me to the same bedroom as before. As I brushed by him and went in, I was reminded of what happened the last time we were alone. "Have you ever met Morgan?" I asked to distract us both from the thought.

"No. Dad doesn't like me around when she comes."

"He meets with her?"

Tynan bent his head and his hair covered his eyes. "Sometimes."

"Strange." I sat on the bed and threw my purse on the nightstand.

He sat down at the other end. "Do you feel better now?"

"I think so."

"That was weird."

"Yeah."

Tynan brushed his bangs out of his eyes. "Is there something going on between you and Daley?"

"What do you mean?"

"You two were pretty intense down there. Daley's my brother. I don't want to get in the way if you two are into each another."

I just had a magic harp prophesy I'm gonna do a lot of really bad things and then nearly bled out with magic and he wants to talk about his feelings?

"Nothing's going on," I said instead.

"You frightened us," he said softly.

"I'm sorry."

Before I could react, Tynan reached out and pulled me against him. Without knowing exactly how it happened, his arms were around me and my head was tucked under his chin. "I won't let anyone hurt you." His heart beat thudded next to my ear and I heard the echo of Viviane's.

Be still and silent.

Tynan's lips brushed my hair, but I didn't need my colors to know I didn't feel the same way he did. When I didn't respond, his grip loosened and I slipped away, ignoring the hurt on his face.

"I'm going to get cleaned up. And I'm starving. Could we get something to eat?"

Tynan smiled in relief. "I'll get a bunch of stuff to bring back here and we can make a picnic on the bed and watch TV."

I stifled a sigh as I realized he had no intention of leaving me alone. "That would be great."

Tynan was already on his way out the door. "I'll be right back. See if you can find anything good on."

I'd stuffed a change of clothes in my purse in case I ended up staying the night. Taking my t-shirt and yoga pants into the bathroom, I started to pull off my shirt and then stopped as something caught my eye. The bracelet had slipped down my wrist and revealed a red burn the same shape as the wheel charm. It didn't sting anymore when I probed the damaged skin, but it would probably scar. Undoing the clasp, I put the bracelet away in my makeup bag and dabbed some foundation on the red mark.

Twisting my hair into a loose bun, I was just coming out when Tynan returned carrying a tray heaped with food and two bottles of orange soda. For the next half hour, we watched a show about teenage werewolves that Tynan found completely hilarious. When I pretended to fall asleep before the show finished, Tynan turned off the lights and slipped out.

As soon as he was gone, I flipped onto my back in the darkness and stared up at the ceiling, rubbing at the mark the wheel charm had made on my wrist. Lightning illuminated the room, but no thunder followed. Curious, I got out of bed and went to the window.

As my eyes adjusted, I saw flashes of lightning outlining Daley as he stood with his arms raised on the edge of the forest bordering the yard—real lightning, not the kind I saw when I sensed his power. He was alone. As I watched, the bolts came faster and faster until the light was almost continuous. The lightning wasn't flashing around him, it was striking him.

There was no thunder. Daley was thunder incarnate.

CHAPTER TWENTY THREE

I held Mom's hand as we walked towards the iron gates of Windfield Farm. I knew from memory that we would walk through them and down the road to the Larsen's home. Mom would knock on the door and a boy with messy blond hair would open it. That boy and I would look at one another and know we were going to be friends forever. That would be the beginning of my life as I remembered it; there was nothing else before.

But as we walked, I did something I couldn't remember doing in real life. I gazed up at the tall, dark-haired woman who held my hand and wondered who this stranger was and where she was taking me.

I woke before dawn and it took a moment before I realized where I was. The dream had left a bad taste in my mouth, but at least my head didn't hurt as much—the binding seemed to be holding back my headache along with everything else. I couldn't get back to sleep so I decided to get up.

I crept out of the room and down the stairs. A huge, stone-floored kitchen running along the back third of the house was easy to find. Feeling through the cupboards in the darkness, I found a glass and then squinted at the sudden glow when I opened the fridge.

"Ah, it's you, *mo leanabh*. I wondered who was scurrying through the house like a little mouse."

I gasped and nearly dropped the pitcher of juice in my hand. Twin spots of amber ringed with red glittered in the gloom; Thomas Redcap was sitting at the table sipping something from a mug.

"What are you doing here?" I was glad to see him now that my heart was no longer in my throat. Despite disappearing and leaving me with more questions than answers—and probably only because he rescued me from L'Inconnue—his unexpected presence was strangely reassuring. I poured some juice and sat down beside him.

"I was invited. Or at least, I came with someone who was invited: your dear, sweet Auntie Morgan."

"Why?"

"When your queen calls, you answer."

"Your queen?"

He shrugged and took a drink. "The closest thing to one this side of the Wall. Due to my slightly more extensive experience dealing with you, *mo leanabh*, I was given the pleasure of accompanying your dear aunt. I thought you would be happy to see a friendly face, under the circumstances."

"Taliesin called Morgan to help me bring my abilities under control?"

Redcap finished his drink with a satisfied sound. "There's no one more powerful than Morgan Le Fay."

"I keep getting told that Taliesin and Morgan are at war and yet they seem pretty cozy."

Redcap chuckled as he pushed back his chair and stood. "Oh, you don't know the half of it. I'll be seeing you at a more hospitable hour. Until then . . ." He touched his cap and brushed past me.

"Redcap?" He paused and looked back. "What are you? I mean, what exactly is a 'redcap'? And don't tell me it's someone who likes to wear red baseball caps."

His face changed. It was strange how young he seemed one moment—as young as Daley—and then almost ancient the next. "What I am is the last of my kind. My ancestors killed for the joy of it and ate the flesh off the bones of their victims to absorb their memories. They dipped their caps in blood to strike fear in the hearts of their enemies. I have never dipped it in blood, but I wear this old cap to remind myself."

"Remind you of what?"

Redcap stared at me for such a long time that I thought he wasn't going to answer. "Of what happens when you don't change with the times, *mo leanabh*. My people are dead, hunted by men of conviction like Taliesin. I survive because I have embraced the world as it is, not as I wish it to be. I learned that lesson the night my mother was killed. She refused to accept that the old world is no more. Both Taliesin and Morgan are in danger of learning that hard lesson the same way."

He grimaced. "There's something you should know. Viviane has gone from me, poured out as surely as her ashes were poured out on the water. In all the history of my kind, once gained, no one else has ever eluded us." He disappeared down the dark hall.

As I returned to my room, I was glad for the heads up about Morgan. I wasn't sure what I thought about the woman. She was estranged from Mom, but she came to mourn her. She was Taliesin's enemy, and yet he turned to her for help. She was the villain in most of the stories written about Arthur, and yet according to Taliesin, she was Arthur's great love.

And she makes some very unfortunate fashion choices.

After a quick shower, I redressed in my slightly rumpled clothes from the day before, but left the charm bracelet in my purse. The house was still quiet so I decided to explore the main floor. I was just about to open the double doors off the foyer when I heard the voices of a man and a woman from behind them.

"I am glad you chose to contact me."

"You were the obvious choice and I welcomed the excuse. Truthfully though, I did not expect you to arrive so . . . expeditiously."

"Should I have delayed?"

"No." Silence and movement. "It has been a long time."

The woman sighed. "Too long. If only you would relent, we would not need to be parted."

"Dear one, you know that is not true. However this plays out, we are destined to be parted."

"If only . . ."

"If only."

Silence again and I had enough of a teenager's imagination to guess what the owners of the voices were doing. *So that's what Redcap meant by his crack about Taliesin and Morgan.* I backed away from the door and retreated to the study. As I waited for everyone else to get up, I searched for something to pass the time. The bookcase was a bust. The owners of the house were self-help nuts, and while I definitely might need help, none of the books were interesting. One on the desk stood out from the others because of its age and worn condition and I guessed it was Taliesin's. I couldn't be any guiltier of invasion of privacy than I already was, so I picked it up and opened it.

It was an art journal filled with drawings, writings, and snippets of poetry. I knew I should probably put it back, but I'd read somewhere on the internet that scholars had been studying the remaining fragments of the works of Taliesin the Welsh warrior-poet for hundreds of years, so why not me? I sat down with the book on my knees.

The poetry was OK, but what held me in place violating my host's privacy were the beautiful drawings in pencil, ink, and watercolor. Notes in the margin indicated the names of the subjects, but I didn't need them to recognize Tynan by his hunched shoulders and lock of hair falling over one eye, and Miko by her ponytails and crooked smile. Daley was drawn in black ink with his arms raised to the sky. Beside him was a girl with a river of dark hair falling over her shoulders and a chain around her neck with a gem encased in filigree. The note in the margin said *Daley and Melusine.*

I forced myself to turn the page. A fragment of poetry was followed by the sketch of a wolf in fine pencil strokes, its fur ruffled by an unseen wind.

I have fled as a wolf cub.
I have fled as a wolf in the wilderness.

I flipped through the pages. Among the images of those I recognized—Rowan, Boudica, even Mom—one was repeated over and over: Morgan Le Fay.

I came to the last page. On one side was the full-length image of a smiling man dressed in armor. Tall and broad-shouldered, confident and powerful, I didn't need the dedication at the bottom to tell me it was Arthur. On the other side, another man's face looked back at me—a face of cruel angles, wintry eyes, and silver hair.

I knew that face.

Underneath the drawing was written:

Cernunnos, Lord of the Grey Lands of Avalon.

CHAPTER TWENTY FOUR

I was still staring at the page when Taliesin and Morgan entered the room. "Rhiannon, you surprised me. How long have you been waiting here?"

I couldn't answer. I had no idea how long I'd been staring at the portrait of my father.

Morgan frowned and took the book from my unresisting hands. She was dressed in a wiggle skirt, crisp shirt, and black pumps and her hair cascaded over her shoulder in controlled waves. I guessed the more conservative getup was for Taliesin's benefit.

Examining the picture, she turned to the bard with a smile. "A good likeness. When did you do this?"

"Years ago, when first we met at Camelot." He took the book from her and placed it on the desk.

I don't blame him for not wanting her to see all his stalker pics.

Morgan glanced at me. "Cernunnos is my brother and Viviane's too, so he is, in a way, your uncle."

"No," I said.

The porcelain skin between her eyebrows furrowed delicately. "'No' what?"

"He's not my uncle."

"True, he would not likely appreciate being called such."

"No. That man is not my uncle."

Morgan rolled her eyes. "Fine. Forgive my attempt at civility. You are right, he is not your uncle . . . ,"

"He's my father."

Stunned silence and then they both began to speak at once.

"You must be confused . . . ,"

"Nonsense, child, my brother has no . . . ,"

"You grieve for Viviane, so perhaps you . . . ,"

"To think that you, a foundling my sister took pity on, would dare claim kinship with the Lord of the Grey Lands!"

"Shut up, shut up, shut up!" I yelled. My head felt like spikes of metal were drilling through it.

Taliesin swayed. "Calm down, Miss Lynne. You are making it difficult for me to hold the binding. We will be quiet now, I assure you."

Peter ran into the room, followed by Thomas Redcap at a slower pace.

"Are you all right?" From the look of Peter's hair and wrinkled sweats, the intensity of my emotions had pulled him out of bed.

"What's going on?" Redcap asked.

Morgan gestured in frustration. "It is not enough that somehow this child wormed her way into my sister's life, but now she is claiming to be Cernunnos' daughter."

Redcap cocked his head at her and smiled. "Of course she is."

The woman's mouth gaped open like a fish. If it hadn't felt like my brain was being bashed in with a rock, I would have laughed.

"Look at her. The hair and eyes are different, but think of the fine cut of your brother's face, the arch of his eyebrows, the set of his shoulders. Think of what Taliesin told you of her abilities. Putting aside the color manifestation—which is something new, I admit—who has ever taken the power of a Cŵn Annwn before? They are *his* creatures, you know this. Not even you could do such a thing."

Morgan turned to the bard. "Could it be possible?"

Taliesin shook his head. "I do not know. We all thought that of you four, only you had ever brought a child into the world, and then only because of the earth magic."

Redcap leaned against the wall and snorted. "You're both missing the most interesting question. Viviane found her—or was given her—and has been hiding her from Cernunnos all this time. Why? Viviane broke faith with both Arthur and her brother. Why would she want her brother's child?"

Taliesin frowned. "A weapon?"

"Or perhaps a gift."

"I still don't believe it," Morgan said, folding her arms across her chest.

Redcap laughed. "Well, I think you'd better start. Viviane instructed the child to scatter her ashes on a lake right after a blue moon. Oh, and did I mention that L'Inconnue de la Seine came all the way from Europe through watery Paths to wait for her? I'd already guessed what the girl was before we came here."

Peter sat down on the couch. "What's he talking about?"

Redcap seemed to be enjoying himself. "Let me illuminate. Viviane allowed what was left of her power to dwindle until death so she could hide herself and this girl from her brother. Why would she make such a sacrifice? Viviane and Cernunnos were alike, cold and unfeeling. Seduced by the power this world gave to her, Viviane turned her back on her brother and bound her power to the worship she received from humans. When that worship faded, so did she. Fated to finally die, she gave what was left of herself in the care of a child. A child she instructed to throw her ashes into a lake. A lake made special by Viviane's love for it."

"A sacred pool," Morgan murmured.

"Yes, a sacred pool where she could be reborn in renewed power. Perhaps L'Inconnue felt the approach of Viviane's remains and was angry a greater water goddess might encroach upon her territory."

Peter shook his head. "How does that prove this Cernunnos guy is Rhi's dad?"

Morgan was pacing now. "When Viviane and I made our allegiances here, my brother swore revenge upon us. We were three sisters born of magic. Of all the creatures I have met through the long ages of the world, only he has the power to unmake us—or perhaps make us. If even a particle of Viviane's body remained and a portion of her spirit lingered, Cernunnos might be able to raise her up and restore her. Magic could birth Viviane again, but he would never do this for her."

"His child might have the same power," Taliesin said gently.

Everyone was watching me. I wanted to disappear but I forced myself to respond. "He's the silver-haired man. I saw him once when I was little. We hid from him. Mom never told me, but I guessed he was my father."

Taliesin sighed. "I had heard rumors that Cernunnos could cross the Wall in some manner. Viviane was known for her powers of concealment, just as a lake appears to be one thing on the surface, but its depths are hidden."

Morgan was Amazonian and I had to crane my neck to look up at her as she accosted me with questions. "What did you do when you scattered the ashes? Did you say anything? Did Viviane give you any other instructions?"

"She asked me to scatter her ashes in the lake, that's it. That's what I did."

Morgan glanced at Redcap and he nodded. "After L'Inconnue tried to drown her, Rhiannon threw the ashes into the lake and then passed out."

"And you saw nothing after that?"

"No, but Viviane has gone from me. It's not impossible that it was part of her plan."

The woman looked worried and it made me angry. "I'm not saying I believe it's possible, but don't you want your own sister back?"

Morgan turned away and Redcap answered. "Viviane was the Lady of the Lake and Arthur worshipped her before he came to understand who and what she really was. Still, because of that, she has power over him. If she were restored in her full strength, who knows what she would do; her allegiance was always as uncertain and as changeable as the waves."

Morgan made an impatient gesture. "It doesn't matter now. Either Viviane didn't know the nature of the spell she needed, or she died before she could show the girl what to do."

"So you admit that Rhiannon could be Cernunnos' child?"

"It is possible and impossible all at the same time. It would explain a great deal about my sister's behavior, though not my brother's. Which then begs another question—who is this child's real mother?"

My dream told the truth; my birth mother had abandoned me to Viviane.

A strangled yelp interrupted my thoughts. Peter had picked up the journal from the desk and was now staring at the portrait of Cernunnos with his finger on the page. He lifted it to show me what was written at the bottom. One word was scrawled in the corner in pencil. I'd missed it before. I'd been too busy staring at my father's face.

"C'mon! Merlin? Really?" Peter asked plaintively.

CHAPTER TWENTY FIVE

"Yes, he was known in my time as Merlin." Taliesin took the book from Peter's hands and closed it before gesturing for him to take his seat. "I had forgotten how powerful that name has become in this modern age, but I assure you, he was no kindly mage with a pointed hat and long beard. I have shown you the story before in broad strokes, but these are the finer details. Perhaps it will help you to know that Cernunnos was also Anubis in Egypt, Hades in Greece, and Pluto in Rome. When he tired of this world, he alone was not diminished by leaving his worshippers. His power seemed endless."

"Then a whisper of an unknown magic reached his ear. On a small and insignificant island in a cold sea, a young king named Arthur struggled to unite a nation. Despite what the storybooks say, there was no sword in any stone. It was Viviane who gave him Excalibur—a mysterious talisman of earth magic—and he became the Earth King. Cernunnos came to him and named himself Merlin—even I did not recognize him as one of the old gods of my people. He guided Arthur as his friend, but he sought to control and limit him as well."

"Arthur's power could not be contained and when he no longer heeded his mentor, the Lord of the Grey Lands sent Morgana to ensnare him with her beauty. You know the rest." He took Morgan's hand. "Instead, she told Arthur the truth. She changed her name to Morgan le Fay as a warning to her brother that she had come into her own power, but I remember her by the name she bore when first we met." Morgan pulled away, visibly moved. "She and Arthur had a child—a boy—and named him Mordred. They made plans to invade Avalon even though the Lady of the Lake turned against them for it and reclaimed Excalibur."

"Cernunnos was forced to resort to deception. He appeared to Mordred as Merlin and convinced the boy his father meant to rule both worlds as a tyrant—a truth wrapped in a lie. Mordred demanded Excalibur from Viviane as his birthright."

"In the midst of the last great battle on the borders of Avalon, Mordred stabbed his father through the heart with the sword and then fled and was never seen again. Excalibur was destroyed and the Lady of the Lake took what remained and hid it away. The Earth King could not be killed by his own magic, but instead fell into an enchanted sleep. Morgan le Fay honors the oaths she made to him on the day they met and guards him still until she can find the key to waking him."

Morgan brushed a tear from her face. "Thank you, my dear bard, for seeing me with such charity despite all that has passed between us."

"Always," he whispered.

With a sigh, she walked over to me and placed her cool hands on my temples.

"What are you doing?"

"I am helping you. My gift is the ability to sense the power in others. I guide them in accessing it and am able to take some for myself to shape with incantations for my own purposes."

That sounds like the politically correct way of saying she steals it.

Morgan laughed softly. "Do not look so worried. I can also draw my magic from places and objects of power, and for those I train, it is a gift given willingly in thanks. You, however, donated so much raw power to the heavens yesterday that even the efforts of Taliesin's electrically charged protégé could not clean it all up. Now hush. When Taliesin releases the binding, I will help you regain control over yourself."

"How?"

"By going into your mind."

Hell to the no.

Without warning, indigo disappeared and sparkling color rushed in. I must have closed my eyes because everything else disappeared. Disoriented, I felt like I was drowning.

"Rhiannon! Calm yourself. Keep your eyes closed and concentrate on me and me alone."

I forced myself to obey. To focus, I placed my hands over hers and her form appeared in my mind in colors even more chaotic than the ones flowing around me. Unlike Daley and the Cŵn Annwn, the outline of color around her seemed fractured and disjointed.

"I can see you."

"And what do I look like in your mind?"

"Colors all around you and through you, hundreds of them."

I felt her hands shift as she turned to speak to Taliesin. "She must be seeing what could be described as my aura. I had thought such an ability was only a foolish tale told by charlatans, but it would explain how emotion, power, and essence are visible to her." Her voice addressed me again. "What else do you see?"

"Color everywhere."

"And where does this color come from? Are you seeing the rest of us here in this room?"

I paused. "I don't think so. I mean, I sort of have a sense of people sometimes, but it doesn't come clear until I touch them. At least, that's what happened before."

Redcap's voice was close. "Here, let me try." His hand brushed my shoulder and I gasped as a fleeting vision of him lined in warm gold and blood red flickered across my mind.

"I saw you!"

Morgan gave an unladylike snort. "Yes, the redcap's nature is very vibrant. I am not surprised you could see him so easily."

There was silence. I tried to open my eyes, but I couldn't feel my body anymore.

It is beautiful, how you see it. My vision of the woman solidified and her voice was now coming from inside my head.

You can see what I see?

I am inside your consciousness. For the moment, I perceive what you perceive. My mental impression of Morgan sighed. *As I can also perceive that you are indeed his daughter. While your colors hold no meaning for me, I can sense the echo of my brother's soul in them. Of your true mother . . .* She paused *. . . there is something almost familiar about it, but I cannot capture it.*

Color swirled around me like a rushing stream. *What is all this then?*

I do not understand what it is, let alone what it means, but it does seem to have a source.

A source? We aren't anywhere! We're in my mind!

Yes, but this is your mental picture of a true reality. She pointed to an ebony strand spinning through the others, leaping and diving like a fish. *I do not like the look of that. What does it feel like to you?*

I only had to think of the color to have it in my hand. The headache I'd endured all summer spiked.

It's pain. My pain.

Follow it.

Releasing the ebony, I imagined myself sinking deeper into myself. Morgan disappeared. Following the dark flow, I arrived at a wall of ice edged in silver. Color stained with ebony leaked from a broken area in the center.

Viviane created this spell, but it is failing. Morgan's voice was faint and far away.

You can see it?

No, you are too far within yourself for me to reach, but I can sense her touch.

What is it?

Some sort of barrier, I believe. What do you perceive?

I approached it cautiously. *It's damaged.* I remembered how I felt something break when the harp screamed the prophesy at me. Panic rushed through me once again. *Where are we, Morgan? My brain? My soul?*

Who can say? It is a question more for science than magic. What I can tell you is that my sister created this to protect you from something. She was silent for a moment. We do know that at least some of what you perceive is power.

I noticed colors similar to Daley's and the Cŵn Annwn. Was this only a mental representation of what I'd done to them? What about all the other colors?

Morgan continued. *But if that is true, why would Viviane try to protect you from it? Why would she not want you to have power?*

I thought of the ebony and how it tainted all the rest. Where it touched the icy barrier, the surface appeared rotten and putrid.

Maybe because of the pain.

There was urgency in Morgan's voice now. *If you are right, then whatever is seeking its way in—whatever you take in—also wounds you. It is beyond me to remake my sister's construct, but I can strengthen it.* She murmured words in a language I didn't understand. *Take this and bind the corruption.*

A ball of light materialized in front of me. With a thought, I guided it to the weeping lesion.

What will happen? Am I healing something in my mind or in my body?

I do not know.

Anger sliced through me and a bright red separated itself from the other colors in response. Viviane had made this barrier to block my full abilities, I was sure of it. I had a sudden intuition that this particular shade of red—if I could grasp and shape it—could be used to ignite the flesh of an enemy. White horror filled me and the terrifying color paled and faded away.

As the spell spread across the barrier like an ointment, I surged up through myself back into consciousness. When Morgan slipped her hands out from under mine, I opened my eyes, blinking at the light.

"Were you successful?" Taliesin asked.

Morgan sat down on the edge of the desk and crossed her long, slim legs. "Perhaps. I believe Rhiannon draws power from those around her like a sponge; you were not far wrong when you suggested the *leanan sidhe* as having similar abilities. Viviane created a barrier to try to keep the girl from doing so, yet over the years she has unknowingly collected remnants from those she has encountered. She sees them as colors, though I have no idea of the reality of this or if she shapes them as she perceives them. Though this ability must be her heritage from my brother, I believe Rhiannon is part human and cannot safely contain the power she is heir to."

She looked at me. "I think Viviane was trying to protect you from yourself and perhaps those of power around you too. Why she did not tell you—did not teach you how to control it—I cannot say." Morgan's eyes were round and pale as moons. "With Viviane's death, the spell is failing. I have done what I can, but you will need to be vigilant or you will be a threat to both yourself and others. I will seek for answers concerning this strange ability and will help you where I can; we are blood and I am bound by that."

Her eyes became fixed, unblinking. "Remember this always: blood magic is the greatest magic of all."

A strange tingling went through me as if her words were the echo of something I was supposed to remember.

Morgan Le Fay stood and kissed Taliesin on the lips before turning and walking out the door.

Redcap winked at me as he followed her. "Until we meet again, *mo leanabh*."

Tired and depressed, I said my goodbyes and went home. Later that night as I lay in my own bed staring up at the ceiling, I thought about what I'd seen before I returned to the conscious world.

Morgan's spell seemed to heal the barrier, but a single ebony spot remained.

CHAPTER TWENTY SIX

The world fell into a pattern: days at school and nights and weekends at the mansion. And while I sometimes felt a prickle up my back as if someone was watching me, there were no more howls, paw prints, or bathtubs full of seaweed.

October arrived rainy and cold. Leaves flared briefly to early, vivid life and then were struck down into the gutters. Binnorie's prophesy wasn't mentioned and neither was my parentage. I assumed everyone who'd missed the big news had been told that Cernunnos was my father, but no one mentioned it. Perhaps they were all being polite.

And maybe they're just afraid the wrong word might set off the ticking time bomb.

Taliesin had assigned my training to Boudica and after a week, I wondered if it was to punish her or me. She wasn't openly hostile, but I could feel her dislike. Boudica was of the wax on wax off school of training and I repeated seemingly insignificant tasks until I wanted to go *Karate Kid* all over her ass. I practiced holding still for as long as I could. Once I achieved thirty minutes of complete stillness, we began again with me balancing on one foot. I was still struggling to achieve even one minute in that position. She had me solve complicated puzzles and then break them up and do it again until I wanted to scream. Apparently no one trusted me to try to access even the orphaned colors that remained behind Viviane's barrier until I demonstrated some discipline.

I just got better at faking it.

One of the best things about the mansion was the indoor pool and as the weather got worse, we all spent a lot of time there. The sight of Taliesin in Hawaiian print swim trunks was disconcerting.

Rowan in his Speedo made me want to gouge my eyes out.

Miko was afraid of the water and the closest she would go was to sit in her bikini on the edge of the shallow end, showing off her pierced navel in the center of her toned tummy. Peter did back flips and belly flops to impress her. Tynan swam solitary laps while Daley would practice a dive or two and then dry off and leave.

Tynan.

Things had gone awkward between us. Tynan was gorgeous and clearly into me, but he wasn't Daley.

Isn't the handsome guy with a secret past and hidden sadness practically the foundation of modern pop culture?

Because Daley was sad—I'd seen proof of it. I often stayed overnight in the room that was now unofficially mine. About a week after Binnorie's prophesy, I was almost asleep when a flash of lightning jolted me awake. When no thunder followed, I knew it was him. I tried not to look, but I couldn't help myself and I slipped out of bed and went to the window. Daley stood at the edge of the property staring up at the sky and I was shocked to see moonlight reflecting off tears on his face. The tingle of his electricity on my arms was almost like touching him and for a moment he was outlined in color. Ashamed of myself for spying, I was about to turn away when I noticed an iridescent aqua webbing across him. It was the same color I encountered when I took his power, but it clashed with the others; it didn't seem to belong.

I returned to my bed, but I couldn't sleep. The strange color made me uneasy and restless.

I wasn't the only one struggling to figure things out. According to Miko, Tynan's abilities had become even more unpredictable and unstable. He had lost the ability to call a Cŵn Annwn from the Wall. We found that out when Taliesin tried to arrange another test of my abilities. After a week of moping around the mansion, he created fire from air when he snapped his fingers. Rowan clapped him on the shoulder and declared the mystery solved—Tynan was a pyromancer. The next day, he couldn't make a spark no matter how hard he tried. Again, Rowan clapped him on the shoulder and promised they would figure it out eventually. And so it went—Tynan would exhibit a powerful ability that would just as quickly disappear and Rowan would try to make him feel better about it. Taliesin would remain noticeably silent.

The one constant was that Tynan could sense the Paths. He confided in me one night that back in Las Vegas he'd even travelled a couple of feet down one before losing his nerve. He made me promise not tell anyone and I agreed, but I resented being forced into what felt like a lie.

A couple of weeks before Halloween, Boudica and I were sitting by the pool in bathing suits and t-shirts while Peter, Tynan, and Daley horsed around in the shallow end. Their object was to keep a beach ball from hitting the water, but it was really an excuse to dunk one another and elbow each other in the face as they launched themselves after it. Peter had started the game and it was good to see the other guys laughing and having fun; my best friend's sunny nature was infectious. Taliesin and Rowan cheered them on while Miko sat on the steps leading into the pool gripping the metal handrail as if her life depended on it.

Boudica pulled off her t-shirt and threw it on the small table between us. "For all his long years, Rowan is still like a child. He takes such pleasure in simple things." The words might have been affectionate, but her tone was strangely neutral.

I decided to risk asking something I'd been wondering about. "I thought all the earth magicians were human. Why are Rowan and Taliesin still alive after all these years?"

Boudica shrugged, muscles rippling under pale skin scattered with freckles. "No one knows in Taliesin's case, but Rowan has bound himself to the bard by oaths sworn on both magic and his faith. He will remain on this earth as long as Taliesin does."

"So when Taliesin dies, Rowan dies too?"

She shrugged again. "Perhaps when the bard is gone, Rowan will begin to age again—though likely some battle or other will do them both in at the same time."

I shivered despite the moist, warm air. There was something cold in the woman's voice.

As if she doesn't even care. Or worse.

We sat in silence for a minute, but eventually I couldn't help myself. I had to ask, "And what about you?"

She lifted a pale eyebrow. "You mean, what is my status among the immortals?"

I squirmed under her frosty gaze. "I guess so, yeah."

"No one has told you then?" I shook my head. "I was the queen of the Iceni," Boudica declared proudly. Rowan glanced over in concern, but I smiled back and he relaxed.

She was waiting for me to respond, but I didn't what to say. Scowling, she jabbed her finger at me. "Don't they teach you children anything? The Iceni were of the Celtic bloodline. My kingdom was roughly where Norfolk is today. In *England.*" I could feel myself flush at her obvious contempt.

The woman sighed. "When my husband died, I was the rightful heir, but Rome had already placed its yoke around the neck of Britain and didn't recognize the right of women to rule. Rome took my kingdom, flogged me, and raped my daughters. So I waged war upon Rome. In the end, I was defeated. I took poison with my daughters, but to my horror, I awoke and they were dead. I fled and didn't know what I was until Rowan found me. I learned from Taliesin that my abilities in war and my immunity to the poison were my heritage as a descendent of the *sidhe* warriors who once served Cernunnos.

"*Sidhe?*" I repeated. It sounded like *shee*.

"I suppose, in your modern lexicon, you would call them elves, but they were nothing like the languid actors prancing around in your movies. The *sidhe* were warriors so beautiful and bright that it hurt to look at them directly. And so in love with battle that no full blooded members of that race remain— a little like your friend the redcap, though nowhere near as messy. The *sidhe* could sever the head of an enemy with one stroke and almost no blood, so clean and hot were their blades, so strong their arms."

Her lips twisted. "I didn't know which of my parents to thank for my unwanted life. They both died when I was young. I suspect it was my mother for my clearest memory is being taught by her how to lift a sword. Sadly for my poor daughters, their blood was too diluted by their father's to survive the poison as I had. I'm not immortal, though I've aged very little since that time. A dose of poison strong enough to account for what I am would have killed me, and I would have adjusted my portion if I'd known. By the time Rowan brought me to the bard, I'd relearned the desire to live—for vengeance, if nothing else." Boudica's voice became low and almost sensual. "I enjoyed watching the great Roman empire fall at last."

I felt sick. I wished I'd never asked.

Boudica smirked as if she understood how her story had affected me and it only increased her contempt. As she stood and walked to the deep end to execute a perfect dive into the pool, I could see the white of old scars criss-crossing the skin on her back.

Miko wandered over and plopped down into the chair Boudica had vacated. "Was she telling you her story? I caught the end of it."

I nodded. "It's sad."

The fairy pulled her knees up to her chin. "I don't know why she joined Taliesin. I don't think she likes any of us, not even Rowan. It's terrible what happened to her, but she's wrong inside. Did she tell you what she did after she lost her kingdom?"

"She said she waged war on Rome."

Boudica had joined the boys in their game and Daley was now sitting on the edge of the pool watching. His necklace shimmered aqua against his bare chest.

Miko dropped her voice so no one else could hear her. "When she conquered a Roman city, she destroyed it. She slaughtered almost eighty thousand people, even the women and children, and what she did to the bodies . . . well, it was awful. At least, that's what the history books say. Of course, when she was defeated, the Roman legions were just as bad, but it's not a Roman I have to sit across the table from every night."

I shivered again; I'd seen some of the darkness running through Boudica. "I feel sorry for her."

"Sure, feel sorry for her if you want, but don't ever trust her. I doubt she's even remotely sane. But then, who am I to talk about trust." The fairy was staring at her phone with a strange expression on her face.

"Who's that?"

A dusky blush spread across her cheeks. "No one important. Just an old friend who wants to hook up." She slipped the phone back into her bikini top and I laughed.

"That's an interesting place to keep it."

"Might as well fill it with something." She nodded her chin at Boudica. "We can't all be as well endowed as some people." The woman's *attributes* were definitely impressive, but my gaze strayed back to Daley.

"Oh Rhi, don't even think of Daley that way."

I forced myself to look away. "What are you talking about?"

"You know what I mean. Daley will break your heart."

"I'm just curious. Why does he always wear that necklace with the aquamarine stone?" From Taliesin's book, I knew it once belonged to the girl named Melusine.

Miko frowned. "The stone is clear."

I sat up straight as I realized that the color I saw the pendant as was the same as one of the colors I saw surrounding Daley. "Stay here for a minute."

"What are you doing?" Miko hissed.

"Checking something out."

I walked over to the shallow end. Rowan smiled and Taliesin nodded as they passed me on their way out. I almost lost my nerve at the shock that ran through me as Daley looked up. Electricity sparked across my skin. I'd asked Miko, but no one else was affected by Daley's power the way I was. The charm bracelet was still in my purse, but the red scar on my wrist burned.

"Hey."

"Hey," he replied.

That was the extent of the conversation. I stood there awkwardly. The beach ball hitting me in the face came to my rescue.

"Sorry, Rhi!" Peter yelled.

"It's OK." But instead of throwing the ball back in, I offered it to Daley. Frowning, he reached for it and I made sure our fingers connected. Hoping it would be enough, I closed my eyes.

For a moment, there was nothing, but then the stone burned aqua and I saw tendrils escaping it, entwining with Daley's lightning. They connected him to a beautiful girl with a river of dark hair.

CHAPTER TWENTY SEVEN

"No. Friggin. Way."

I'd dragged Miko away from the pool and we were sitting across from one another on her bed. She'd decorated her room with posters of Japanese rock bands and pink pillows. She was twisting one of them now in her small hands.

Tell me again what she looked like."

We'd been through this twice already. "Pretty. Long, black hair. White dress with swishy sleeves."

Miko's eyes were wide. "That's what we buried her in."

"What?"

"We buried her in a white dress with long sleeves."

"Who?"

"Melusine. Daley's girlfriend."

I had to know. "How did she die?"

Miko grimaced. "When Melusine first joined us, everyone was so excited. She was an actual descendent of the first Melusine—an ancient water elemental who could turn into a kind of dragon. Our Melusine wasn't a pureblood and hadn't learned how to access her powers, but it would have been a real game changer for us if she could. Unfortunately, the

original Melusine was also a man-eater—not just literally—
and ours was the same. By the time she came to us, she'd left
a pile of broken hearts behind. One of them eventually caught
up with her."

It took me a moment to understand what Miko was saying.
"She was murdered?"

"Some kid walked up to her in the middle of the street and
shot her. He put another bullet in his brain before Daley could
even react."

"That's awful."

"It gets worse. The kid left a suicide note in his pocket.
Melusine had been texting him, promising they would get
back together and getting him to send her money. When he
ran out of cash, she told him she was done with him. Daley
went out of his mind with grief. He took the necklace off her
dead body and he's worn it ever since. He's forgotten what
she was really like."

"What was she like then?"

"Beautiful, vain, charming, manipulative—just like most
sirens, loreleis, nixies, and mermaids." Miko smiled her
lopsided smile. "And fairies too. But Melusine was from that
whole class of Greylander whose sole purpose seems to be to
seduce and destroy men for the fun of it."

I didn't remind Miko that my closest magical counterpart
might be a *leanan sidhe*. "She seemed sad."

"She might have cared for Daley," the fairy conceded, "but
there's no way of knowing if he truly loved her back. That's
the only part of her magic she was ever in control of, but
Daley refuses to believe it. He refuses to remember how they
fought all the time or how jealous and unhappy she made
him."

I went to the window. The picture of Daley's face raised to the moon was an image my mind kept turning to no matter how hard I tried to banish it.

A pillow hit the glass and I turned and raised an eyebrow at Miko.

"Sorry. I wasn't aiming for you. I'm furious I didn't see Melusine's spirit had attached itself to that stupid necklace. Seeing the truth is supposed to be my specialty!"

I sat back down on the bed and leaned against the headboard. "So what are we going to do about it?"

"Hauntings aren't good. Ghosts forget the details of who they were in life but not the big emotions. Since that's all they've got, those emotions just get bigger and bigger until they spill over into the mortal plane. Add magic into the mix and it could get ugly."

"So if ghosts exist, I guess it's proof there's life after death. I suppose it's our duty to help her move on to wherever it is she's supposed to go." I didn't want to examine too closely why I wanted her gone so badly. "Do you think Daley can see her?"

"Nope," Miko replied without hesitation.

"Why not?"

"If Daley could see Melusine, he'd be happy."

CHAPTER TWENTY EIGHT

I sat cross-legged on my bed at the mansion with a magazine, but *10 Ways To Add Sparkle To Your Holiday Wardrobe* couldn't hold my attention. Giving up, I tossed it across the room at the dresser, but it missed and slid down the front to join the sweater, boots, three t-shirts, two pairs of jeans, and several textbooks on the floor. I was spending less and less time in my own home, but my two rooms were starting to look the same.

Peter had run out of excuses to give his parents and usually left before dinner. Missing him, I lay back and concentrated on the connection between us—a thread the color of new grass. As we both trained, our bond strengthened, and I was able to sense him without being near him. I'd also learned how to block that awareness. I never again wanted to catch even a hint of what he was feeling when he was making out with Miko. After that first horrifying experience, Taliesin taught me how to create a mental barrier to give us both some privacy. It was like imagining a pane of glass reflecting the bond away.

I tossed onto my side restlessly as I was reminded of my disappointing interview with the bard.

"Yes, I am aware that Melusine is still with us," was his calm reply.

"What do you mean you're 'aware' of it?" Miko squeaked. "Why haven't you done anything about it?"

Taliesin sighed and glanced at the fridge behind us; we'd cornered him in the kitchen on his way to get a snack. "What would you have me do? Take away Daley's only comfort in grief? Should I be that cruel?"

"You've been cruel before."

Taliesin nodded. "Yes. But Melusine has not yet posed a threat to any of us. You remember how Daley's sadness threatened to overwhelm him after death. You also know of how I first found Daley, but I will tell the tale again briefly for Rhiannon's benefit." He sat down at the kitchen table and gestured for us to join him. "Six years ago I went to consult with the Seer of New York." He glanced at me and I remembered that the Seer of New York was Morgause, my mom's and Morgan's sister. It felt strange to think that I had another aunt out there, although an adopted one.

"She told me to seek out the Hudson River Psychiatric Center and that my journey to knowledge would begin there. Since the Seer is rarely so specific—or coherent—I immediately went in search of the place. It was very strange. Part of the facility was still in use, but the rest was abandoned and filled with ghosts. I could not see them, but I could hear them answer when I asked why the Seer had sent me to them. Their whispers led me to Daley who was starved and half-crazed. He had been sent to the facility for observation, but in his confused state had run away to join the spirits. They are like lightning, after all, being insubstantial and yet powerful. I do not know how long he was alone with them. If Daley remembers, he does not say."

The magic in the bard's voice transported me. I could see barred windows, rotting wood, and Daley huddled in a corner in the dark.

Taliesin continued, "Daley's stepfather drank and his mother did nothing to protect the boy from the man's rage. One night, Daley fought back. It was also the night of a great storm. Without meaning to, he tapped into the power that is his birthright and struck his stepfather down with lightning. When the house caught fire, Daley's mother refused to leave her husband's side. Daley tried to save her, but they were separated by flame." The bard sighed. "I took him in as my son, but it wasn't until we found Tynan that he began to heal. Daley's great need is for a family to replace the one he lost. He was going to ask Melusine to marry him."

"What?" Miko gasped.

"When she died, I was afraid we might lose him to the shadows again. Rowan began to sense that the girl's spirit was still with us, but it seemed to help Daley and allow him to function. We hoped he would eventually let go and shed the ghost on his own." The bard's smile was grim. "I know we cannot let the situation carry on indefinitely. The more a spirit loses touch with its own identity, the more it believes that we, the living, are its enemy. But let us wait and see, for Daley's sake."

I tossed again and punched the pillow as I tried to get comfortable. Taliesin wanted us to stay out of it, but he couldn't see the web of Melusine's possessive desire.

She's not going anywhere.

I gave up and got out of bed; maybe a quick run would clear my head. Easing into the hallway, I closed the door carefully behind me.

"Where are you going?"

Startled pink starbursts blinded me, but I heard Tynan laugh softly. "Sorry, I didn't mean to scare you."

As my eyes cleared, I forced myself to smile. "It's OK. I couldn't sleep so I was heading down to the gym."

"I was going to go for a walk. Why don't you come with me?" I couldn't think of a way to say no so I followed him downstairs to the doors that opened onto the back terrace.

There was frost in the corners of the glass. "Maybe I should grab a jacket."

"You won't need one." Opening one of the doors and stepping out, Tynan motioned for me to join him. My reluctance must have shown on my face as I came out. "Don't worry. Look at what I can do." He made a motion with his hand and the chilly air around us swirled, picking up dried leaves.

Coughing at the dust of the leaves as they disintegrated, I was about to tell Tynan to stop when I realized the air was now dry and warm. I looked at him in surprise. "That's amazing."

He ducked his head but I could see the white of his teeth as he smiled. "What color is it?"

Warm air flowed over my skin and I closed my eyes briefly. "Auburn with orange sparks. But how?"

"I'm agitating the atoms around us to create heat. At least, I think I am. I've never understood where science and magic meet." He kicked at the remains of the leaves as they fell to the ground; the warm wind was gone. "It doesn't matter. I won't be able to do it again tomorrow."

A hint of warmth stayed with me as I followed him out into the yard. "It must be frustrating."

"If I knew who my real parents were, maybe I could make sense of it."

"You honestly don't remember anything from before Taliesin found you?"

Tynan shoved his hands in his pockets. "My first real memory is waking up in a bed at the ranch. Daley was watching over me."

"Don't you think it's strange that you and Daley were both found in New York?"

He shrugged. "Not really. New York's a magnet for anything paranormal. All the great cities of the world are. There's lots of Paths in them too. If I somehow got lost on one, I could have come from anywhere in the world." His fists clenched. "How can I find my destiny when I don't know who I am?"

I turned away and looked up at the moon—it was almost full and it filled the sky with cold light. "I don't believe in destiny. Knowing who your parents are might not give you any more answers than you already have."

Tynan came up behind me and put his arms around me. I wasn't short, but my head still came under his chin and I felt enveloped, trapped. "Finding out Cernunnos is your father is a good thing, Rhi." His breath was warm on my hair.

"Really? He sounds pretty scary to me. Even his own sisters are afraid of him."

"It's better to know who you are than to be left guessing like me." I tried to ignore a flash of irritation.

Tynan just can't let go of his own deal.

The hard pounding of his heart against my back reminded me of the day Mom hid me from my father. She'd hidden me from the world. My birth mother had abandoned me to her. They never asked me what I wanted. Tynan wanted to make decisions for me too—wanted to make me feel something I didn't feel.

I untangled myself from his arms as gently as I could and tried to change the mood. "Ty, I need to talk to you about Daley."

The air around me ignited with a boom and I was hurled to the ground. Hot pain prickled across my arms and the smell of burning hair filled my nostrils. "What the hell!" I screamed, but Tynan was shouting back and his voice was unnaturally amplified.

"Daley! Always Daley! Don't you know he can't see you with her around? He can't see anyone anymore. She will never let him go!" The house lights were turning on and it was only a matter of seconds before everyone found us.

"Can you see her?" I demanded. "Can you see Melusine?"

Tynan seemed to sink into himself. "She haunts me."

Daley and Taliesin ran out. Ignoring me, the two of them half dragged, half carried Tynan into the house.

Rowan rushed to my side and hissed through his teeth when he saw my arms. "Are you all right?"

"I think so."

Taking my hands, he helped me to my feet as he examined me. "It's just your forearms and they're scorched, not burned. I have something that will fix them." He looked at me with gentle eyes. "Please forgive him. He has these episodes sometimes, but he won't remember anything in the morning.

He likes you so much, and that's the problem; it reminds him of Melusine." Rowan spat on the ground as if her name tasted vile. "It wasn't enough she bewitched Daley, she had to toy with the boy too. Ty's broken and Melusine dug her pretty little teeth into that break whenever she could. She even tried to come after me once, but Bo holds all my heart."

Leading me into the house and down to the kitchen, Rowan retrieved an amber-colored glass jar from the fridge. The ointment in it smelled like wet grass. "Starweed for burns," he explained as rubbed it into my skin, "but I've increased its potency." When I ran my hands over my tingling forearms, they were smooth and hairless, but the pain was gone.

Once I assured the druid that his medicine had worked, I gathered my things and went home. I wasn't mad at Tynan anymore. Knowing his history, I couldn't be surprised he wasn't stable. At least I had the answer to one of his problems.

The bitch has to go.

CHAPTER TWENTY NINE

At school the next day, I marched straight up to the one person who could help me—Lacey McInnis.

In less than three months, Lacey had tumbled from the top of the food chain all the way to the bottom. The other Bumblebees had been tolerant of the new Lacey for a while, but once she quit cheerleading, they moved on. With her stringy hair and sloppy clothes, the rumor started that she was hooked on meth.

I knew what she was really hooked on.

I leaned against the locker next to hers. "So, how's the witch training going?"

Lacey lifted an eyebrow that hadn't seen a tweezer for a while. "What are you talking about?" As she pushed a strand of dirty hair out of her face, I was shocked to see the growing length of black tattoos creeping up the underside of her arm.

"C'mon, a moron could have figured it out. You keep having all these super-secret study sessions with Cailleach, and you've gone all Courtney Love all of a sudden. The answer is obvious to anyone who even guesses that magic exists."

Sighing, she closed her locker and leaned against it. "What do you want?"

"I need your help."

Lacey looked at me like I was crazy. "You need my help? You're the flavor of the month everyone's all excited about and *you* need *my* help? Do you know how hard it's been for me to achieve anything in magic? How much blood I've spilled from my own veins? I've basically given up sleeping and eating. Even with all that, I wouldn't be anywhere without Cailleach helping me. And do you know what's funny about that? Do you? Cailleach came here for you! When she found out you were already training with Taliesin, she decided to find a new apprentice. I said yes." The last was defiant.

"Good for you."

She stared at me for a second before responding. "What?"

"I said, 'good for you'. Why should you be the one left in the dark?"

Lacey's eyes went dead. Maybe she believed me. Maybe she was just too tired to fight. "What do you want?"

"Let's get out of here." I was skipping again, but my new birth certificate was my get out of jail free card. Lacey closed her locker with a bang. I thought she was going to say no, but then she nodded and began walking for the exit. I had to hurry to keep up with her.

We drove in my car to a donut shop a couple of blocks away and I bought us both blueberry muffins which we took to a table in the corner. After a slow start, Lacey devoured hers. I pushed mine over and she started pulling it apart and popping pieces in her mouth. Her wrists looked fragile with the dark knots and swirls of the tattoos enclosing them.

"When was the last time you ate?"

"Not sure," she mumbled between bites.

"Aren't your parents getting worried?"

"Cailleach put a whammy on them so they only see what they want to see. So," she said, brushing the crumbs away and changing the subject, "why do you need my help?"

"It's something I think I need a witch for." Either that or a priest. "It's kind of an exorcism," I added.

That caught her interest. "Cool. Demon?"

"Ghost, but a magic one."

"Still cool. Way above my pay grade though. We would need Cailleach's help."

I told her the whole story. I even threw in the detail about Melusine coming on to Rowan to make sure I sealed the deal.

Lacey shook her head. "Wow. She sounds like a real piece of work. But if she's not hurting anyone, why don't you do what Taliesin says and let her fade away?"

"He can't see her. I can, and believe me, she's not letting go of Daley without a fight."

"But what makes you think she's so dangerous? She couldn't even stop herself from getting shot."

A thread of mauve unease wormed across my vision and I hesitated. When I didn't reply, Lacey fidgeted and I knew I was losing her. Hoping I was doing the right thing, I said, "Melusine was the direct descendant of the original Melusine. She could turn into a dragon."

Lacey leaned forward, her face filled with excitement. "So she could turn into a big old ghost-dragon any second?"

"I don't know, but I don't want to wait around and find out." And I wanted Daley and Tynan out of Melusine's scaly little paws.

"Sounds interesting." She laughed brightly and was the Lacey I'd known almost all my life again. "Who am I kidding? It sounds awesome! I'm in. But I know what Cailleach's going to ask—what's in it for her?"

"She's interested in me, right? Well, I'm interested in me too. If she still wants to, I'll train with her. I'm not making a lot of progress right now. Maybe she can help me find some answers." I was betting dangling that bait would be enough to snag Cailleach.

Lacey started to leave. "Where are you going?" I asked.

She turned and lifted an eyebrow at me. "I'm going to contact her." I looked at her phone sitting on the table and she laughed again. "Haven't they taught you anything? I need water and a basin. I use a scrying bowl when I want to talk magic with Cailleach. That way, no one else can listen in."

I could feel my cheeks go warm. "Of course," I murmured to cover my ignorance, but by the look on Lacey's face, she wasn't fooled.

After a few minutes, the girl returned and the fleeting energy some food had put into her was gone. Slumping down in her seat, she wouldn't meet my eyes. "Cailleach has agreed to help, but she's naming the time and place as a condition."

"OK, when?"

"All Hallows Eve—Halloween. Are you going to the dance?"

"What dance?"

Lacey rolled her eyes. "The *Halloween* dance." The "Stupid" afterwards was implied.

"I don't know. Why?" Eastdale always held its dance the Friday before Halloween. It had been one of Peter's and Lacey's first dates.

Lacey's face clouded and I wondered if she was remembering the same thing. "I'll give you the rest of your instructions then."

"Why?"

"Because Cailleach says so, that's why. A spell like this is delicate and takes planning. She'll let you know what she wants you to do when she's ready."

As we left, I could tell Lacey was pleased to be back on top of our personal little food chain. I blinked away angry red specks—the dance was just a few days away and I could endure it until then. When I dropped her off beside her own car, she drove away without saying good-bye.

When I went back to the mansion, Rowan met me at the door and told me Tynan had no memory of attacking me and the ability he'd shown was gone too. Still, I was glad he was out target shooting with Peter and Daley in the makeshift range at the side of the property. I'd been surprised when Peter told me he was learning to shoot. Guns were useless against advanced magic beings, but apparently they worked just fine on a lot of lower monsters and most of the Protectors were packing.

I found Miko in her room and told her about my plan to get Lacey's help. To my relief, the fairy was all for it. We both decided to leave Peter out of it. He was spending a lot of time with Daley and my best friend didn't exactly have a poker face.

I felt bad about it, but not as bad as I should have.

The one wrinkle was Melusine. Each day I spent at the mansion, I became more attuned to Daley's power. I was beginning to be as aware of him as I was of Peter—as if we had our own bright bond. But I could feel Melusine through it too. I could see her all the time now, hovering around him, whispering in his ear. When I closed my eyes and tried to sleep, she was still there, shimmering in aquamarine. Once I tried to touch the color of her power. As it passed through my fingers, my hand brushed Daley's shoulder and we both jumped as electricity arced between us. Daley stared at me with dark, unreadable eyes. I looked at Melusine.

The day before the dance, Melusine turned and looked back.

We were all in the kitchen. Yelping in surprise, I bumped into Peter and he dropped the plate he was loading up with Rowan's brownies. Melusine pressed herself against Daley and stared at me, her eyes filled with meaning. He seemed oblivious.

For the rest of the night, she made sure I saw Daley was hers by pawing and kissing him whenever I was around. Then she confirmed my suspicion she wasn't confined to the vicinity of the necklace—or my awareness of Daley's power—when she appeared in the air above me as I lay half-asleep in bed. Screaming, I tumbled to the floor in a tangle of blankets and pillows.

Tynan's room was next to mine and he rushed in. "I heard you scream. Are you all right?"

"I'm fine. It was just a nightmare." I sent the same message down the green bond that vibrated with Peter's concern.

Floating in air and wrapping her white legs around Tynan's waist, the ghost flicked a silver tongue into his ear. Tynan's cheeks flamed and he excused himself.

I couldn't wait for Halloween.

When I shuffled down to the kitchen for breakfast the next morning, I was surprised to find Peter sitting with his elbows on the table, running his thumbnail between his teeth. He looked up when I came in and laid his palms flat against the surface, but he didn't smile.

"I want to know what's going on."

"What do you mean?"

"Don't mess with me, Rhi. I can feel it in here." He tapped his chest. "You're hiding something and I want in."

I sat down. "I didn't want to drag you into it."

"This thing between us—this bond—it doesn't give us a choice, does it. I go where you go."

I sighed and nodded. "I'm sorry. You're right." I told him everything about Melusine and the plan to get rid of her, including Lacey learning magic from Cailleach.

"Don't you think you should have told me all this days ago?"

I felt a twinge of guilt as the bond between us pulled and strained. "I know. I'm sorry."

Peter slammed his fists down on the table and I gasped at the violence of it. I'd never, ever seen Peter lose control.

Is there a Protector version of 'roid rage?

He flattened his hands against the table again, but they were shaking. "You and me for always, remember? No matter what, I have your back and you have mine. Right?"

A sudden chill crept up my spine. "Even if I'm wrong?" I asked softly.

214 · HEATHER HAMILTON-SENTER

"Even if you're wrong," he replied without hesitation. "The way I see it, you pick a side and stick with it. Maybe sometimes we'll be right and maybe sometimes we'll be wrong, but if we stick with each other, it'll even out in the end. If this is your plan, then I'm with you."

"What about Taliesin and Rowan?"

Peter smiled and the man filled with coiled aggression who'd assaulted the furniture a moment ago was gone. "I've known those guys for like, what, five minutes? What do you think?" I leaned over to give him a fierce hug.

"You and me," he said when I released him.

"You and me." I agreed, but in my heart I knew I was capable of choosing something else.

I pushed the thought away. "Do you want to go to the dance tonight?"

"The Halloween dance? Are you joking? Why?"

"Lacey wants me to meet her there so she can give me the rest of Cailleach's instructions."

"Why doesn't she come by and give them to you? Or text you?"

Peter was right. Meeting Lacey at the dance seemed unnecessary, but I didn't want to risk putting her off by being difficult about it. "I don't know, but let's just go with it, OK?"

"Fine. But you know you have to dress up, right?"

I stared at him as he smirked at me.

Kill me now.

CHAPTER THIRTY

I checked myself out in the mirror again.

"C'mon, what's taking so long?" Peter had been asking some variation of that for the past half hour. Taking a deep breath, I opened the door and refused to look at his face until he said something.

"Wow."

I could feel my cheeks burning. "Is it OK?"

Peter laughed. "OK? Are you kidding me? Don't get me wrong, Rhi, because I just don't think of you that way, but you're like *totally* hot."

I couldn't help grinning. "Don't be an idiot."

Dragon or no dragon, when Peter told me dressing up for the dance was mandatory, I wanted to scuttle the whole plan. He and Miko convinced Tynan and Daley to go too and it became a whole group date thing again.

Because that turned out so well the last time.

I fidgeted in my costume. Going as the Little Mermaid had seemed like a good idea at the time. Streaks of red hair paint enhanced the highlights in my hair and I'd scrunched and fluffed it into a mass of curls. A green bikini top was covered in sequins from the craft box hidden in the back of my closet. Rummaging through Mom's wardrobe, I'd found a long green skirt so tight that I couldn't imagine how she'd ever walked in it. It was made of a ruched material, and when I cut slits in the bottom edge, it fanned out to suggest a mermaid's tail. The skirt hung low on the hips and it was sheer enough to show my legs and bikini bottoms in the light.

I felt naked.

Peter was dressed as Superman and it was the same costume he wore when he took Lacey the year before. I didn't think it was the smartest idea, but it was too late to change now. Our school had a strict policy about dances—show up at the starting time or you didn't get in.

"Tynan's going to pop a gasket."

"That's not what I want." I rummaged through my purse until I found the charm bracelet. I was starting to feel silly about hiding something so pretty. I fastened the silver chain around my wrist, but I still twisted it so the charm was on the inside and dangled against my palm. "I'm not interested in Tynan that way."

Peter's pale eyebrows shot up in surprise. "I thought you liked him."

"I do, but . . . he's got issues."

As we walked to the Celica, I threw Peter the keys—there was no way I could drive stick in this outfit. As I eased into the passenger seat and the seams of my skirt strained, I prayed to make it through the night without a wardrobe malfunction.

Putting his key in the ignition, Peter paused and looked at me. "Is it Daley?"

"I don't know," I murmured.

Peter sighed as he started the car and pulled away from the house. "Maybe Tynan has issues, but so does Daley. I talked to him about Melusine."

"You what?"

"Don't worry. I didn't tell him anything, but Daley's my friend. I just wanted to know how he still felt about her. He's got to be aware of her on some level."

"What did he say?"

Peter hesitated before answering. "That he will never love anyone the way he loved her." Something crushed my heart in its icy fist. "I'm sorry, Rhi."

We were approaching the gate when a flash of something caught my eye. "Stop for a second."

Peter hit the brakes. "What? What is it?"

"I'm not sure, but I thought I saw something running around the back of your house."

He peered out the window. "A coyote?"

"I couldn't tell." Coyotes were pests, but not usually dangerous to people. They'd go after dogs or cats though and the stud farm had plenty of those.

Peter put the car in park and got out. As I watched, I noticed how muscled he was and how he walked with a kind of dangerous grace.

We're all changing so much.

He disappeared behind the house for a couple of minutes and then returned, got in the car, and drove away without saying a word.

I stared at him. "Well? Did you find anything?"

He was breathing fast, but his voice was steady. "Paw prints—lots of them—all around the house."

"Like the ones in the guesthouse?"

"Yup."

"Coyote?"

"Too big."

My mouth went dry. "What about your parents? Shouldn't we warn them or something?"

Peter shook his head. "They've gone to a show in Toronto and they're staying overnight in a hotel downtown. Old Tom was going to lock up the horses and go visit his daughter in Port Hope, so he's probably already gone too. We'll take care of things at the dance and then get the others to come back with us. I think we're going to need their help."

"Is it another Cŵn Annwn?"

"I don't know, but there's more seaweed piled up behind the house. It was like some kind of crazy nest."

What nests in seaweed hundreds of miles from the nearest ocean?

"I heard something howling a few days ago but I thought it was Tom's dog."

"Let's just do what we need to at the dance and get back as soon as possible."

We were quiet until we reached the school and parked. Shuffling inside in my skirt, I presented our tickets to one of the students sitting at the table outside the gym.

"Hey, Rhi! Love your costume." It was one of the Bumblebees dressed as a sexy nurse. I was pretty sure her name was Angela, but they all tended to mash together into one black and yellow swarm. Apparently none of them remembered they used to be almost completely unaware of my existence.

I felt bad that I hadn't really returned the favor.

"Thanks," I said as Sexy Nurse stamped my hand. "I like your costume too. Have you seen Lacey yet?"

Sexy Nurse exchanged a look with Sexy Little Red Riding Hood, another Bumblebee. "Oh, we've seen her. Maybe you can talk some sense into her. We've all tried."

"I'll try too," I said and that seemed to satisfy them. Sexy Nurse gave me a smile and a wave while Sexy Red stamped Peter's hand like she was kissing it.

I was too eager to find Lacey to wait for him to disentangle himself. As I entered the gym, the noise of the music and the color of the flashing strobe lights hit me with so much force that I thought my own colors had burst out of me and splattered all over the walls. My vision blurred, but I steadied myself and looked for Lacey.

She wasn't hard to find.

Swaying to the music, Lacey was dressed in black leather pants and a vest that pushed her breasts up past PG-13 territory. A studded choker and teased hair completed the biker chick look, but I knew the black tattoos crawling over her bare arms and shoulders were real.

As I approached, her eyes flew open, though I doubted she could hear me over the music. I would have expected her eyes and lips to be made up to match her outfit, but she wasn't wearing any makeup at all. In fact, her face was ashy pale. She shouted something, but I shook my head and pointed to my ear to show I couldn't hear. Grabbing my arm, she pulled me to the far exit and down the hall to the backstage entrance of the auditorium.

"No one will bother us in here." I followed her through the wings and onto the stage. It was pitch black except for the light above the stage manager's table. I couldn't see where the stage ended and the chairs began and I had a strange impression of nothingness—as if the rest of the world had disappeared.

"Scary, isn't it." I could hardly see Lacey, but her voice carried. "All those people—it's terrifying. But once you get going, it's such a rush." I wondered if she'd even auditioned for this year's show and her next words answered me. "I'll miss it, but Cailleach says performing is a type of magic. Until she frees me, all my magic is bound to her."

"What do you mean, 'frees you'?"

Lacey's laughter was harsh. "Don't you know yet, *Rhiannon*?" She stressed my name strangely. "None of us are free. Taliesin wants something, and if you don't give it to him, he'll just take it. Arthur and Morgan are worse. If you go to them, Arthur will enslave you the same way he did her. If you fight them, you'll die. You can always join your father I guess, but maybe there's a good reason your mother was hiding you from him." I was surprised by how much she knew and was glad the darkness hid my face. "At least Cailleach has promised to give me my freedom once she has what she wants."

"What does she want then?"

Lacey laughed again. "It doesn't matter. What do *you* want?"

"I want Melusine gone."

"Why?"

We'd been over this already. "Because she's dead. Because she enchanted Daley when she was alive. Because she could hurt him. She could hurt all of us."

"And because you love him."

The words rang out through the stage and the auditorium like a bell.

"Yes."

Lacey walked back into the glow of the stage manager's light and I left the abyss of the stage to join her. She handed me a piece of paper with elegant handwriting on it. "I'm glad you were honest with me. It makes everything so much easier. Cailleach's powers rise at Samhain—Halloween—and she'll meet you at that address and that precise time. This is your spell, so you need to find all the items yourself. Don't pawn it off on Peter."

I didn't like her tone. "Of course not."

She tapped her fingernails against the table a couple of times as we stared at each other. "Can I give you a piece of advice?"

I was starting to lose patience and a thread of angry scarlet wormed its way across my vision. "What?"

"Leave Daley alone. Be happy with Peter and Tynan. Cailleach says even the redcap has a thing for you. Isn't that enough? Why do you need Daley too?"

Scarlet frosted with ice. "This is for Daley's own good and everyone else's safety."

Lacey backed away into the darkness. "You're *his* daughter—what can you know about 'good'? Maybe someday, someone will decide to put you down for their own safety, for everyone's 'good'. Maybe they already have. Something's stalking you, Rhi . . ."

My name whispered and echoed across the stage, but I knew Lacey was already gone.

CHAPTER THIRTY ONE

I opened the stage door and walked out of the darkness, squinting at the transition to the fluorescent lighting in the hall. Clutching my list, I stumbled around a corner and walked straight into a couple making out against one of the lockers.

The girl pushed away in surprise. She was wearing a mask with feathers draping down her neck and a black-feathered ballet skirt, but I would have known her anywhere. It was Miko.

The guy with her wasn't Peter.

I didn't get a good look at him as he took off out the back door, but I caught a glimpse of white teeth when he turned to smile at me. I remembered the text she received that day by the pool and the old friend who wanted to hook up some time.

Apparently that's exactly what they did.

We stared at each other—Miko covering the side of her face with her hand and me crushing Cailleach's instructions into a ball. The paper was sweaty and ragged, but it was better than doing what I wanted to do.

It was better than punching her in the face.

"It's not my fault," she whispered. "I tried to tell you—you can't trust a fairy."

I turned and walked away.

"He promised me wings." I could tell she was crying, but I didn't stop. I could feel the red rising inside me was too dangerous for me to be around her. Almost blinded by angry crimson, I went back to the dance to find Peter.

"Rhi? Are you OK?" I was surprised to discover I'd almost walked right past Daley without seeing him.

"No. No, I'm not," I said, but I knew he couldn't hear me. He stared at me for a moment, then reached out and pulled me into his arms.

"What are you doing?" I yelped. The music had changed abruptly to a pop ballad and my voice was loud in the sudden quiet. Daley smiled. My embarrassment increased as I realized my arms were somehow around his neck and his hands were warm on the curve of my bare waist. We were dancing, sort of.

If you call me swaying back and forth in this stupid skirt dancing.

"You looked a little unsteady." He glanced over his left shoulder at my hand. "What's that?"

I crushed the paper into an even smaller ball. "Just something I need to take care of." I took a look at him. "What are you supposed to be?" He was wearing jeans, a black t-shirt, and a black leather jacket.

"Just me."

I shivered in his arms. That's all he needed to be—just Daley. Costumes might be mandatory, but I doubted anyone would have dared to try and stop him from getting in. "Why are we dancing?"

He shrugged. "It seemed like the thing to do." For once there was no challenge, no twist of suspicion in his voice. "A better question is what am I even doing here?"

There was no sign of Melusine and the necklace was tucked away under his shirt, so I relaxed a little. "I really don't know. I thought you'd bail."

Daley laughed and my heart skipped a beat; I'd never made him laugh before. I wanted to tell him everything—about Melusine, about me, even about Miko—but then his irises darkened and I could have sworn fine blades of lightning were flickering across them. Pulling me closer, he frowned as if he didn't understand what he was doing. My body was molded so closely to his that when a rumble of distant thunder vibrated through me, I wasn't sure where I ended and he began.

Daley closed his eyes as if he couldn't look at me anymore, but he leaned in and his mouth brushed mine. Gasping as electric sparks arced across my lips, I pulled back and that's when I saw them.

Melusine and Tynan standing together staring at us.

Shoving Daley away, I focused on Melusine's fury because I couldn't bear to look at Tynan. He was dressed as a pirate, like a little boy.

Daley stiffened and turned. "Ty . . ."

Melusine's face hardened as she realized Daley still couldn't see her. Iridescent scales rippled across her skin.

I braced myself to face the dragon.

The stench of seawater and rotting fish filled the air. People stopped dancing and looked around, making faces at the smell. A moment later, the fire alarm went off and kids started running for the exits. Teachers struggled to keep things under control and I was surprised to see Thomas Redcap among them.

Miko had to push against the crowd to reach us. "I pulled the alarm to get everyone out." I refused to respond to the pleading in her eyes as Peter joined us.

I haven't decided if I'm going to tell him his girlfriend is a lying skank.

Peter's pale eyebrows shot up as he wrinkled his nose. "Do you smell that?"

I nodded. It smelled like something that nested in piles of rotting seaweed.

The gym was now almost empty. One of the teachers began to walk towards us to herd us out, but Miko made a slight motion with her hand and he turned and ran out the nearest door.

"He thinks we're following him," she explained.

"Thanks Meek," Tynan said.

"Glamour is the only thing fairies are good for." She seemed so sad that I was tempted to forgive her, but one look at Peter, oblivious in his dorky Superman costume, and I just couldn't.

I caught his eye. "Can you see anything?"

"Nope. I'll cut the strobes." He went over to the abandoned DJ equipment and fiddled with the knobs until the colored lights stopped flashing.

"There." Daley pointed to the far side of the room. "By the wall. Something's moving." Melusine drifted to his side. The dragon had subsided.

Miko frowned as she concentrated. "It has a type of glamour, enough to make it almost disappear in shadow, but it will have to come out to attack." She swayed, but Tynan caught her and steadied her. When she pulled away, her costume was dark and wet around the neckline and something that looked like blood stained the sleeve of Tynan's shirt.

We all jumped when the door to the gym crashed open, but it was just Redcap. "I see you've cornered the Dobhar-chú," he commented as he sauntered towards us, "but this one has friends hiding in the corners." I caught the fleeting impression of movement on the far edges of the room. "Water-hounds are cautious killers. I've been following this pack ever since I caught their scent."

"What are they hunting?" It had to be asked, but I already knew the answer.

Redcap winked. "Why, you, *mo leanabh*, of course. They've been hunting you."

CHAPTER THIRTY TWO

Terror presented itself in its usual cold white, but I wasn't sure anymore that I could trust what I felt/saw. Ignoring it, I stuffed the crumpled up paper in my fist into the only place my costume would allow—my not-so ample cleavage. A couple of quick rips and the slits in my skirt opened up past my knees. Redcap's smile had turned into a bit of a leer, but at least I could move freely.

Daley put his hand on his brother's shoulder. "Call Dad."

Tynan nodded and pulled out his phone.

Redcap seemed amused. "Good idea. I'd forgotten the bard has some expertise in canine matters."

Peter walked back to us, never taking his eyes off the prowling shadows. "What's a water-hound?"

"A very vicious creature," Redcap replied.

"Like the Cŵn Annwn?"

Redcap shook his head. "No, nothing like. The hounds of Avalon are dangerous but noble creatures. The Dobhar-chú honor nothing. They kill for the joy of it. Dobhar-chú means water-hound, but they aren't hounds at all. They're monsters born in the depths of the sea, but as long as there's enough water to keep their hides moist, they can make their nests almost anywhere."

I thought of the wet carpet in the guesthouse and the small stream that ran on the edges of Windfield and behind the main house.

"The Dobhar-chú will study their prey and wait till they have the advantage. They probably followed you here in the hopes of taking you by surprise in the confusion and noise." He ogled my body and his mouth twitched. "And when you're hampered by that quite fetching outfit."

I flushed and crossed my arms over my chest. "Why are they after me?"

Redcap shrugged. "Likely they've been conjured by someone to eliminate you."

"Who?" He shrugged again.

Miko pointed. "That one's bigger. It might be the leader." I could see the shape of the creature, but nothing else.

"Can you do anything about its glamour?" Daley asked. Melusine stood close to him and she seemed more solid than before.

The fairy's face was strained. "I'm trying to break through, but it's hard." She swayed again and then straightened her shoulders. There was a moment of change, as if the earth shrugged under my feet, and then everything looked subtly different. Miko had broken the Dobhar-chú's glamour.

"Fairies are good for something," she muttered as she fell to the ground.

"Miko!" Peter cried as he rushed to her and pulled her limp body into his arms. Her feathered headdress fell off and I could see the two small puncture wounds on the side of her neck and the thin stream of blood leaking from them. There was a hiss of indrawn breath—Daley's—and my attention returned to the shadows.

But the shadows were gone. Instead, four enormous creatures stared at me.

Redcap whistled softly. "They hunt in mated pairs. Someone most certainly wants you dead to send two sets after you."

I was almost submerged in a torrent of white fear. Redcap was right; they were nothing like the beautiful and terrifying Cŵn Annwn. The largest was as long as Tynan was tall. Dark and slimy, rotting seaweed was matted in its wet fur and its claws and teeth were yellow and dripping. The smell of dead fish made me want to gag.

"Dad's on his way," Tynan said.

Daley grunted. "I'm not sure he'll get here in time. We'll have to take care of this ourselves."

Tynan hunched his shoulders. "I don't have anything in me today."

"You're bigger and stronger than anyone else here except Peter. Stay between Rhi and the Dobhar-chú."

I felt a flash of acid purple irritation; I didn't need a six foot four babysitter. "Why don't you just zap it?" I made a gesture to indicate throwing lighting.

"My abilities are limited inside. If I can lure them out. . ." He gasped and stared at my arm. Before I could react, he grabbed my wrist.

"Ow!" I cried as he twisted it to catch the light. The silver wheel charm dangling from the delicate chain sparkled with pale fire.

"Where did you get this?" His fingers dug into my flesh.

"You're hurting me!" I tried to pull away and keep an eye on the Dobhar-chú at the same time, but Daley's grip was unbreakable. Tynan and Peter watched us in confusion.

Redcap frowned and put his hand on Daley's. "You're hurting the girl. Let her go. Now!"

Daley was taller, but Redcap's face was dangerous. Daley released me and I glared at him as I rubbed my bruised wrist.

Stepping between us, Redcap gave me a reassuring smile and took my hand gently to lift it back up to the light. "Is that what I think it is?" he murmured.

Daley answered him. "It is. I've been searching for it all my life! I would know it anywhere."

Redcap raised an eyebrow at me. "Where *did* you find it?"

"Guys," Peter interrupted, "I think we have more important things to worry about right now."

I glanced over at the beasts; they were definitely closer.

"Actually," Redcap replied, "this is indeed quite important 'right now'."

I was starting to panic and yellow fluorescence surged through me; the creatures were getting ready to pounce. "It's Viviane's. I found it with her things. Satisfied?"

"Yes, quite." Before I could move, Redcap snapped the charm off the chain and presented it to Daley with a flourish. "Our Rhiannon may have found the Wheel of Taranis in Viviane's jewelry box, but I believe it belongs to you."

The moment Daley's fingers touched it, the charm expanded until it was the size of a small shield. His hand fit around the edge and between two of the spokes as if it had been made for him.

Which I guess it probably was.

With a mighty heave, Daley threw it against the windows on the outside wall of the gym and they shattered. The scar on my wrist burned and I felt the wheel's power as it soared into the sky, searching for thunder and lightning.

The Dobhar-chú attacked.

CHAPTER THIRTY THREE

I was wrong about Melusine—the dragon hadn't entirely subsided. As the Dobhar-chú leaped at us, Melusine swept shining claws across the closest one's belly. It surged through her insubstantial form and collapsed on the ground with its guts spilling out. The ghost disappeared and the other Dobhar-chú skidded to a stop on the smooth gym floor.

The Wheel of Taranis whizzed through the air and returned to Daley's hand like an electrified boomerang. Pointing it at one of the beasts, he gestured and lightning spun out of it and ripped a long gash along the creature's back. Even though it was wounded, it never made a sound. Daley raised his arm to strike again, but the beast sprang and knocked him to the ground. The Wheel fell out of his hand and skidded across the floor.

Tynan struggled to pull the Dobhar-chú off his brother as Daley held its forelegs to keep the gnarled claws from slashing his chest. The third beast circled Peter who was still crouched beside Miko. Redcap used his own sharp nails to rake its flank while Peter punched it with his fists.

That left the last, the biggest, facing me. I had to keep my eyes open, but I tried to sense its essence. I almost had it and there was nothing pure about it—the Dobhar-chú's colors were moldy and putrid—then it slipped away. I needed to get close enough to touch it. Wet eyes gleamed with intelligence and I knew it had orchestrated this moment, separating me from my friends to tear me apart.

Three howls pierced the air and the Dobhar-chú lifted its ugly, dripping head to look past us. A white form sped past me so fast that it was almost a blur. With a great leap, it launched itself at the monster. The two creatures—one black and one white—fought in frenzied motion and eerie silence. When my friends dispatched their own attackers and the beasts lay dead, they gathered beside me to watch.

"What is it?" Peter held Miko tenderly in his arms, but he still flanked me, ready to fight.

"It's a Cŵn Annwn," Redcap answered and then frowned, "only, somehow it's not."

The Cŵn Annwn was smaller and was losing the fight. Daley lifted the Wheel, but I put a hand on his arm to stop him—there was no way to strike one animal without hurting the other.

I shook off the static electricity that accompanied every contact with Daley. I didn't know what to do. I couldn't get close enough to touch the Dobhar-chú and take its power. The Cŵn Annwn would die and it would be my fault; I would never be able to hide from the shame of what I'd done to it.

Hiding—that was something I knew intimately. Closing my eyes, I conjured up Viviane's voice.

Rhiannon, listen to me. We cannot be seen. Hide in the shadows and be still and silent.

The veil of blue mist that appeared in my mind had broken apart almost into nothingness. Acting on intuition, I searched among the orphaned remnants of color in my mind. Similar tones spoke of sadness and loss, but this one was very specific. I was about to give up when I sensed a small amount and called it to myself. With a thought, I added it to Viviane's mist and repaired it. Giving it a mental push, I opened my eyes.

A substance like filmy cloth lay in my hands.

Redcap approached cautiously. "What is it, *mo leanabh?*"

"The spell Viviane used to hide me, but I've changed it a little." Before he could question me further, I threw the veil of blue over the Dobhar-chú.

Viviane used this to hide me from the world. Let's see how you like being hidden from what you need to survive.

Slipping past the Cŵn Annwn, the color molded itself to the other creature's skin. The hound of Avalon backed away, sides heaving, as the Dobhar-chú tried to claw the veil off. The spell was created by Viviane from her strengths—the hidden depths of water and the dark side of the moon. The Dobhar-chú needed water to survive, but with this spell, I was the master of water. I hid every cell of the creature from even the tiniest molecule of moisture. Thrashing and struggling, it made the first sound since it revealed itself—a sad, strangled whine. Even through the blue, I could see the creature dry and contract until it was a desiccated husk. When I released the spell, the Dobhar-chú's body collapsed in on itself and crumbled into dust.

Something brushed my leg and I looked down, but I was too sick of myself and what I'd done to be further surprised. A grey wolf approached the Cŵn Annwn. The two animals touched noses in silent communication and then the Cŵn Annwn gave three howls. As the air shimmered, the grey wolf disappeared and Taliesin stood in its place.

I remembered the passage in the bard's journal: *I have fled as a wolf cub. I have fled as a wolf in the wilderness.* I remembered that Goodfellow had said, "Many a year he once padded through my forests, as silent as the wind." Taliesin was a shapeshifter. At least, that's what I guessed he was. He certainly didn't fit the profile of a snowboarding werewolf.

The bard approached and the Cŵn Annwn followed, limping. "I would like you to meet Seolan. He is the hound of Avalon whose power you took. He has returned to the state of his birth before Cernunnos transformed him and has been rejected by his pack." Taliesin scratched the dog behind his large ears and the animal leaned against him in satisfaction. "Seolan is an Irish Wolfhound. They were once the hunting dogs of the nobility of that land and he is still formidable, but now mortal. By taking his power, you have declared dominance over him. He accepts you as the leader of your pack and seeks to be allowed into it. To please you, he has been hunting the Dobhar-chú while they have been hunting you."

Taliesin gestured and the dog took two steps forward, long nails clicking on the gym floor. I kneeled down and placed my hand on his head. Closing my eyes, I searched for his colors, but nothing of the supernatural creature he once was remained. He was just a large dog with white hair threaded with grey.

Seolan lowered his head to his paws and looked up at me with deep, liquid eyes.

I wanted to run. I wanted to wrap myself in a veil of blue so dark no one would ever find me. What I'd done to him was unforgiveable. I'd stolen from him the joy of the hunt, the wild sky, and the warm gift of belonging. I'd taken his life out of curiosity and ignorance and left a smaller, greyer one in return. I was the monster here.

But Seolan forgave me. I saw it in his eyes. Throwing my arms around his neck, I pressed my face against his silky hair and cried for the first time since Mom died. Seolan waited patiently while I purged myself of all my grief.

"Guess I missed the fun."

Miko was awake. Rubbing her neck and grimacing at the fresh blood smeared on her hands, the fairy stepped towards me as if she wanted to say something and then stopped, eyes wide.

"I feel funny . . ." She convulsed as shudders rippled through her body. There was a wet, ripping sound and wings sprang from her back as delicate and translucent as I'd imagined fairy wings would be.

But they were also black and had the thick ridges and jagged edges of the wings of a bat.

CHAPTER THIRTY FOUR

Daley and I sat on the landing at the top of the stairs. After a tense drive home, Miko and Peter had gone to her room.

Then the yelling began.

Everyone else was hiding from the drama and even Seolan had run away into the forest behind the house. With her wings appearing like that, Miko had come clean and confessed she'd let her Ex infect her with his bite. Peter's deep anger had been frightening and I'd had to block my awareness of him through our bond.

I watched Daley from the corner of my eye. The wheel charm had shrunk back to its original size and he was rubbing it absently.

Redcap had called it the Wheel of Taranis. I wanted to know more, but Miko's transformation had been so stunning that I didn't notice when he slipped away.

Did Mom want me to find it? Why did she have it? Was she hiding it from Daley?

"I should have known. I should have stopped this," Daley said bitterly.

"How could you possibly have known?"

He shoved the charm in the pocket of his jeans and dragged his fingers though his hair. "Miko always had a thing about not having wings. I thought it was enough that she was Binnorie's keeper, that she had a purpose. I guess not. She must have been desperate to do what she did. I should have known," he repeated. "It was my responsibility."

"No, it's not. You're not her keeper or her judge, no matter what Taliesin says."

His body sagged. "I guess Miko and Tynan have been talking about me."

I put my hand on his shoulder, but the jolt that shot through it made me gasp and sparks of power danced between my fingers. "Do you see that?" I whispered.

He put his hand over mine and the sparks flew higher. "Yes." Sliding his fingers down my arm, Daley laughed softly as electricity raised the fine hairs. Shivering, I pulled away, but he grabbed my hand to stop me. Tracing the lines of the scar on my wrist with his finger, he looked at me and blades of lightning flashed through his eyes.

It was hard to be so close—the sting of his power hurt— but it was harder to stay apart. As I pressed myself against him and he put his arms around me, the tremble in his body was like silent thunder.

Ice touched my back and I was wrenched away. Skidding down the stairs on my behind, I hit the ground with a thud. Daley stared at me for a moment in stunned surprise and then came after me.

"Are you all right? What happened?" He helped me to stand.

I tried to cover my embarrassment with a laugh. "I'm OK. I must have slipped somehow." Movement caught my eye.

Melusine hovered above the spot where we'd been sitting and she was smiling. The ghost had pushed me. When she waved at me coyly, light caught the luminous claws on her fingers. Daley followed my gaze. "What are you looking at?" I was saved from answering by the sound of a door crashing against the wall. Peter stomped down the stairs and his face was so filled with fury that even Melusine swished out of the way.

Miko ran after him. "I'm sorry!" Her wings were retracted and she looked pale and fragile.

"Save it!" Peter snarled as he pushed past Daley. With a growl, he turned and drove his fist through the window beside the front door. I jumped back as shards of glass hit the floor around him. Miko's scream brought the bard and druid running.

Rowan approached Peter like he was an animal that might bite. "Steady, lad. Don't move too fast or you'll do more damage."

Ignoring him, Peter yanked his arm out of the jagged break in the window. He wasn't even scratched. When he looked at me, his eyes were bleak. "We're all changing so much," he whispered, echoing my earlier thoughts.

Miko was crying, but Peter just continued to stare at me as the anger drained out of him. Through our bond, I let him feel that I was with him, always. He nodded, knowing I would come with him, and then opened the front door and walked out.

"Rhi?" the fairy said softly.

"Go away, Miko." I couldn't look at her, but I heard her obey.

Taliesin walked away without commenting, but Rowan hesitated. "Coming into one's power is different for everyone, and change is,"—he paused and his face was sympathetic—"inevitable." After a moment, he followed the bard.

Melusine had already drifted off to wherever she went when she wasn't stalking Daley. He was clutching her pendant and wouldn't meet my eyes. "Goodnight," he murmured and then climbed the stairs to the bedrooms. I was left standing alone in broken glass.

The wood floor creaked and pink splattered across my vision as my heart jolted in surprise. Not quite alone—Tynan lurked in the shadows behind the stairs.

"Good night, Rhiannon." His voice was strange—darker, older—and the colors it conjured in my mind were disturbing.

I couldn't manage a reply as I let myself out.

CHAPTER THIRTY FIVE

Halloween and *trapped* were the first thoughts to penetrate my soggy brain. *Headache, hungry,* and *morning* followed. Pushing myself up on my forearms, I scraped back the tangled hair from my face to see why I couldn't move.

Seolan was lying across my legs. I'd heard him howl a few times and knew he was close by, but hadn't seen him since the night of the dance.

The dog moved off when I shifted. Giving him a tentative pat on the head, I kicked away my blankets and got out of bed. How he got inside was obvious when I went into the living room. I always left the kitchen window open a little, even when the weather got cold. It was wide open now and the screen was on the floor. Muddy paw prints dotted the kitchen counter, but I couldn't be mad; they blended in with the dirty dishes and empty takeout containers. I pulled the window almost closed but left the screen out.

The movement intensified the pain in my head. Bottles of pills were stashed in every room now—I'd tried everything legal looking for relief. The drug of choice in the kitchen was aspirin. Popping two in my mouth, I swallowed them without water, then decided to take two more. I wasn't going to let a headache spoil the day.

It was October thirty-first— Samhain—and I was finally going to get rid of Melusine.

Since the dance, the ghost had grown bolder. She roamed the mansion freely and I'd endured a number of increasingly solid pushes and slaps when I wasn't expecting it. After she raked my arm with a luminous claw during dinner and I had to pretend I'd somehow cut myself with my own knife, I lied about having a cold and stayed away from the mansion for a couple of days.

I still needed to pick up the items for the spell. Scrawled across the bottom of the page of instructions Lacey gave me was a note that elements collected as close as possible to Samhain had more inherent power, so it was a good excuse to skip school. After a half-hearted attempt to tidy up, I pulled my hair into a loose bun and left the house. Seolan slipped out with me and bounded off down the laneway into the trees, but not before nuzzling my hand with his nose. I had a feeling he'd be back.

It was nice to have someone to come home to.

I spent the day gathering everything and then grabbed some food from the only roadside taco truck in Oshawa. It meant a trip to the edge of town, but the extra fortification was worth it. I had just enough time to wolf down two soft tacos before the dimming sky told me it was time to go. I arrived home to find Seolan sleeping on the couch and the wind whistling through the open kitchen window. I turned up the heat and closed the window just enough to keep the worst of the cold out in case the hound wanted to leave the house while I was gone.

By the time I was showered and dressed, it was almost dark. Gathering my purchases, I was just putting them into one bag when Peter opened the front door and stuck his head in.

"Hey, I have Mom's van so I thought I'd pick you up."

"Thanks." I followed him outside. Pulling the door closed firmly, I checked on the sprig of holly above it. It was still green.

As we walked to the van, I could feel Peter worrying about seeing Miko. The last few days had been difficult. She'd called and texted, but he hadn't answered. When she started texting me, I ended up as the go between relaying messages.

I wasn't sure what he was more afraid of: getting mad at her again or forgiving her. I knew what I would do, but for Peter, who was raised with a strict moral code, forgiveness was the only option. Except he'd confided in me that he wasn't sure he could.

Climbing into the van, I put the plastic bag on the floor and Peter started the engine. Turning on to the main road, he had to be careful not to hit any of the trick or treaters who were beginning to filter through the gates. Mr. Larsen gave out full-size chocolate bars on Halloween and that info had spread like wildfire through the new subdivision behind us. Most kids were willing to walk a fair bit—or to get their parents to drive them and drop them off—to trick or treat at a full-size house.

"What's in the bag?" Peter asked.

"Two dozen birthday candles, a can of cream soda, a bag of glass marbles, gingerbread man cookies, and a picture of an oak leaf. It was supposed to be an actual leaf, but I couldn't find one so Lacey said a picture would be fine. I had to go to the library and pull one out of a book." I felt rather bad about it.

Peter's pale eyebrows disappeared into the light fringe of his hair. "Really? Lacey and that teacher are going to conjure up some major mumbo jumbo and that's what they need?"

"Yup." I didn't want to admit it, but I'd been wondering if Lacey had given me the list to waste my time out of spite. I couldn't even imagine how any of it would be useful in banishing a ghost.

"What's our cover story then?"

"Miko's worked it out. She's telling Tynan and Daley we're having a sort of magic intervention for Lacey at Cailleach's."

"We're going to her place?"

I shook my head. "Lacey said it was a neutral location that wouldn't make Melusine suspicious."

"Nice." Peter grinned and I could feel his renewed tension through our bond. He was so tightly sprung now that he always seemed ready to explode into action. That terrible anger was gone, but I couldn't lie to myself anymore that a Protector was a glorified bodyguard. A Protector was a warrior.

When we arrived at the mansion, I grabbed the bag and climbed into the middle row after a look from Peter. Miko slipped into the seat I'd vacated, but after a murmured greeting, they were silent.

I was surprised when Tynan got in the van and sat in the very back. Daley eased in beside me. Melusine floated into the empty spot beside Tynan with an acid look in my direction.

"So," Peter said, "where are we going again?"

I checked the map on my phone. "Go north on Holt Road. Right before you get to Conlin, turn at King Lane."

He nodded. "That's not too far, maybe 5 minutes."

I checked the clock on the dash: 5:45. By the time we turned on to Holt at 5:52, my stomach was wound tight around a knot of marigold and I was having serious second thoughts about the whole thing. The sun hadn't fully set, but there were no streetlights and it was dark and eerie—particularly with a ghost in your car on All Hallow's Eve.

Peter stopped the car and put it in park.

"What's wrong?"

"What was the address again?"

"King Lane, corner of King and Holt."

"That can't be right. Holt ends here."

I took off my seat belt to look over the dash. Peter was right—the road had come to an end and the headlights showed an overgrown path in front of us. I checked my phone again. "Holt's supposed to go all the way to Conlin Road."

"Well, it doesn't." He grabbed the phone. "Wait a sec while I check something."

I glanced over at Daley. Melusine had her arms wrapped around his shoulders from behind and her claws had become translucent fingers again. The helpless longing of her pose and Daley's constant caress of the necklace made me feel guilty, but also seriously creeped out.

And then Melusine's eyes opened and there was so much menace in them that I couldn't wait to exorcise her pretty little behind.

"Cool." Peter said as he passed the phone back to me.

"What?"

"It's a trap street."

"What?" Tynan repeated from the back.

"A trap street." Peter twisted around. "You're kidding me, right? Do you guys seriously not know? A trap street is a street that doesn't exist. Map makers put them in so if somebody copies their map, they can tell. I read about them online, but I never thought I'd find one."

Peter was in geek heaven, but I wondered if this was another element of the spell. Names were important. Maybe magic flowed freer in a place that didn't have a real name to bind it.

Daley was impatient. "We must have the wrong address. Somebody call Lacey."

I checked the clock: 5:59. "There's no service," I lied as I put the phone in my pocket.

Tynan leaned forward. "There's probably something up ahead we can't see, maybe a private road. If Lacey's got as deep into witchcraft as Rhi says, then we should at least try."

"Ty's right." Miko pointed. Easy to miss in the darkness, Lacey's car was parked just off the path.

Daley shrugged and the ghost hopped on his knee and nestled into him.

Peter pulled forward a few more feet and then put the van back into park. "I think we're walking from here."

As I got out, Miko linked her arm through mine and pulled me ahead of the others. Her skin was cold and clammy and I suppressed a shudder of revulsion as I shook her off.

Her face went blank. "He knows," she hissed and I shivered again at the new sibilance in her voice.

"Daley?"

She shook her head. "Tynan. He was getting suspicious so I had to tell him everything." She glanced over her shoulder to make sure no one was close enough to hear. "He wasn't surprised."

"He remembers seeing Melusine?"

"I don't know. He's not happy though. The only thing that convinced him was telling him Melusine wants to hurt you and is getting strong enough to do it." She wasn't wrong. The long scratch on my forearm was proof.

The fairy looked scared. "And there's something else. I heard Binnorie singing yesterday when I was in the hallway outside my room. I've never heard her sing on her own like that." She hesitated. "I don't want to tell you . . ."

"Miko . . ."

She sighed. "She was singing that the dragon was going to peel your skin off like a banana."

My heart thumped in my chest and yellow alarm pulsed with it, but I ignored them both. I checked my phone again: 6:02. The path ended at a small clearing with a picnic table off to one side. Lacey and Cailleach were waiting for us.

"Give me the bag," Lacey demanded and I handed to her.

The others arrived and Peter put the camping lantern he was carrying on the table. The light illuminated a lit cigarette balancing on the edge and Melusine flitted over to it, gazing at it longingly.

"Melusine used to smoke in her room when Daley wasn't home," Miko said with wonder in her voice. "She knew he wouldn't like it if he ever found out."

"You can see her?"

Miko nodded. Melusine was getting stronger.

Cailleach's eyes were black pits in her face. "Belief begets reality. The god of thunder's belief in his love for the dragon girl has tethered her to this world, but it is your belief and

desire for her which has brought her back to the brink of life."
The woman wasn't looking at me or Daley with her unblinking, round eyes.

She was looking at Tynan.

"What's she talking about?" Daley asked.

Tynan's eyes were fixed on the ghost. "Melusine is with us. I can't always see her, but I can feel her. She misses you. She misses me too. Sometimes I talk to her so she won't be lonely."

Daley tried to put his hands on his brother's shoulders, but Tynan shook him off. "Ty, I know you cared for her—maybe more than you should have, but that's OK. I wish it wasn't true, but she's gone. We have to accept it."

Tynan's face changed and his voice became darker. "Try telling that to Rhi."

Daley frowned and looked at me. I pointed to where Melusine hovered around the cigarette. "Melusine is here. Her spirit is tied to her necklace, but she needs to move on. You can't see her, but I can. You don't know that she's changing, becoming something more than just a ghost. Lacey and Cailleach offered to help us, but we were afraid that if we told you, you wouldn't come."

Sparks began to flicker around Daley's head and thunder boomed in the distance. "You know what you should do, Rhiannon? You should mind your own damn business."

Miko rushed forward. "It's true. I can see her now too."

A gasp to my left. "Holy crap!" Peter said, "So can I."

"Me too," Lacey said calmly.

Daley clenched his fists. "Why can't I see her then?"

That's a good question.

Cailleach advanced and Melusine moved away until she hovered between Tynan and Daley. "The collective power of our belief in the girl, aided by the Path close by, is making her more solid by the minute. What we have come to do, we must do quickly or we will have no control over her at all."

I checked my phone again: 6:04.

I closed my eyes. Maybe the bond between Melusine and the necklace was keeping Daley from seeing her. Extending my senses, I found the spot of blazing aquamarine centered over Daley's heart. Wisps crept from it and connected to his colors.

It was worth a shot. I opened my eyes and put out my hand. "If you want to see her, give me the necklace." Thunder boomed, closer now, but after a brief hesitation, he slipped the necklace off and gave it to me. The wheel charm had been threaded onto the chain as well. I removed the jewel and then passed the chain and charm back to Daley.

What I'd once thought was a precious blue stone in silver was just white glass surrounded by silver-plated wire. Placing it on the picnic table, I smashed it with the base of the lantern, shattering the glass and twisting the metal.

"What are you doing?" Daley yelled and then stopped as he saw Melusine's ghostly form for the first time. "Mel?"

Lacey laughed as she rummaged through the contents of the bag. "I meant regular candles, not birthday candles." But she pulled them out, so I guessed they would do. Marking out the edges of a short walkway with the candles, she then made a circle with the marbles at the end of it. She lit the candles with the cigarette and took a long drag before snuffing it out.

Lacey smoking is almost as disturbing as standing five feet away from a ghost that wants to peel me like fruit.

Cailleach gestured and Lacey addressed us in the same voice she used to belt out show tunes. "At the setting of the sun, we embrace Samhain and the world stands on a knife edge between light and dark, life and death. Cailleach, the divine crone and great queen of winter, rises in her power and the door to the Otherworld opens. I pass through the candles for purification and the circle of stones is my protection from all hostile spirits." Lacey promenaded through the candles and Cailleach watched as if she were judging her performance at a beauty pageant.

Lacey held up the picture of the oak leaf. "The veil is thin and like the druids of old, we summon immortality by the power of the sacred oak." She burned the picture in the flame of the last candle. A thread of slate-grey flashed across my eyes and seemed to wind through my skull and down my spine. Talk of immortality didn't sound like an exorcism. Yellow warning flickered on the edges of my sight.

Lacey scattered the ashes in the center of the circle and poured the can of soda on top. "Food and drink to appease the spirits who walk free this night. It would normally be milk or wine, but milk is too weak for this casting, and sending you to buy wine might have drawn too much attention. It doesn't really matter; it's the looks that count. Most spirits aren't too smart. Sorry Melusine." Lacey giggled and her pupils were dilated.

Melusine drifted away from Daley and wafted into the circle. As she brushed ghostly fingers at the liquid puddled on the ground, her claws returned and an impression of pearly scales rippled across her hands.

"What's happening?" Daley whispered.

Tynan replied before I could. "Melusine is haunting you and we're sending her on."

Daley rounded on his brother. "What?" The thunder crashed closer this time.

"It's what Rhi wanted."

Daley grabbed me. I gasped as his nails dug into my skin and electricity followed. "What are you doing?"

"Melusine doesn't belong here. We're doing this to protect you!"

"Shut up!" Lacey's voice was unnaturally amplified. "You're interrupting my casting!"

Daley's hair and face sparkled with electricity as he shook me. "What gives you the right? Who made you Melusine's judge and executioner?"

"Daley, she's already dead!"

"I won't let you take her away from me again!" Daley's fingers emitted electric shocks and I cried out in pain.

With a murmured incantation, Cailleach gestured and an invisible force pushed us away from one another. "Enough! This casting is bound by the circle of stones and none may disturb it. See." She pointed. "The spirit is already caught."

"Mel . . .," Daley groaned. The ghost reached for him with claw-tipped fingers and then pulled back as she encountered an invisible barrier at the limit of the stones. Daley stared at her in desperation and a hot wind began to swirl between them. Tynan stood behind his brother with a sad expression on his face.

I felt as if someone had thrown cold water over my head. Had I truly believed Daley would thank me for ripping his dead girlfriend away from him? Was I really that stupid? Ugly honesty the color of dead worms smacked me in the face.

I'm doing this because I'm jealous of Melusine.

Miko touched my arm. "This doesn't feel right. Make it stop."

I looked at Peter and he shrugged. "Your call." But I could feel his true emotions through our bond. Peter currently wasn't very fond of supernatural exes and would be just as happy for me to send Melusine on her merry little way.

Despite my less than pure motives, I knew the ghost was a threat, but the colors of this magic were dark and reminded me of the Dobhar-chú. Cailleach watched me closely as I approached the stone circle. "Lacey, stop. I don't want to go through with this." She ignored me as she crushed the gingerbread men and scattered the fragments on the ground.

"Spice cake in the shape of the god of death to feed him as he returns to the underworld," Lacey intoned.

"Stop!" I tried to cross the circle, but it was like hitting a brick wall. Falling hard on my back, the air was knocked out of my lungs and searing pain flashed into my head.

This has gone to hell.

I forced the pain away as Peter helped me to my feet. "This isn't right. There's got to be another way." Lacey hesitated, but Cailleach gestured and she flinched.

"C'mon Lacey, we're friends . . ."

"Friends! Are you kidding me? How could I be friends with someone who sneaks around in the shadows? I've always seen you for what you really are." Her voice broke. "You took away the only guy I ever cared about. And do you want to know what the worst thing about that is? Do you? You didn't even want him! You were going to do the same thing to Melusine. You think you have power, but I have power now too. And wait till you see what Melusine's really like once she's reincarnated into her true form." She smirked. "Actually, maybe you'd better skip that part. I have absolutely *no idea why*, but she doesn't like you very much. Isn't it funny how you have that effect on people?" Lacey's face had hardened into an echo of Cailleach's.

Dismissing me, Lacey put out her hand and Melusine raked a claw across it. Lacey winced and then made a fist. Drops of blood dripped on the ground.

Blood magic.

The strands of their hair rose and mingled together as the spell gained strength. Lacey began to chant and Cailleach joined her:

I am the wind on the sea.
I am the roar of the wave.
I am the bull of seven battles and the hawk upon the cliff.
I am dew and flower, fish and lake.
I am the mountain made flesh.
I am the word and the point of a weapon.
Fire bursts from my head and the moon is ordered by my
will.
Return from Tethys' kingdom, O beast of the sunset,
And receive my enchantment of wind and spear.

I wanted to hide from the mess I'd made—run and hide until the world was black and white and choices were easy— but I'd bungled everything in the worst way possible and I was going to have to somehow fix it. If Viviane's frozen wall in my soul was keeping me from accessing real power, then it was time to bring all barriers down.

I descended through myself to that bruised and damaged place. Morgan's spell had healed most of the wound, but the dark spot in the center still remained. Mom—Viviane—had built this wall in my mind to protect me from the power I was heir to—a power that was maybe too powerful for me to contain. I needed that power to make things right.

I wanted it too.

I believe fear is white and thickly veined with blue the color of the sea. I believe it is an icy edifice which keeps me from my true self.

But ice melts.

The wall was a symbol of everything that had been denied me. I could see power as color and there was enough crimson rage to call up a fire capable of destroying it. I brought Viviane's wall down, damning all consequences. As the colors of her spell dissipated, a dark emptiness was revealed—the corruption that had been breaking through the barrier. I had a moment to register its full horror and then color poured through it from somewhere outside myself. I reached for the surface of my mind before I drowned in it.

I had done something terrible.

When I opened my eyes, flames of magic still danced on my palm. "Daley," I whispered. He saw the flames in my hand and understood. Joining me, he gestured for Tynan to flank us, but Tynan had backed up to the edges of the clearing, slinking into the darkness like the figure in my dream. I turned back to the witches and their ghost. In response, Cailleach moved behind the circle, but Lacey and Melusine were oblivious.

"Lacey, I'm not kidding. You need to stop. Now!" I flicked my wrist and sent a tongue of flame out to test the boundary of the stones. It held. Lacey lifted her arms to the sky and Melusine's ghostly form began to solidify into living flesh.

We were running out of time. I could sense Peter at my back, ready to fight. There was a ripping, flapping sound and I knew Miko had unfurled her new wings.

"Well done, little witch, but you need to go back to the kiddie table and let the grown-ups take it from here." A woman in a white coat and gloves stepped into the clearing with someone unexpected in tow: Boudica.

"What are you doing?" Daley demanded, but Boudica ignored him.

Morgan glanced at the flames in my hands, but didn't hesitate as she strolled up to the circle and faced Cailleach. Lacey and Melusine stood uncertainly between them.

"Well, Crone, I see you have found a new protégé. Have you not yet learned that they will only take what you have to give and then take their freedom?"

"As did you, my child."

Morgan flinched. "I left my brother, not you. Do not blame me for choosing love."

"You chose a human over the one who protected you from the time you and your sisters came into being. You chose the earth king and now you are bound to him and to your own ruin." Cailleach sounded sad.

Morgan nodded at Boudica and the woman drew her sword. The sound it made as it left its sheath was like the hissing of snakes.

Cailleach was trapped, but she regarded Boudica with contempt. "I see you have found a she-dog to do your bidding.

What did you offer her to take her from Taliesin? Beware, for this one will sniff after whoever holds the bone."

"I know what you intend to do with this dragon in the making and I cannot let you give my brother so great an advantage. Do not make me choose between the love I bear you and that for my husband."

Cailleach cocked her head and her round eyes blinked once. "If you were truly choosing love, then you would choose another. Abandon this foolish quest to wake the earth king. I bear a message from your brother. He will forgive all past trespasses if you make peace with the bard and live the rest of your long years with him. But be warned, Cernunnos will not allow you or Arthur to challenge his power again."

Morgan sighed and her voice was soft and ragged. "As you say, I am bound and bound again. My fate is stretched upon an unstoppable wheel and I must follow it or be pulled under."

"Then you will remain as Cernunnos made you," Cailleach replied cryptically, "and will never be made whole." She bowed her head. "Do what you must, my child."

Morgan gestured and Boudica struck so fast that nothing earthly could have stopped her. Lacey screamed as the Crone's head rolled into the circle, dark eyes open and staring. The flames in my hands sputtered and died as I struggled to not be sick. Boudica smiled as she wiped the blood on her sword onto the grass.

Morgan turned away from the body on the ground. "Cernunnos corrupts all who cannot escape his influence. He sought to raise a dragon from the last of the bloodline of Melusine to use as a weapon against us. My brother wishes to dominate this world as he does his own; to cast us all into everlasting twilight. Arthur is the only one strong enough to hold against him. This is what Taliesin cannot accept. Can you not see that we must be united against the true evil?" Put that way, it sounded reasonable, but she said it looming over the severed head of a woman she loved.

So what does she do to people she's just fond of? Daley confronted her. "And what about those who won't kiss Arthur's boot? What about all the people in this world who just want to live their lives untouched by magic?"

"What of them? They are not your people. Would they fare better with the host of monsters my brother will send once he is ready to attack?"

Lightning sizzled in the air above Daley's head as he pulled the charm off the chain and it became the Wheel of Taranis in his hands. "Arthur is a tyrant."

If Morgan recognized the Wheel, it didn't frighten her. "That's Taliesin talking," she sneered. "Arthur will bring order to the ranks of all magic users and then, with their help, to the world. He will bring peace and freedom to this world and to the Grey Lands, our true home."

Tynan stepped out of the darkness. "Our father believes there can be a middle ground; a path between chaos and tyranny."

Morgan shook her head in frustration. "Taliesin would . . ." And then her eyes widened. Striding over to Tynan, she murmured an incantation and a ball of light appeared in her hand. Holding it up to Tynan's face, she looked at him with desperate eyes.

"My son!" Morgan le Fay cried.

CHAPTER THIRTY SIX

I was wrong. This has gone so far past hell that I'm looking at hell in the rearview mirror.

"Did you know?" Morgan screamed as Boudica shook her head in confusion. "We leave now! Bring the boy and the dragon."

Boudica gave a whistle and two horses burst into the clearing, one white and one black. I would have been trampled if Peter hadn't pushed me out of the way. A stray hoof caught him in the leg and he fell.

Lacey stood in front of Melusine and began chanting, but Morgan gestured and the stones creating the magic circle flew apart. Boudica pushed Lacey out of the way and she hit the ground hard and lay still. Almost solid now, Melusine didn't resist when Boudica heaved her up onto the black horse and then mounted behind her.

"Mel!" Daley cried, but she just smiled and leaned back against Boudica. Thunder boomed and a bolt of lightning flashed, but the horse dodged it easily. If Daley used the greater power of the Wheel, he might hit Melusine.

"Look!" Miko pointed. Tynan was on the white horse and Morgan was behind him. Putting her arms around his waist, she rested her cheek against his back.

I ran to them and grabbed the reins. "Ty, what are you doing?"

The wind whipped Tynan's hair across his face and I couldn't see his eyes. "I felt it was true when she said it. My soul knows it." His voice darkened. "Taliesin always sent me away when she was coming, never let me be near her. He was hiding me. Morgan's my mother. I have to go with her." I gasped in pain as he tore the reins from my hands. He gestured and a grey gash ripped through reality. Beyond it I glimpsed twisted trees like the ones in my dream—a dream of travelling on a Path. Morgan's horse jumped through the portal and Boudica's followed.

I ran after them. Miko screamed something through the rising storm of Daley's fury, but I ignored her. Throwing myself through the opening, I whimpered in pain as I skidded across the ground and had to stop myself with my raw hands. I was just getting to my feet when Daley hit me from behind. We lay there for a moment, entwined in ways that felt intimate, before he pulled away. Standing, he brushed his hands off on his jeans as if their contact with my body had soiled them. I stumbled to my feet and hoped my burning cheeks would cool before he noticed.

"Where are they?" Daley's voice was swallowed in the thick silence of the Path. The air felt dead and resistant to speech and movement.

"I don't know. They should be right here." Without a Guide to change it into something more familiar, the Path took its true form. The ground beneath our feet was too smooth and uniform. The twisted trees were bare, but dense and impossible to see through, and they curved above our heads and blocked the sky. It was like being in a grey tunnel. I was reminded of what Morgan said about Cernunnos casting the world into everlasting twilight.

"We need to find Tynan. He's our only hope of getting out of here."

White fear made it difficult to think. The Paths were deadly to those without the talent to travel them. "Why did you follow me?" I whispered.

The flashes of lightning in Daley's eyes were the brightest things on the Path, but the expression on his face was unreadable. "We need to get Melusine and Ty back."

There was no sign of the portal we'd come through. "I can't hear the horses."

Daley took a couple of hesitant steps. "The sound is strange here. They could be just ahead and we might not even realize it."

"I'm going to try something." Closing my eyes, I extended my awareness along the Path and was rewarded almost immediately. Without Viviane's frozen barrier blocking the way, I was filled with fresh color. I still had almost no idea what to do with any of it, but I could sense the powers of those around me more easily. Morgan was a rainbow of fireflies dancing across a silver lake. I could tell she was too powerful for me to challenge. I tried Tynan, but his colors were even more chaotic. Clashing hues chased one another so fast that I couldn't focus on any of them.

I moved on. Melusine was a surprise. I expected fire now that she was in her dragon form, but she was still aquamarine, sea-foam, and iridescence. A pale rope the color of bone surrounded her and disappeared into a far darkness. I shuddered. The dragon might be rising, but Death hadn't relinquished its claim on the girl.

Running out of options, I found Boudica. In my mind, I could see the aura of her power as a fierce gold fouled by blackness.

I opened my eyes. "They're just ahead." I didn't wait for Daley as I began running down the winding Path, but I knew he was following. The trees made it difficult to see more than a few feet ahead. Without warning, the Path took a sharp turn and we skidded to a stop in front of an immense form.

Melusine had completed her transformation.

The dragon's head was long and tapered, and while it somehow kept something of the girl, it was also completely inhuman. Its serpentine body was covered in scales of mother of pearl and four powerful legs were tipped by luminous claws. The creature's wings were small and obviously not useful for flight. In fact, they almost looked like gills. Tynan and the others had to be somewhere behind her, but Melusine towered over us and blocked the way.

"Mel!" Daley cried. "You don't have to do this. Come back with me."

I heard the dragon's answer in my mind, and by the shocked look on Daley's face, so did he. "Why would I want to do that? You have no idea of the power I now command. Death and the witch have freed it in me. I have become *Otohime*, the luminous jewel, and I will take my rightful place among the gods."

"Please, Mel. I love you."

The dragon's sinuous neck extended until the creature's snout was inches from Daley's face. Its mouth gaped open and translucent fangs dripping with venom were exposed. "Melusine," he whispered.

"Our love was just a little thing." The dragon sounded amused. "It pleased me to have you. Tynan too." There was no sound, but the dragon's movement gave the impression it was laughing. "Do you begrudge your brother a few kisses, a few sweet embraces when your back was turned?" Daley's face darkened but there was no thunder on the Path. "Don't be sad. You served the purpose all men are made for, and quite well, I might add. I would have stayed with you if death and glory hadn't come calling, but your place in my story is finished and it's time for you to go. Say goodnight, my love."

All the light and electricity that belonged uniquely to Daley seemed to dim and grow cold. Closing his eyes, he bowed his head.

I could tell that Melusine was preparing to lunge. Pushing past Daley, I sank my hands into the scales around her neck, shuddering as my fingers dug through them like the scales on a fish. The dragon reared, but I held on, feet dangling a few inches off the ground. I didn't need to close my eyes to find her colors. Ignoring the chill of Death's pale rope, I closed my fingers around her aura and the soft, wet scales oozed through my fingers. Filling my hands with aquamarine and iridescence, I pulled. Melusine howled as skin and power was ripped from her. I landed on my feet with a thud.

I had a moment of triumph, but her power slipped through my fingers like water. Shaking my fingers clean of iridescent slime, I backed away as the dragon advanced, snarling and huffing. I looked to Daley for help, but he'd slumped to the ground and either didn't realize or didn't care I was in imminent danger of being shredded. Using Viviane's spell to create a blue veil, I threw it at the beast, but it slid off and dissipated. Melusine was more powerful than a spell spun from moisture and mist and her mouth widened into a parody of a smile.

I needed more power. If I couldn't find it inside myself, I would have to get it somewhere else.

I didn't dare close my eyes, but I could sense Boudica somewhere ahead on the Path. Tynan and Morgan seemed to have disappeared, but I fought back grey despair and concentrated on the woman. Boudica was a queen. Despite the darkness surrounding it, the gold of her aura told me she had the power of command and the ability to bend others to her will.

I can use that.

Melusine's neck lifted up like a snake ready to strike and I knew it was now or never. Darting to the side, I slipped around her, but my heart stopped for a moment as I felt the displacement of air as the dragon's teeth snapped together behind me. I'd only barely avoided having my head chomped off.

Melusine's struggle to turn her enormous body around on the narrow corridor gave me a head start. Two turns of the Path and I found Boudica running her hands across her horse's neck, murmuring calming words. She'd been left back to babysit the dragon, but the horse seemed to have other ideas and was pulling on the reigns, eyes rolling. Distracted by her efforts to control her mount, she was unaware of my arrival until I barreled into her and knocked her to the ground. As she let go of the reigns, the horse panicked and ran off.

Now that I was touching her—straddling actually—I could feel the gold of Boudica's power emanating from the thick choker at her neck; it was the symbol of Celtic royalty and she'd unconsciously centered her entire being on it. Before she could catch her breath and push me off, I grasped the two ends where they met in the middle of her throat and pulled. There was a small resistance, and then the choker broke apart and her color flowed into me.

There was probably a moment when I could have stopped—a brief moment when I knew that I was taking too much—but I let it pass. Filled with a pleasure so visceral, so transcendent, I took her power. And when that was gone, I took her very essence, even the darkness. Throbbing with color, I tossed the broken choker aside and stood. I wasn't even aware of Boudica as I stepped over her to face the dragon. Melusine had stopped and was watching me as if she was curious as to what I had done, but I wasn't interested in her anymore either.

It was Death I needed to talk to.

I didn't stop to think of how impossible it was to do what I was doing. Filled with so much power, I felt like I could order the stars to dance. Instead, I closed my eyes and commanded Death to take Melusine.

And Death obeyed.

Melusine screamed—a sound that pulsed between the roar of a dragon and the pitiful cry of a woman who died too young. As death's pale rope tightened and pulled her into the black abyss, I joined my scream with hers. Pleasure had twisted and erupted into flames which licked the inside of my skull. I fell, but strong arms caught me and held me tight.

"There you go, *mo leanabh*, I've got you."

I knew that voice. "Redcap? What are you doing here?"

His breath was soft against my ear. "What I always do, Rhiannon; come at the call of a Great One's death."

There was a sensation of movement I couldn't make sense of and then cold grass brushed my cheek as Redcap eased me down onto the ground. I opened my eyes as he brushed the hair back from my forehead, but even that light touch brought fresh agony.

Taliesin's face swam into view. "Is she injured?"

"I'm not sure. I can't see a wound."

A wail shook the trees and they whipped and waved in response as it began to rain. I turned my head and forced myself to focus through the pain. At first, I couldn't understand what I was looking at. Rowan was holding something in his arms and rocking it back and forth. I blinked and white horror surrounded it.

It was Boudica, beautiful and cold, eyes wide and staring.

CHAPTER THIRTY SEVEN

I pieced the details together of how I got there as I lay in the hospital bed. I remembered Rowan refusing to be parted from his wife's body. I remembered him ripping the cross from his neck and throwing it into the grass before Taliesin and Daley restrained him.

I remembered the screaming.

Now that the pain was dulled by a drug being dripped into my veins, I realized I was the one who'd been screaming. I also remembered Daley calling me a vampire, but I knew that wasn't what I was. I was something worse. Boudica was a queen. That gold lined with darkness was her very soul.

And I'd yanked every bit of it out.

Peter stayed by my side until the drugs kicked in. He had a nasty gash on his leg that had to be stitched—Morgan's horses must have been supernatural to have the power to injure him—but I could feel through our bond that he was already healing. He told me how Miko had called Taliesin and the bard had contacted Robin Goodfellow. They'd arrived via another Path shortly after Daley and I disappeared. How Redcap appeared was part of his own particular mystery.

When Peter's parents came to take him home, I pretended to fall asleep so they would all go and leave me alone. When the room was quiet, I surrendered to indigo. The drugs weren't the only thing restraining me, but I couldn't blame Taliesin.

I woke up the next morning when someone tapped me gently on the shoulder. It was the doctor on call. Pushing myself up in the bed, I pulled the blanket around my flimsy hospital gown. My stomach sank as I realized it was the same doctor I'd seen at the walk-in clinic—the one whose yellow aura showed how worried he was about my headaches.

"Hello, Miss Lynne. Do you remember me?"

"Dr. Calder," I said to prove I did.

"You were supposed to come back and see me."

I shrugged. "I was fine so I didn't think I needed to."

He raised an eyebrow as he checked my chart. "And yet it says here you were brought in screaming in pain and had to be put under heavy sedation to calm you down."

"My headache got bad last night, but I've been handling it."

He held up the chart. "Clearly you haven't. I'm going to arrange for you to have some tests."

"What kind of tests?"

"We'll do a neurological exam to check your hearing, vision, balance, and reflexes, and then an MRI to get a look at what's going on in your head." After a few reassuring platitudes, the kind doctor who oozed yellow concern left to continue his rounds.

I sank back into the pillows and tried not to think about the corruption in my mind. Morgan and I had tried to heal it, but clearly we'd failed. The pain must mean that what I'd done to

Boudica had made it worse. I knew something now, something terrible.

Mom hadn't made the barrier to protect me. She'd made it to protect everyone else. And I'd destroyed it.

Rhiannon, hide in the shadows and be still and silent.

I didn't need to close my eyes anymore to conjure the veil of blue mist. It was tattered and torn, but I knew I could repair it and make it stronger than Viviane ever could. It was only a spell—a product of thought and imagination—but I could feel it as it settled on my skin. I touched my face as it molded against me like fine silk, cool and smooth. I could sweep it over myself and disappear into the shadows forever. I could hide from what I'd done.

A tremor ran through the mist and I strained to hold it. Taliesin's indigo was trying to stop me from accessing power, but with the barrier in my mind gone, I was stronger. Concentrating, I saw something I'd missed before. The texture of Viviane's spell was different from Taliesin's, but the color was just a lighter version of the same. I laughed, but it was an ugly, broken sound.

I've been bound in blue my whole life.

A blast of anger like a desert wind passed over me and dazzling shades of scarlet and crimson erupted from my hands. They flowed through me from some source outside myself—I didn't know where and I didn't care. The flames burned through Taliesin's indigo and evaporated Viviane's shadowed mist.

And then I struggled for air as magic fire consumed the oxygen in the room.

Panicking, I commanded the flames to recede, but they ignored me. I'd lost control the same way I did with Boudica.

The flames flickering across my skin didn't burn, but that didn't mean I wouldn't suffocate. I started to lose consciousness.

No. Not again.

I forced my mind down to Viviane's barrier, but instead of an icy edifice, there was only a dark tunnel leading to some unknown place. Color rushed through it towards me.

A shift and my perception changed. I was floating in a lake of color and bright drops of rain pelted me. Each one carried a message, but as the rain beat harder, the lake churned and I began to drown.

Another change as my mind struggled to comprehend the reality of what was inside me. I was suspended in a night sky and the multi-colored sparks in it were stars. Floating through space, I plucked a golden orb from the darkness, but the stars whirled around me and threatened to crush me into dust.

I was back at the tunnel. The shades of red were gone, exhausted in the flames that had filled the hospital room. Gold swirled around me now and tentacles of ebony reached through it. This was what I'd taken from Boudica. Gathering all my strength, I ejected her colors from my mind. Tweaking and combining Viviane's and Taliesin's spells, I closed off the pathway with a veil of indigo.

At least this time it's my choice.

I opened my eyes and gasped; the flames were gone, but the oxygen in the room was thin. Pulling the I.V. out of my hand, I staggered to the window and forced it open until cold air rushed in and I could breathe normally again.

Once I was able to teeter over to the bathroom and get dressed, I made my escape. I called a taxi once I made it to the hospital entrance. When it dropped me off at Peter's house and Mrs. Larsen opened the door, I threw myself into her arms.

She patted my back and brought me into the kitchen where Peter was eating breakfast. "What are you doing here?" she asked. "Why didn't you call us to come get you?"

"It was just as fast to catch a taxi. I must have knocked my head again, but they did some tests and said I could go home."

Mrs. Larsen clucked her tongue. "It's always dangerous driving on Halloween. I'm just glad you kids weren't killed. I hope they throw the book at that driver. Imagine drinking and driving on a night when all those children are wandering around!"

I glanced at Peter and he gave a slight nod—car accident was our cover story.

"Yeah," he agreed, "it's lucky we were in Daley's Yukon. The van would have been totaled." I was glad Peter hadn't had to trash his mom's minivan to sell the lie.

"Why don't you sit down and I'll get you something to eat."

I shook my head. "That's OK. I just wanted to let you know I was home. I'm going straight to bed."

"Well, call if you need anything."

I agreed and Peter hopped after me to see me out. Closing the front door, he walked to the porch stairs and sat down; he was pretending for his parents' sake that he didn't heal unnaturally fast.

"You really scared me. I could feel you screaming right here." He tapped on his temple. "I thought my head was going to split open."

I sat down beside him. "Welcome to the club. I'm fine now though. I've got it under control." I sighed and slumped over my knees. "I messed up."

Peter draped his arm over my shoulders. "We messed up. And maybe we didn't even do that. Melusine wanted to kill you—Miko told me—and Lacey and Boudica betrayed us. You tried to rescue Ty and Boudica got in the way." His voice hardened. "That's what happens in war."

"How are Daley and Rowan?" I was afraid of the answer.

"They're hurting. Rowan's out of it. Taliesin and Goodfellow saw enough to guess what happened when they pulled you out of the Path. Melusine attacked and Boudica got caught in the crossfire, and then Morgan escaped with Tynan. Is that about it?'

"Yeah." I didn't add that I'd ripped Boudica's life and magic away to give myself the power to defeat Melusine.

"Rowan won't accept that Boudica was a traitor. Miko says he's locked himself in his room with her body and won't come out."

Bile burned the back of my throat. "What do we do now?"

Peter pulled up his pant leg and picked out a couple of stitches. The skin around them was already smooth and perfect. "Taliesin wants me over there tomorrow. Should I put him off?"

No more hiding. "No. Besides, Morgan has Tynan and we have to figure out how to get him back."

"She called him her son. What does that even mean?"

I didn't have an answer and after a quick hug, I went home and did what I should have done in the first place.

I went to work.

CHAPTER THIRTY EIGHT

A crackle of accusatory thunder woke me up. I got out of bed and opened the blinds, but I knew what I would find— clear blue sky. This was Daley's thunder.

Dressing in jeans and a t-shirt, I swept my hair into a tight ponytail and searched in my closet for the largest bag I could find. It was easy now that most of my clothes were littered all over the floor and I found one from my gym days in middle grade. Pulling Excalibur out of my underwear drawer, I dropped it in.

I'd spent the rest of the previous day researching all the Arthurian lore I could find online. A lot of it was confusing and contradictory, but I felt better prepared to face Taliesin. I picked up Peter in front of his house and instead of going to school, we drove to Taliesin's rented mansion.

As we parked, I grabbed Peter's hand and squeezed it hard once. "Follow my lead." He nodded. Hefting the bag over my shoulder and marching up to the front door, I opened it and walked inside. I'd been treating the place like home for weeks, so why stop now?

"Taliesin!" I yelled.

278 · HEATHER HAMILTON-SENTER

After a few seconds, the bard appeared at the top of the stairs. "Miss Lynne," he acknowledged, "I am glad to see you are recovered, but now is not the best of times for you to be here. I would ask that you go home until I send for you."

"I don't think so, Tal." He scowled at my tone but didn't respond.

A small pink and black projectile ran down the hall and hit me with a fierce hug. "Hey, Miko," I responded as I disengaged myself.

She backed away at the coolness in my voice. "I was worried about you. I've never heard anyone scream like that before." She looked at Peter as if asking for permission to go to him. He gave her a small smile, but something in his face must have told her to stay put. The fairy wrapped her arms around herself and I could see the tears in her eyes. She didn't seem to understand that Peter might accept what she'd done, but it was going to take him some time to forgive it.

I felt the pull of his electricity before he even arrived, but as Daley entered the foyer, I ignored him and focused on Taliesin as he descended the staircase.

"How long have you known?" I demanded.

"Known what, Miss Lynne?"

"How long have you known that Tynan is really Mordred?"

Miko gasped. "Then it's true? Tynan is Morgan and Arthur's son?"

I nodded. "Not just their son. Mordred is the one who betrayed Arthur and put Excalibur through his heart. He's the reason Arthur is sleeping. Am I right?"

Taliesin did something I would never have expected—he sank to the bottom step and sat there looking old and crumpled. "Yes, Viviane gave Excalibur to Mordred. Whether for Cernunnos who had deceived the boy, or for herself, I do not know. I can only guess that her purpose for you is to continue her work of vengeance."

Daley stared at Taliesin as if he didn't recognize him. "And what about Ty?"

"I have not known, not for sure." The bard rubbed his eyes. "But I had begun to fear it. The destruction of Excalibur broke Mordred's mind and he was never seen again, but he was known to be a master of the Paths. Tynan thinks I do not know, but his ability to sense them first aroused my suspicions. There were stories of a Path that led through time, but I thought they were fantasies. Due to my estrangement from Arthur, I had never seen Mordred, even as a baby. I doubted it could be possible, but still, I never risked Morgana seeing him. She is bound to Arthur even at the expense of a son."

"What about Boudica?" I asked. "Did you know about her?"

"I swear I did not. Rowan refuses to believe it, but I saw and heard enough to know she betrayed us."

I faltered in my righteous anger. "I didn't mean to kill her. It was an accident."

Daley barked a laugh and his hair crackled with sparks. "Didn't you? Isn't that what your kind does? Leanan sidhe, succubus, whatever you are—you take what doesn't belong to you. At least the mystery of Rhiannon Lynne is solved at the expense of two lives."

"Maybe it's true. Maybe that's what I am. But I didn't do it on purpose. I had to stop the dragon."

And people die in battle all the time.

I pushed the thought away, but my own coldness shocked me. "The Melusine you loved was gone. You knew what she'd become and yet you bowed your head and practically asked her to bite it off."

"Daley!" Miko gasped.

Thunder boomed, but I couldn't stop. "Maybe the girl Melusine loved you once, but the dragon Melusine wanted to kill you. I wasn't going to let that happen. I couldn't." Something flickered in Daley's eyes, but he turned away.

"Is Melusine truly gone?" Taliesin asked.

I forced my attention back to the bard. "I think so. She was bound to Death and I told it to take her."

Taliesin stared at me, but I didn't explain. He didn't need to know all my secrets. Standing, he declared, "You are fearsome indeed, Miss Lynne, to command Death itself."

Peter stepped forward. "So we're agreed it's a huge mess, right? What are we going to do about it? How are we going to get Ty back from Morgan?"

"What can we do?" I was shocked at the sound of the bard's voice; rough and broken, its power and beauty were gone. "He is her son. She has more right to him than I, though I doubt she can love him after what he did to his father. Tynan is lost to us."

"Wrong answer," I murmured. "We're getting Ty back."

"How? Morgana will never trust me again and she is more powerful than you can imagine."

"I have something she's going to want more than a son." I upended the bag and dumped its contents onto the floor with a crash of metal on marble. The remains of Excalibur gleamed in the sunlight streaming through the windows.

Taliesin fell to his knees, touching the twisted gold and silver with reverence. "Can this be what I think it is?"

"Take it and make a trade with Morgan. What can she do with a hunk of useless metal anyway?" The bard didn't move. "Take it," I insisted.

"He can't, kiddo." Rowan shambled down the stairs, reeking of alcohol.

Fear is white and thickly veined with sea-blue.

The druid gave a low whistle. "Well aren't you just full of surprises. Who would have thought you had Excalibur hidden in your handbag?" The others looked at me in shock as they caught on and Rowan laughed wildly. "That's right, this hunk of junk is the greatest earth totem ever created. Says something about us, doesn't it? Excalibur has latched on to our dear little Miss Lynne here. I think it knows we aren't really her friends—that we aren't exactly on the same side. Don't believe me? I'll prove it to you." Rowan kicked at the metal hard enough to break a toe, but Excalibur didn't move. I flinched for him, but the druid was beyond physical pain.

"Where did you find it?" Taliesin whispered.

I shook my head. "I didn't find it. My mom . . ." I paused and corrected myself, "Viviane left instructions for Goodfellow to get it from where she'd hidden it and then to give it to me."

Miko poked at the metal with a black-nailed finger. "How could he lift it then?" With horror, I realized she wasn't wearing nail polish anymore—her fingernails were actually black.

Taliesin touched her shoulder and she backed away. "If Viviane intended it for Rhiannon, then the agent of its journey would be given the ability to complete that mission. Viviane was the Lady of the Lake and Excalibur's first master."

"Can Morgan use it?" I asked.

Taliesin hesitated before answering. "I don't know. Perhaps. Her powers are older than any earth totem. She might be able to break its will."

"Then she'll want it bad."

The bard rubbed his face and I saw he hadn't shaved. "If Arthur is awakened, Excalibur could be used to defeat us! How can we give our enemy the key to our destruction?"

"We don't know what might happen in the future, but we do know that Tynan needs us right now! You've said yourself he isn't safe with Morgan. Call her, Taliesin."

"Make the call, Tal," Rowan said over his shoulder as he shuffled back up the stairs. We watched him leave in silence. We knew what his steps were taking him back to.

CHAPTER THIRTY NINE

Taliesin arranged the exchange. Rowan was finally persuaded to let his wife's body go and Boudica was to be cremated at sunrise in the woods at the back of the property. Morgan would meet us there.

Time crawled by. Rowan spent the day preparing the area in the tradition of the druids—he'd left his Christianity back in the clearing with the cross he ripped from his neck. The other men retreated to the garage to fashion a rough coffin. Miko and I had nothing useful to do, so we watched TV and listened to music. None of it distracted me enough, but I didn't want to go home. I fell asleep around midnight, but a nightmare of an avenging queen riding a ghostly dragon woke me up before dawn.

After a long shower, I dressed in the clothes I'd brought with me: black skirt, black boots, black sweater. Miko and I waited at the bottom of the stairs for the men to carry the coffin down. Rowan shambled behind it, but he seemed sober. I expected him to accuse me or tell me to go, but his eyes slid past me as if he'd never seen me before. As we passed through the yard and into the woods, Goodfellow was waiting for us in the shadow of the trees. Rowan looked at him in confusion.

We entered a clearing where a pyre of wood was surrounded by leaves and herbs scattered on the ground. Tynan and Morgan stepped out of the trees to meet us, but Tynan's head was down and his hair hid his face. Shrouded in a velvet cape, Morgan was finally dressed the way I would have expected Arthur's consort to dress. The men laid the coffin down on the pyre and backed away as Taliesin and Morgan shared a long and meaningful look.

"Let's get this over with," she said coldly.

He gestured to the coffin. "For Rowan's sake, let us first lay Boudica to rest."

Morgan shook her head. "The woman's soul has gone from this world and has nothing to do with me now." Her voice caught. "It is you who has broken my heart. I have always accepted that you will fight me in the end, but I never believed you would deceive me. You hid my son from me! What was once between us is finished."

Taliesin's face was stricken, but he bowed his head and gestured for me to come forward. I'd wrapped Excalibur in one of Mom's long scarves and Morgan gasped as I loosened the material to show her.

"So it is true! Viviane had it all along."

"Take it," I said. "It belongs to me and I'm giving it to you." Morgan put out her hands and I placed Excalibur in them.

She exhaled. "I was not sure I would have the strength to hold it. Even now, its weight is almost unbearable. But you have given it to me freely and it accepts me grudgingly. Once

BOUND IN BLUE · 285

Excalibur is in its true master's hands, it will burn bright again."

I ignored her and held out my hand to Tynan. "C'mon Ty, let's go."

He turned to Morgan and whimpered, "Mother?" He sounded like a little boy.

The woman's face was unreadable. "See, my son. Your friends are here."

"I have no friends." Tynan slapped my hand away so hard I stumbled and fell against the coffin.

It slid off the pyre as if it had no weight at all.

"What mischief is this?" Morgan cried and then whispered an incantation. With terrible strength, she pulled off the lid and threw it aside.

The coffin was empty.

Everyone froze except Rowan. He was wandering around the clearing as if he'd lost something.

"That's impossible!" Daley said. "We put Boudica in the box ourselves just minutes ago. We carried her here. I felt the weight."

There was yelling and arguing, but I was watching Rowan. He was touching the grass and trees with frantic fingers. "Tal."

"Where is she?" Morgan screamed.

"Tal!" Rowan shouted.

But the bard was focused on the woman he loved. "Morgana, I swear to you, I do not know."

"Taliesin! Listen to me!" The trees swayed and bowed at the druid's command. "This is the wrong place!"

Goodfellow stepped into the clearing and understanding sent white shivers across my vision.

The Green Man can make a Path look like whatever he wants.

Goodfellow raised his arms and the trees around us were replaced by stone walls stretching up into darkness. We were in some kind of cave. Lanterns hanging from iron hooks illuminated a crumbling archway and a stone sarcophagus with a man's figure carved on the lid.

Everything seemed to happen at once, captured in images stacked on top of one another like pages in a book.

Boudica raising her sword, her armor shining gold in the torch light.

Miko flying at her on black wings and being batted aside like a dark butterfly.

Morgan facing the Icenian queen with Excalibur in her hand.

Rowan falling to his knees.

Taliesin reaching for Morgan.

Tynan using his power to throw Taliesin against the cave wall.

Peter cradling Miko to his chest.

Tynan embracing the carved image on the lid of the sarcophagus.

Heart pounding, I forced myself to focus on the two women facing one another. Boudica was muscular and the sword in her hand was deadly, but Morgan was taller, and even in its ruined state, Excalibur was infinitely more dangerous.

Rowan lifted his arms to his wife. "Bo!" he cried. "You came back to me!"

Boudica sauntered over and gave him a vicious backhand that drove him to the ground. When he moaned, she kicked him in the head until he lay still. "Weakling," she muttered. Rubbing her knuckles, the woman turned to me. "Thank you for releasing me from your mind, or wherever it was you put me. I was aware of myself, but couldn't feel my body, and it took me a while to figure out what happened. I was getting a little worried my 'death' might become permanent. You and the Redcap have a lot in common, but at least he waits till his victims are dead before stealing their souls. Still, it all worked out pretty well. Things were getting ugly between you and Melusine and I was happy I didn't have to risk my ass over that little bitch."

I stared at her. "But you were dead. They put you in a coffin."

Boudica shrugged. "I've been working with Morgan for a while, but only to get intel." I glanced at Taliesin sprawled near the wall and she laughed. "Not for that self-righteous dick." She smirked at Morgana. "Sorry, *Morgana*, but you know he is." When Morgan didn't respond, Boudica shrugged again and turned back to me. "Your father says hello, by the way."

I flinched as she pressed her finger against my temple. Eyes glittering, she lifted her sword in warning and I froze. "Cernunnos has special *insight* into what's going on in that pretty little head of yours—practically insider knowledge." She flicked me hard with her finger and laughed when I gasped. "When he realized what you did, he preserved my body until my soul was free. Goodfellow controls what enters a Path and where it goes. Rowan had no idea he'd conveniently prepared my crematorium at the mouth of one.

Morgan wanted Excalibur and the boy. She thought Goodfellow was with her, but he belongs to us. When she revealed the destination, he scooted my body ahead of you all. I really do need to thank you. I've been trying to find Arthur's tomb for years without tipping her off. I was almost ready to give up."

"Why?" Morgan's voice was so quiet, I could barely hear her.

Boudica whirled around. "How can you, of all people, even ask that? I was a queen! I ruled before Arthur sucked at his mother's teat. Why should I bend my knee to an upstart king or the rogue bard who spurned him? Cernunnos promised me my kingdom and look where we are—in Arthur's tomb with Excalibur ripe and ready for the picking." She glanced over her shoulder. "So, thanks again, Rhi. I'm actually quite sorry I sent the Dobhar-chú after you, but the little witch insisted and your father wanted to see what you would do."

Red rage smeared across my sight, but I forced myself to smile. "So what did dear old Dad ask in return then, *Bo*? To prance around in a French maid's costume and bring him his slippers?" It was a random shot, but when she scowled, I knew I'd hit the bull's-eye.

Morgan's laughter echoed off the stone walls. "Really, Boudica? You would endure my brother's cold hands and the certainty of death when he tires of you for a petty kingdom?"

Boudica swung her sword lazily as she walked towards Arthur's stone coffin. I recognized the action from when I'd watched her training—she was getting ready to attack. "Oh Morgan, it's almost sweet how naïve you are. Cernunnos didn't offer me a spit of land in the middle of the sea. He's giving me the entire world. The only price is Arthur's head."

Lightning ricocheted through the cave and struck the woman, throwing her across the floor. Daley emerged from the shadows holding the Taranis wheel.

Boudica wiped a trickle of blood from her mouth as she stood. Her armor wasn't even singed. "That was a mistake, godling."

Daley shrugged. "I may not want Morgan to wake Arthur, but I'm not going to let you murder him in his sleep."

"Hit her again!" I screamed.

Movement caught my eye. Morgan had joined Tynan and they stood together looking at Arthur's effigy.

Boudica sneered at Daley. "I'll deal with you later, boy." She approached Morgan cautiously with her sword raised.

I ran to Daley. "Why did you stop?"

He lifted the wheel. "It needs to recharge and I'm too far underground to harness any of the elements. It doesn't matter though. That's *sidhe* armor she's wearing. Its magic protects her."

Boudica pointed her sword at Morgan. "Witch, I have a message from your brother." When she opened her mouth wide, a voice from another world came out of it. The effect was obscene.

"Dear sister, you stand on the edge of the knife. Forsake the earth king and all will be forgiven. Advance, and there will be no mercy, no peace. I will hound you through the eras of your immortality until you go mad and beg for death. I will not warn you again."

The voice scraped away at the barrier between my mind and pain. Morgan didn't even look up as she whispered something and gestured at Boudica. The woman was flung across the cavern like a doll and disappeared into the darkness behind us.

I looked back at the tableau of mother and son, finally reunited. For the first time since I met him, Tynan seemed peaceful and happy. "My son," Morgan whispered, tears streaming down her face as she pulled him close and kissed him on the cheek.

Tynan jerked strangely. He looked down at his mother and opened his mouth, but no sound came out. As Morgan pulled away, I saw the jagged length of Excalibur jutting out from under his ribs.

When Tynan fell, I did too. I thought I heard Daley yell, but it was cut off abruptly. Crawling on all fours to where Tynan lay pumping out blood and life, I screamed for help, but everyone was frozen.

"What have you done?"

Morgan stared at me as if I should understand. "I could not risk them interfering. They will be fine. They are only caught momentarily out of time." The pupils of her eyes were dilated and the irises were almost colorless.

"Not them! Tynan! Your son!"

"You mean Mordred," she corrected absently as she bent down and drew Excalibur out of his body like a knife out of butter. Bright blood was on the metal and she used it to draw on the chest of the effigy. "Four circles for the four elements: air, fire, water, earth. When I draw the fifth at the center, I will bind them with the all-encompassing illumination that commands them." She focused on me again and frowned. "You can't think that any of this is what I wanted. If I had met Taliesin first, so many things would have been different. I was a creature finally freed and Arthur was my salvation. I swore unbreakable oaths to him and was caged again, but I was happy to live in a cage forged by Arthur. I made my bargain freely and never guessed I would live to regret it." She looked at the bard where he lay crumpled on the ground. "Will you tell Taliesin? Will you tell him I regret it?" she asked plaintively.

I wasn't interested in Morgan's pain. I pressed my hands to Tynan's wound to stop the blood, but it flowed fast between my fingers.

Morgan sighed. "Let him rest. My son's death was ordained from the moment he raised Excalibur against his father. The son shed the blood of the father, and the father must be raised by the blood of the son. This was the missing spell I have been searching for all these years. I told you once that blood magic is the most powerful magic of all—even my brother is bound by it. Though I was compelled to search, I hoped Excalibur was lost and my son, wherever he was, would be safe."

Her voice hardened. "Viviane's scheming has brought us here." She turned away. "Leave him be. My son is mad. It is better that he pass this way."

She was right—Tynan was damaged—but he was also a boy who had wanted to kiss me and had told me the meaning of my name. Closing my eyes, I searched for the bright green of my bond with Peter. We belonged to each other in a way that was more powerful than blood. I took my hands off Tynan's wound and concentrated. When I opened my eyes, a fine net of peridot green covered the blood on my palms.

With his blood on my skin, I could see Tynan's colors, wild and chaotic, and drifting away. I was running out of time.

Panicking, I placed my hands on his chest. As my spell sank into his body, I imagined the power of this bond encircling his soul. If he belonged to me—if his blood belonged to me—it couldn't be used to wake Arthur. I could deny the power of blood magic.

But I was too late. Morgan drew the last circle before I could bind Tynan and claim him as mine. Throwing Excalibur away as if she couldn't bear to touch it anymore, she cried out:

"I see in the rocky peaks far away, the place of death;
A rough mountain with a misty summit.
Come down from it and launch your ships on the
Fomorian ocean,
Thou son of Uther Pendragon!"

The sword had skittered towards me across the ground. Before I could reach it for it, there was a booming sound and chunks of stone flew through the air—the sarcophagus had shattered. I was thrown backwards, small fragments nicking my arms, but something soft broke my fall.

It was Rowan. Or at least, his body. His head had been severed in one clean cut.

As I scuttled back in white horror, I heard soft laughter coming from the gloom beyond the torch light. "Now I am truly my mother's daughter, the last of the *sidhe*."

While the druid was caught out of time by Morgan's spell, Boudica must have been out of range and had escaped it to complete her betrayal. I could sense her aura. There was still gold in her, but it was now completely overshadowed by darkness. I took a step towards it, but then it winked out. Cursing Goodfellow under my breath, I knew she was gone

There was a cry and I turned to discover that time was moving again. Peter was helping Miko up. Daley had been hit by some of the debris and was bleeding from a cut on his forehead, but otherwise looked all right. Taliesin stirred and I knew he wasn't dead.

Morgan le Fay stood at the side of a man in the middle of the rubble. Tall and muscular, his black hair and neat beard framed a handsome face and eyes gleaming with warmth and intelligence.

Looking upon Arthur in the flesh for the first time, I knew Taliesin was wrong—the Earth King was the savior of the world, not the enslaver. When he laughed with joy and embraced Morgan, joy filled me too. I wanted to bow to him, my once and future king, and beg him to accept me as his. I put out my hands towards him and was surprised to see they were covered in blood. Tynan's blood. Arthur's son lay forgotten on the ground and my heart was my own again.

A sense of dark teal like the shadows on the forest floor caught my attention; Goodfellow was still nearby. I was relieved. Even though he'd betrayed us and had helped Boudica escape, we were going to need him.

Closing my eyes, I searched for the auras of my friends using their strongest colors to find them. Taliesin was bronze like a trumpet. Miko was bright pink, but inky black branched through it like veins. I could easily find Peter through our peridot-green bond. Daley was the deep blue-grey of stormy seas, the platinum of rain clouds, and the red-orange of lightning. Cutting through them was a pale, pure gold.

Excalibur.

CHAPTER FORTY

The sword called to me, but it lay on the ground not far from Arthur and I didn't dare draw his attention to it. The Earth King released Morgan and looked around in surprise. "How long have I slept, my love? And where are we? This is not the chamber at Camelot."

Morgan's eyes darted away. "No, my lord."

Frowning, he peered into the gloom. "Who are these fallen? Is that Taliesin?" I froze as his gaze passed over me, but if he saw me, he dismissed me as no threat. I began to creep towards the sword.

"No, Arthur."

Arthur's face was tender, but his voice was steel. "Why are you lying to me, Morgana?"

"I . . .," she faltered, "I don't want you to hurt him."

With a laugh, Arthur pulled her close again. "For one so fierce, you have a tender heart. I would never harm Taliesin. He was a brother to me once and may still see reason and join us. But why is he here? What are we doing in this cave?" Arthur noticed Rowan's body and his smile slipped away.

"And is that not Taliesin's pet druid? What happened in this place?"

"What do you remember?"

His face darkened. "I remember my son attacking me with my own sword." I froze in case the mention of Excalibur reminded Morgan that it was still there, just out of reach.

"Let us go," she said as she laid her head on his chest. "There is so much I need to explain and this place holds only sorrow."

But Morgan had not forgotten the way into my mind.

"Take it! Quickly! I cannot fight the oaths I have made for long. In a moment, I will be forced to tell Arthur who you are and that Excalibur is here. Understand that I am bound and could not even choose my own son over him. You are my brother's child and heir to his power. Only you have the hope of standing against them both. Remake Excalibur and free me, free us all. If you don't, both our worlds will be consumed in the flames of war."

If I could hear her, then she could hear me. *"I will kill you for what you did to Tynan."*

"My son is not dead yet. Look."

She was right. Tynan's aura was a swarm of multi-colored sparks dancing towards the same darkness Melusine had been tethered to, but he was still alive.

I had to do something fast. Calling up every shred of the power of the spell Viviane had hidden me with, I screamed the familiar words. "Listen to me! We cannot be seen! Hide in the shadows and be still and silent!"

"What mischief is this? Where did they go?" Arthur roared.

The spell had worked. We were invisible to him.

Pushing Morgan away, he began to pace the room like a lion in a cage. As he passed within a few feet of Excalibur, I knew I couldn't guarantee Viviane's spell would hold at close range.

I lunged for the sword. "Everyone! To me!"

Daley was the first to understand. He slung Tynan over his shoulder. Taliesin had regained consciousness and Peter helped him to his feet. Miko was shaky on her feet but moving. I ran for the back of the cave where the Green Man was hiding in the shadows and the others followed. Glancing back, I was shocked to see Arthur following. He might not be able to see us, but somehow he could sense us. Morgan watched and did nothing.

"Goodfellow, get us out of here!"

There was a feeling of pressure—as if my ears had popped—and then I stumbled and fell. Rolling onto my back, my hands still clasped around Excalibur, I looked up at grey branches which hid the sky. We were on another Path. Depending on the Green Man was a gamble, but we were safe.

Goodfellow leaned down and offered me his hand, but I ignored it. "Why?" I demanded as I stood.

He dropped his hand. "I swore my own oaths to Arthur. I thought he would save the forest from the destruction of Man, but he only wanted control over the Paths. Still, as long as he lives, my oaths hold. When Morgan told me to take you to Arthur's tomb, I couldn't deny her, but I swear I didn't know what she intended to do. I gave you Excalibur in good faith, as Viviane asked me to. I didn't know the boy was the lock and Excalibur the key to raising the Earth King."

Ice washed over me as I realized I was the one who had offered to exchange Tynan for Excalibur. I was the one who had set events in motion.

I freed Arthur.

"If you belong to Arthur, why did you help Boudica double-cross us both?"

Goodfellow's eyes were no longer green, but grey with tears. "With Arthur sleeping, I thought I could gain the Lord of the Grey Land's favor. I hoped he would have the power to free me from my oaths." The Green Man straightened his shoulders and regained some of his strength. "I care nothing for the petty conflicts of men and magicians. I seek only to be free."

I looked at the others. All of them except Peter were bruised and bloodied. Daley kneeled on the ground with Tynan in his arms.

"Just get us home."

"One moment, Robin Goodfellow."

White shivers pulsed through me, but I turned to face Arthur. I'd forgotten he could travel the Paths.

The Earth King strode towards us, but gasped when he saw Tynan. "My son?"

"That's close enough," Daley warned and I heard thunder somewhere far away; we must be near an exit off the Path.

"My son is injured! He needs my help!"

As Arthur's plea tore at my heart, I saw him and I understood. We were all filled with paradoxes and inconsistencies, strengths and weaknesses, powers and disabilities—so many colors. Not Arthur. Arthur was pure. He was amethyst and not a single speck contaminated that magnificent, royal hue. His great power was a singleness of being and purpose that promised he could force even destiny to his will.

My soul cried out to accept him as my lord, but Tynan's blood on Excalibur held me firm. Still, I understood Morgan and Goodfellow better.

I bet Hitler was that same damn color.

Lifting Excalibur, I stepped forward and pointed it at Arthur. Even though it was blood-stained and twisted, Arthur's face changed and I knew he recognized it. He looked into my eyes and I knew he saw me too.

No one will ever make the mistake of not seeing me again.

"Who are you?" And what are you doing with my sword?"

The metal was heavy and my arm shook, but my voice was steady. "Who I am doesn't matter right now. What I'm going to do to Excalibur does." Actually, I had no idea what I could possibly do to Excalibur, but the flick of the king's eyes towards the twisted trees off the Path gave me a hint. I raised Excalibur as if I meant to throw it and Arthur lurched towards it.

"Stop! I'll give Excalibur to the trees. You could try going after it, but I don't think you'd ever find your way back to the Path again."

Arthur folded his arms across his chest. "There are some in my time who would cut off your hands for daring to touch a king's sword—even the ruin of it—but it is not my time, is it." It wasn't a question and he didn't wait for me to reply. "Morgana would spare me the truth, but now that I am fully awake, I can feel it for myself. The earth has changed. I am its king and I know its nature. Time has flowed out like wine from a broken bottle while I slept."

"At least you're taking it well." Excalibur's weight was almost unbearable and beads of sweat slid down my back.

Taliesin approached and bent his head. "Arthur."

"Bard," Arthur greeted him. "Let me see my son."

Taliesin hesitated and then nodded. Scowling but obedient, Daley carried Tynan to Arthur.

The king frowned as he examined the wound. "What did this terrible damage?"

He was asking Taliesin, but I waved the sword to get his attention. "What do you think?"

Arthur ignored me as he touched Tynan's face with a gentle finger. "Ah, blood magic. I understand. My son tried to kill me, but he has paid the price for his betrayal and erased his dishonor with his blood." He straightened with a sigh. "Sleep deep, my son." He glanced at me. "You can put Excalibur down. You are weary and I have no interest in it at the moment. Though I would not have it destroyed or lost, it no longer has the power to aid me."

I hated that he could see my weakness, but I put the sword down with relief and flexed my aching arm. Arthur chose that moment to take what he wanted.

Not Excalibur.

Me.

CHAPTER FORTY ONE

My brain went blank the way it does when you dive into cold water and it took me a moment to realize Arthur had grabbed me and somehow moved us to another Path. I braced for an attack, but he released me and walked away. "Keep up. We have only minutes before the Green Man finds us."

When I didn't move, he returned and arched an eyebrow at me. "Despite Taliesin's presence, you seem to be the power behind the forces opposing me. Do you not want to know the truth?"

I haven't had the truth since the day my birth mother dumped me with Viviane.

He seemed to read my hunger for the truth in my face. "Yes, I thought so."

"I need to get back to the others."

"You are worried about my son," he guessed, "but Mordred is as good as dead. I have seen many wounds on the battlefield and his is mortal. I promise you though, time passes strangely on the Paths and you will see my son before the end." With a courtly gesture, he invited me to precede him.

I shook my head. "Forget it. I don't trust you."

He flushed as if I'd hurt him, but then he chuckled and I felt my own cheeks grow warm. "How strange this time must be that you do not recognize the honor I was according you. However, it is indeed easier to converse walking side by side."

I looked up at him; he was even taller than Tynan. "And why would you honor me?"

Arthur laughed again. "My long sleep may have rendered my mind dull, but I am beginning to recover. Though it fills me with great surprise, I recognize in your features the echo of my former mentor's. I called him Merlin. You are kin to him in some fashion."

"You could say that. I'm his daughter."

Arthur stopped dead in his tracks. "Why, the old dog . . ." He immediately sobered. "My memories are addled and out of order. I am forgetting the true identity of my false friend."

"It's OK. I've never even met him."

We began walking again. "You are royal and I accede you honor again. Who is your lady mother?"

"I don't know. Viviane raised me."

Arthur was silent for a moment. "The Lady of the Lake betrayed me and became my enemy."

I shrugged. "Maybe she had her reasons. It doesn't matter now. She's dead."

The king shook his head. "What a strange tale you hint at, but Morgana will tell it just as well. I have not brought you to the Path of Time to waste it."

"Time?"

"As I examined the body of my son, I saw that he has aged only a few years. Mordred knew the Paths almost as well as

Goodfellow and his kin. He must have come this way, though I do not know how he managed it. Other than Goodfellow and myself, I know of just one other who could travel the Path of Time. Her name was Guinevere, but she would not help my son." Arthur didn't know his story was known throughout the world and that I knew the name of his wife.

"This Path seems the same as the other one."

"If you have the gift for it, you can feel the subtle differences." He gestured for me to hurry. "Quick, I sense the Green Man has found our trail and there is something you need to see."

Arthur's strides were almost twice as long as mine and I was almost running to keep up with him when he came to an abrupt stop. "We are here." The Path divided and passed under two archways made from the entwined branches of the trees. Beyond them both, light flickered.

Arthur pointed to the right. "Mordred must have traveled that way and into your time. Can you feel it? I have tried to pass its gate before, but have always been denied."

"His name is Tynan now." I took a step forward, heart pounding. I recognized this place.

"Another name for another existence." He sighed. "I wish I could have left him to it, truly I do, but my son has followed his fate to its inevitable conclusion. Follow me." Arthur passed under the arch on the left, and as I followed him, the light changed without warning.

An unfamiliar world lay before me. To say it was grey would be like saying the ocean was blue—right and wrong at the same time. It was grey, but it was also gleaming silver, flashing chrome, glittering obsidian, and soft dove. Shadowed hills rolled under a stormy sky and fleeting shades of rose, powder, and moth-wing green faded in and out of the scene like mirages. It was all so very beautiful.

And so very, very wrong.

"The Grey Lands," I whispered.

"Yes. Though this is the Path of Time, for me it will only show this one scene. You are looking upon the place as I first did when I was brought here by the man I knew as Merlin." Arthur stretched his hand out and the scene wavered and resisted. "I was completely enchanted. We called it Avalon for the pale pink apples that grew in the orchards and thought it was an island because of the ring of mist surrounding it. And then we thought it was the underworld when we began to sense the taint of evil hidden in its heart. Can you feel it?"

I swallowed. "Yes." It was like a pale flower growing out of a rotting corpse.

Arthur nodded. "Good. Not everyone can, not at first. I freed Morgana, but there are thousands more who languish here and I cannot abandon them."

I reminded myself that Tynan was dying and turned away from the bewitching scene. "Maybe they don't want to be freed."

"It does not matter what they want. I will do what is best for them. That is what a king must do."

Did it ever matter to Viviane what I wanted? Did it matter to Taliesin? What about the mother who gave me up to them?

Arthur was right about the Grey Lands—they were rotten at the core. Maybe someone did need to do something about it, but not this amethyst fanatic. I wasn't going to let him decide the fate of both my worlds.

Because I knew I belonged to the Grey Lands the moment I saw them.

"I'm going to stop you," I muttered.

Arthur turned. "So you are his then? Your father's?"

"I don't belong to anyone."

He dismissed me with a wave of his hand. "Each of us is bound to something or someone."

"I'm going to stop you," I repeated, louder this time.

Arthur laughed, shaking his head. "I am sorry for my rudeness, but you are a child. Not even Morgana can stand against me and there is no one more powerful save her brother. I am the Earth King. I will defeat Cernunnos, and then through blood and marriage, this world and Avalon are mine. But since you value choice, I will honor the nobility of your blood by offering you one: join me or die."

There was movement behind me. I cocked my head to the side as if considering. "Thanks for the great offer, but I'll pass. Oh, and I'd be careful who you say you're married to. Basically everyone knows you already have a wife."

Arthur was fast, but I was faster. I blinked to center myself and fire fuelled by anger leapt from my hands and flared between us. The last thing I saw before Goodfellow grabbed me was Arthur's astonished face and the reflection of flame in his eyes.

CHAPTER FORTY TWO

"That was cutting it a bit close." The others were gone, but Excalibur lay where I'd dropped it. I picked it up and was surprised at how much lighter it felt, as if it had been struggling against the pull of Arthur's power too.

Goodfellow ignored my sarcasm. "I need to close the Path off from the other end before he follows us here. This Path has multiple branches, and with any luck, he won't know which one we took." He glanced back at me. "I'm sorry for my part in everything, Miss Lynne."

I didn't answer because it didn't matter. The only thing that mattered was getting to Tynan in time. The Green Man gestured for me to walk forward and without any transition I stepped into the clearing in the woods behind the mansion. I looked back but Goodfellow was gone.

I ran into the house and the sound of voices led me to the study. Tynan lay on the couch and Daley kneeled beside him, holding his hand. Taliesin hovered over them. Peter and Miko stood by with helpless looks on their faces.

Tynan's face was just like Mom's right before she died.

Daley looked up at Taliesin and his eyes were frantic. "Do something!"

"I can try a binding. If his powers are bound, perhaps his spirit will follow." The bard went still and then his shoulders sagged. "It is too late. I cannot find him."

I put Excalibur down on the desk. "Let me try." The bard hesitated and then nodded.

Someone had bandaged Tynan's wound but it was messy and loose. A pain went through me.

Rowan would have done it right. He would have put ointment on the wound and spoke words over it and Tynan would already be getting better.

Fluorescent yellow panic blinded me for a moment, but I took a deep breath and calmed myself. I'd claimed Tynan in that cave, body and soul. If I couldn't find him, no one could.

I placed my hand on the bandage and blood seeped through it and stained my palm. Shivering with revulsion, I closed my eyes and discovered that Taliesin was right—Tynan's splintered colors shivered in a dance of chaos along a pale rope leading to darkness. A green thread still connected us, but it was pulled tight and looked ready to snap.

Blood magic is the greatest magic of all.

"What?" I opened my eyes and looked around, but everyone stared back blankly. The voice was in my mind.

Blood magic is the greatest magic of all.

It wasn't Morgan's voice, even though she'd said the same thing to me. It wasn't Viviane's either. I had a brief vision of grey, twisted trees and I knew—it was the voice of the woman who had given me away.

"Peter, get me Excalibur." Because I wished it, the sword let him pick it up. Taking it from him, I made a small nick in my palm and my blood joined Tynan's. Excalibur flared gold and then went back to its silent, sleeping state. I lifted my hand, but Taliesin grabbed my wrist. I looked up at him in surprise.

"The gods know I love this boy as if he were the son of my body, but think about what you are intending to do! Blood magic is old, dark magic. Only the greatest among us can wield it, and if you have not noticed, the greatest among us are beings capable of monstrous acts. Arthur was felled by it—held in deathless sleep for centuries—then raised up to unnatural life. Each time it is used, there is a price. Eventually there must be a balancing and an accounting."

I hesitated. "He'll die if I don't do something."

A jolt of angry electricity ran through me and thunder shook the windows. "Then do it!" Daley commanded.

I pulled away from the bard and slammed my hand down onto Tynan's chest.

I must have closed my eyes again because it was dark. Even my sense of his aura was gone. All I could feel was the blood seeping from the cut in my hand and the pulse in my wrist pounding. Louder and louder it pounded—Tynan's had joined it. As the blood spread out from my splayed fingers and mingled with Tynan's, I realized I hadn't closed my eyes at all. Blood was all I could see.

Taliesin's voice pierced me. "For one such as you who sees power, emotion, and thought as color, what does the essence of life look like?"

He was right to ask. Blood was life. Blood was everything—every color that ever was or ever will be. I shook my head; I was too far past speech to explain.

My awareness of Tynan's aura returned, but the green bond between us was too weak to hold him back from Death much longer. I thought I'd claimed him back in the cave, but I was wrong. That was why Morgan's spell defeated me then and Death was defeating me now.

Blood magic is the greatest magic of all. More powerful even than Death.

I concentrated on the blood flowing from my hand and sent it into Tynan's body, forcing the molecules in my blood to meld with his until we were one. Looking into his body from the inside, I was horrified. Tynan's heart was a torn, pulpy mass. As I watched, it faltered to a stop and I knew it would never beat on its own again. As his heart died, I did the only thing I could do.

I gave him mine.

A surge swept through me more painful than anything I'd ever experienced as all the colors stranded behind the barrier in my mind emptied out of me in a great rush. I felt my back arch in a terrible spasm and then Peter's hands on my shoulders holding me down. Waves of hot and cold flowed across my fingers as color erupted from them. The power of my blood could save Tynan, but only if I survived too, and I wasn't sure the pain wouldn't kill me. My heart beat so hard I was afraid it was going to burst.

It was beating for two.

Tynan's life returned to him like sparks over charred and almost cold wood, but it wasn't enough. The trickle of blood from my hand wasn't enough. How much more could I give and still be the anchor he needed? I pushed down the fluorescent hues of panic. I could do this, but I needed more power. I needed the power of a god.

"Help me, Daley."

I felt him hesitate, but then Peter's hands were gone and Daley's replaced them on my shoulders. For a moment it was like being tasered, but then I was filled with thunder, lightning, and storm-painted seas. If he ever mastered all these abilities, he would be as powerful as Morgan le Fay. His platinum was the power to control the wind and I took just enough of it to sweep as much of Tynan's spirit as I could find into his body.

I could do anything while Daley was touching me.

The only color left in me was a trace of Taliesin's indigo binding. It still lingered in the house and had seeped past the barrier in my mind. I used it to bind Tynan inside his own body.

My heart slowed to its normal pace, but the sound was off, as if a second beat followed the first an infinitesimal amount of time later. I thought of an old song I'd heard on the radio once.

Two hearts beat as one.

Taliesin's whisper made me open my eyes, but I couldn't look at him. "You are now bound closer than brother and sister, or parent and child. You will never be free of him until he dies. And he will die the moment you do." I wasn't sure how he knew, but I knew he was right.

I didn't wait for Tynan to wake up. I didn't want to be there when they told him about Rowan. I didn't want to be there when they told him his mother had killed him. Grabbing Excalibur, I left. Peter's concern followed me through our bond, but I ignored it.

Trudging down the driveway, I was surprised to see Thomas Redcap standing at the end of it, frowning. He wasn't wearing his cap and without its constant shadow, his face was soft and young.

He smiled in greeting. "It's good to see you alive and, well, alive after all that has happened, *mo leanabh.*"

"I'm not even going to ask how you know about that. And I'm not your child, Thomas."

He examined me closely. "No, I suppose you're not, Love. Not anymore." His smile turned rakish and his accent thickened. "But that can be a good thing now, can't it?"

My cheeks went hot. "What are you doing here?"

"I haven't the faintest. The death of a Great One called me, but now upon my arrival, I find that all here are living souls."

"Not all of us," I whispered as I thought of Rowan's body lost and forgotten in some distant cave.

Redcap sighed. "Ah yes, the druid. A good man by all accounts, but I do not come for the likes of him. I felt the son of Arthur die."

"Yes, he died," I said. "But then I made him live again."

Redcap's hand darted out to claim mine. Lifting my fingers to his lips, he bit one lightly.

"What are you doing?" I asked breathlessly, but I didn't move my fingers away from where they rested on his bottom lip, one of them bloodied.

He turned my hand over and kissed my palm on the small wound on my hand. I breathed in quickly when I felt his tongue flick at the blood covering it. Golden eyes rimmed in red gazed at me in wonder. "You are a goddess, love. Forgive me, for I couldn't help but try to take a part of you for myself."

Pulling away, I stumbled and dropped Excalibur. It hit the pavement with a dull clank.

I've really got to stop dropping this thing.

Redcap bent to pick it up, but his eyes widened as the rough metal refused to budge. He burst into laughter and the sound was sunshine and apples and warm blood.

"I understand everything now," Thomas Redcap said.

CHAPTER FORTY THREE

Whatever it was that Redcap understood, he didn't share it on the trip up to the lake. He was in a good mood though and enjoying the burger he'd asked me to drive through and get for him. I glanced over at him as he was finishing; he was a neat and fastidious eater.

I shivered as it reminded me of what else he delicately harvested and ate.

Pushing the thought away, I asked Redcap where his car was and why didn't he drive himself if he was so keen, but he laughed again and turned up the volume on the heavy metal station he was forcing me to listen to.

Arthur's awake and preparing to conquer the world and I'm transporting a bloodthirsty Greylander with bad taste in music to cottage country. In the off-season!

I could feel the heat of Redcap's gaze on me as if he couldn't stop looking at me. The nick on my finger and the wound on my hand burned.

When we arrived at the lake, Redcap was out of the car and almost down the hill as if he couldn't wait for whatever it was he was expecting to happen next. "Grab a blanket if you've got one, Love," he called over his shoulder, "and bring the sword." When I caught up with him, he was already sitting on the dock with his eyes half closed against the weak sun. I did a quick check of the drowned trees before stepping back as far from the water as I could.

"Sit down, Rhiannon." There was something in his voice that made my heart beat faster, but then I felt the echo of Tynan's follow it and ice washed over me. "She's down there, yes." L'Inconnue de la Seine.

Placing Excalibur in the center of the dock, I sat down and pulled the blanket over my knees. "Why are we here?"

In a sudden movement, Redcap pulled me back against his chest, grazing my temple with his rough cheek and wrapping his arms around me. "You're cold," he explained.

I held myself stiff for a moment and then relaxed. Redcap would keep me safe from L'Inconnue.

"Do you remember the day we met here?" His breath was warm. "You were a child then. A dangerous child I thought, but beautiful. Now you're a woman and I'm in awe." His lips brushed my ear and my colors swirled in confusion.

"What are you doing?" I whispered.

"Only what you want me to and nothing more," he answered and nipped my ear with his sharp teeth.

"Stop!" I scrambled away from him and grabbed Excalibur.

We stared at one another. He was dangerous—I'd always known that—but I'd been drawn to him too. It didn't matter though. I wasn't ready for what he was offering me.

Redcap sighed and looked away. "I'm sorry, *mo leanabh*," he said rubbing at the shadow of his beard, "I shouldn't have done that. It's just you remind me so much of one I lost long ago."

Something blocked the sun. "Touch my daughter like that again, Redcap, and you will lose something else."

The Lady of the Lake stood on the water with her cloud of dark hair rising in the wind.

"Mom!" I jumped to my feet, torn between amazement and embarrassment. "Morgan said it was possible, but I didn't believe it." Despite all my anger and disappointment, I wanted to touch her, but she was out of reach.

Viviane smiled. "You did well, Rhiannon. I had lost all power, all weight in this conflict over the fate of two worlds. But the moon wanes and dies only to be reborn again, and the tide recedes and then returns. I knew the Redcap would come at my death and consume my spirit and then you would spread my ashes here as I instructed."

Redcap stood and gave her a little bow, but winked at me as he straightened. He wasn't the least bit embarrassed. "I didn't know why I was drawn to this place. And then I met you here and you were attacked by L'Inconnue. She wasn't trying to kill you; she was trying to get us both into the water. The raw power inside you was the spark that lit the flame of the spell and Viviane left me when I jumped in to save you."

"It was some time before my spirit and my body were rejoined, and still not perfectly." Viviane gestured down at herself and I could see the lake through her flowing gown and white limbs. "Perhaps I will never leave this place until the true death of my kind claims me, but I have regained the power to do what must be done."

Moisture ran over my lips and I realized I was crying. Viviane cocked her head at me as if my tears puzzled her. "Do not cry for me, Rhiannon, for I am content. I was one of three sisters, but of us all, I had the least of love within me. It seems to me now that we were each incomplete in some way, but I cannot puzzle out the mystery of it. Much that I was and knew is lost forever. Still, what love I had, I gave to you. Being your mother for a time has given me that gift and I am grateful, but I must now give you a gift which one day you may curse me for."

Redcap motioned for me to approach. "Excalibur returns to the Lady of the Lake," he proclaimed.

I picked up the shaft of lumpy metal and reached out over the water to give it to her. Taking its weight easily, Viviane examined it. "I am glad the Green Man kept our bargain, but it is difficult to again see the totem in this state. In the depths of the sea, I formed Excalibur from metal that fell from the sky, but I did not give it life. That task fell to another. Yet I knew its destiny was to save us from my brother's dominion. I believed Arthur was Excalibur's ordained master, but he disappointed me."

"He's awake," I said.

She smiled sadly. "I know. I felt it. I felt your peril. And yet, here you are."

"Morgan let me go."

Viviane gazed into the sky as if she could see her sister there. "Do not judge Morgana too harshly; she fights her fate as best she can. Love is Morgana's downfall, and yet she has had more of joy with both Arthur and Taliesin than I have had in all my days."

Without warning, Viviane sank into the lake. I tried to look for her in the depths, but the water was strangely opaque. Redcap and I waited in awkward silence and the arm he draped around my shoulders for warmth was now light and impersonal. Finally she emerged, the water streaming from her hair and a magnificent sword in her hand. She offered me the hilt, but I hesitated.

"Take it," Redcap urged me. "Take it before she fades." He was right—Viviane was now transparent. I took the sword and then with the other hand she passed me a jeweled scabbard. Excalibur glittered in the dying light, but I felt nothing from it, not even a hint of the gold I'd sensed before.

She seemed to read my mind. "Yes, Excalibur has been remade, but it must still be quickened. You must temper it in the fire at the heart of the world and then you must find your true mother to guide you in how to use it. I go now to regain my strength. Do not come back here again until the end." She began to fade.

"Wait! What does that mean?" The only mother I'd ever known was leaving me. It hurt worse than the first time because I knew it was her choice, that it had always been her choice.

"Go in peace and remember that as I was able, I loved you." Viviane disappeared into the water.

"Wait!" I yelled as Redcap restrained me from diving in after her.

"Stop!" He shook me hard to get my attention. "Look!"

Where Viviane had disappeared, another figure surfaced, pale and menacing—L'Inconnue de la Seine. The creature had changed. Her hair now flowed over her white shoulders and the ghastly smile had relaxed. Through a splash of bright horror, I saw that her eyes were open and alive.

Redcap pulled me away from the edge. "Viviane has a new daughter now, and she will not let you disturb her mother's rest. We'd best leave before she remembers she once walked on land." We backed away and the creature watched us with gleaming eyes until we were off the dock before she slipped back down into the lake.

I sheathed Excalibur and followed Redcap to the car where he got into the driver's seat without asking and began to drive. The heavy weight of the sword lay across my legs while anger simmered inside me and burned away my tears.

"Why couldn't she tell me? Why couldn't she give me what I needed, just once? I don't care if she's the damn Lady of the Lake! She owes me more than that."

Redcap gave me a concerned look. "I wasn't lying when I told Morgan that things were missing from Viviane's essence. I now believe she used her power to excise certain memories. She no longer has the answers you seek, Rhiannon."

"But why?"

He shrugged. "To protect you in case Cernunnos ever found her, I suspect."

"Does it make me a bad person that I don't care about that right now?"

He sighed. "No, love, it just makes you very young and there's no shame in that."

And there it was, the elephant sitting in the front seat between us.

I wasn't sure how I felt about Redcap. He'd saved my life and I was drawn to him, but he was a monster. Closing my eyes, I leaned my head against the cool glass of the window. The colors of regret filled me, but I wasn't sure if they were mine or his.

I woke up when we pulled up in front of my house and Redcap muttered, "I'll see you in safely." As we went inside, I noticed that either Redcap wasn't enough of a monster for the holly to keep him out, or the plant was somehow sentient enough to know he was with me.

He looked around and frowned. "Viviane lived here?" He seemed surprised and my cheeks went hot.

"What's wrong with it?"

"Nothing. It doesn't seem like her, that's all. This is cozy though." He seemed to be picking his words carefully.

By "cozy" he means cramped, old, and ugly.

Anger swept through me, but there was no color left to call up fire with. "That's just great! I get the second class mother and the second class house. And I suppose you're my second class stalker. Pervert actually. What are you? A thousand years old? More? It's gross. Or maybe you're just a second class monster since you don't even have the guts to eat the corpses you collect. And now I'm stuck with this second class sword! What am I supposed to do with it? Use it as a big, stupid letter opener?" I threw Excalibur on the couch.

Without warning, I was pushed hard against the wall; Redcap had me pinned. One hand held my wrists above my head and the other trailed across my cheek. I winced as his sharp fingernail pierced my skin.

"The Great Ones are always cruel. Never doubt that you stand first class among them, *mo leanabh*. But better an honest monster than one who hides behind a pretty face."

As I stared into his gold and red eyes, I had an impulse to apologize, but the sting of the scratch on my cheek stopped me. There was a low growl as Seolan came out of the bedroom. He was no match for Redcap, but the look in the man's eyes told me we weren't in any real danger.

I was the one who had hurt *him*.

Redcap released me and walked away, his back straight and stiff. He opened the door and hesitated, but didn't turn. "May the next time I see you be at the moment of your death, Great One," he whispered, pulling the door closed behind him with a soft click.

CHAPTER FORTY FOUR

I sat down on the couch and tried not to cry. I knew I'd acted like a brat. Confused, Seolan paced nervously and then jumped on the couch beside me. When he put his head on my knee, I stroked his soft head and felt a little better.

I looked around with new eyes; the place really was shabby. Worse than that, it didn't feel like home anymore. Home was with the people I cared about, and with the exception of Seolan, they were all back at the mansion. Even Peter continued to train there—in fact, had thrown himself deeper into it than ever—though things between him and Miko were strained and uncertain.

I gave the hound a quick hug and then pushed him off to go pack some clothes. I left Excalibur on the couch where I'd thrown it. Maybe Taliesin would know what I was supposed to do with it, but for the moment, I wanted to get as far away from it as possible.

Seolan followed me outside to the car. I thought about taking him with me, but he nudged my hand and ran off into the darkness. The hound came and went as he pleased and I hadn't even had to feed him yet. I suspected his second home was the main barn and he was either stealing food from Old Tom's dog, or Tom had taken him in as a stray.

The windows of the mansion were dark when I pulled into the driveway. Taliesin had given me my own key and I slipped it in the lock and opened the door. I could sense Peter and Tynan through our separate bonds. Tynan was sleeping. Peter was in the gym even though it was late. He didn't seem to care anymore if his parents were worried about where he was at night.

I sighed. He was right. We were changing. Maybe too much.

Hoping I wouldn't run into Taliesin, I went up the stairs and knocked on Daley's door. He opened it with a surprised look on his face and then pulled me into the room.

"Where'd you go? Tynan's been asking for you."

"I'm sorry. How is he?"

Daley sat down on the bed, running his fingers through his hair. "Confused. He says he doesn't remember anything."

I sat down beside him. "Do you believe him?"

"I don't know. I can't wrap my mind around any of it."

Even with the lights off, there was still light in the room—the Wheel of Taranis in its larger state was hanging from a hook on the wall and glowing with stored power. Daley followed my gaze. "Viviane wanted you to find the charm, but did she expect you to give it to me? I wonder if she's laughing at us from wherever goddesses go when they die."

For some reason, I was reluctant to tell him about what had happened up at the lake. "Do you still think I'm a *leannan sidhe* or some sort of vampire?"

He scrubbed at his face with his hands. "Whatever you are, you need to come with us and fall into rank with Taliesin. We're at war now."

It wasn't what I wanted to hear. Redcap had unsettled me, made me feel somehow wrong. Despite what I'd called him, I felt like the monster.

I pounded my fist on my knees. "I don't care about any of that! I don't care about Taliesin's war." The electricity between us surged through me, igniting colors in my mind and my body. What I wanted to say was that all I wanted was for Daley to take me in his arms, but I didn't dare. Instead, I leaned in and kissed him.

I had a moment of fluorescent panic when he pulled away, but then his lips found mine and it was replaced with rose and magenta. Winding his fingers through my hair, Daley pulled me closer and the thunder vibrating between us told me he wanted this as much as I did. Opening and closing, rising and falling all at the same time, I sank into him, blinded by lightning and deafened by thunder.

I was slapped back to reality when Daley pushed me away and jumped off the bed. "What do you want from me?" he choked. I couldn't speak, but I suspected the answer was in my face when his breath caught and branches of light flared across his eyes. He turned and faced the window. His shoulders heaved with a couple of deep breaths and when he spoke again, his voice was steady. "This doesn't mean anything. It's only electricity. I loved Melusine. I know why you did what you did, but I can't forgive you for it, even if I do see my lightning reflected in your eyes."

Cold filled me until I was numb and colorless. I wanted to laugh, but I knew it would come out wrong, twisted and ugly.

If there's a god of love somewhere, he or she must be laughing their asses off. Tynan, Taliesin, Redcap, Daley, Me—we all love the wrong people. We're all bound to the wrong people by bands of crimson and flame. Consumed by fire.

By the fire at the heart of the world.

I heard her voice again—the voice of the mother who'd abandoned me. Something teased at my brain. There was something I needed to remember, and it wasn't about love.

Not this sort of love anyway.

The fire at the heart of the world—I tasted the words, searching for the colors hidden in them. For a moment, I was overwhelmed, but then the fragmented memories of the day she left me clicked together like the pieces of a puzzle. I finally knew what I had to do.

Standing and walking over to the door, I looked back at the young god of thunder silhouetted in the light of the moon streaming through the window. "Tell Taliesin that Viviane is alive and has remade Excalibur. Tell him Excalibur is mine."

Daley's face was shocked, but he remembered his duty. "We need you, Rhiannon. We need Excalibur. Are you with us?"

I left without answering.

CHAPTER FORTY FIVE

I entered the clearing carrying Excalibur in its scabbard in one hand, a flashlight in the other, and a blanket draped over my shoulder. Kicking the candles and other witch debris out of the way, I shrugged the blanket off onto the grass and dropped the sword on it. As I put the flashlight on the picnic table, a gleam of something metallic caught my eye and I knelt down to pick it up.

A cross on a broken chain.

I put it away in the pocket of my jeans, not for faith, but in remembrance of a good man who made flowers grow.

Shrugging out of my coat and rubbing my arms to warm them, I settled myself on the blanket, but it was no barrier against the freezing ground. For a moment, I regretted leaving the warmth of my home, but this was a place with no proper name to bind it; the spell I was going to cast needed all the help it could get. Unsheathing Excalibur, I used the scabbard to prop the sword blade side up. I was shivering violently now and it took a few tries to balance it properly. As I reached the point where cold is indistinguishable from heat, I closed my eyes.

The fire at the heart of the world.

The words were the key that turned the lock on my memory. I was on the Path of Time and the trees were as strange and menacing as I'd experienced before. If they were the ghosts of the forests of the world, they resented all of us. Strong arms carried me and I imagined I felt in them the desire to keep me and protect me. Perhaps it wasn't possible to do both. I looked up and saw Tynan following us. With his long, dark hair and pale skin, he was as haunted looking as the trees.

Who are we running from?

The golden-haired woman stopped and turned to speak to him. "We must separate now and hope that Merlin is confused by our trails. He has no power to pass this way, but he has the patience of a spider. If he discovers what times we have fled to, he will wait for us in them even if it takes countless years. I have taken steps to conceal my daughter. The best I can do for you is to take away the memory of your former life and give you a chance at a new one. Merlin has no interest in you beyond a means to strike at Morgan and will not exert himself overmuch to find you."

Tynan's face was stricken. "Must I leave my mother?"

"If you value your life you must. Your greatest peril is if Arthur survives the wound you gave him and seeks his revenge. You will be safe in the future."

There was a flash and Tynan jumped back into the gloom. I looked around to see Viviane stepping out of a bright light.

The golden-haired woman put me down and looked at me intently. "Rhiannon, you bear a power in your blood from both your parents that cannot be denied. Blood is life. Blood is everything. It is the magic of water, fire, and air combined within the earth of your flesh. When the time is right, Excalibur must be reborn. All our hope rests in you."

The place around my heart hurt; I was too young to understand that it was breaking. I threw my arms around the woman and buried my face in her skirts, but she disengaged me firmly. Kneeling down to face me, she put her hands on my shoulders. "I know it is difficult to understand why I must leave you. I do not want to. But someday you will know what to do with the power you are heir to. Perhaps then we will find each other again."

Viviane stepped forward. "What the child knows, others may divine. What even I know may be forced from me."

"I trust you will take means to never let that happen." There was danger in the woman's voice and Viviane bowed her head in response. "But you are right, as always." Pulling out a small knife from the pocket of her robe, she nicked her finger and blood welled up from the spot. When she touched my forehead, her blood burned and I began to cry.

"When the time is right, remember this and what it means: *the fire at the heart of the world.*"

"Blood magic is the most powerful magic of all," Viviane murmured, taking my hand and pulling me away.

"Blood magic is the most powerful magic of all," my mother agreed. "Pray she need not spill it all to save us."

The memory had been waiting all these years to reveal itself at the right time and place, triggered by the key phrase. Almost losing my nerve, I said a quick prayer to whatever god might exist outside of a world that was lousy with them.

In one swift movement, I slammed my right wrist onto the razor-sharp blade and dragged my arm back.

A deep parallel cut began to stream hot blood. Trying not to focus on what I'd done to myself, I leaned over and slit the other wrist. Because of the awkward angle, that cut ran diagonally across the scar the Wheel of Taranis had left behind.

I'm the child of blood. It flows out like the sea.

Falling back, I pulled Excalibur onto my chest with difficulty—my hands didn't work right anymore. I wanted to cry, to regret what I'd done, but then the pain was replaced by a sweet lethargy. As my blood flowed over Excalibur, I couldn't remember why I was there and I was too moved by the beauty of the cold stars above me to care. Even Peter's alarm running through our bond or the distant sense of Tynan's own heart faltering as mine slowed couldn't reach me.

It took much longer to die than I expected.

Hovering above myself, I examined my body, amazed at how much blood could come from two small, well-placed cuts. Without vanity, I decided the dead girl on the ground was quite lovely even with the vacant eyes and moon-pale skin—beautiful dead things again. The thought reminded me of what was supposed to happen next, but I was surrounded by a pale rope that slowly dragged me towards a far off darkness.

I was disappointed to realize I was wrong.

A sudden shimmer, a breath of warm air, and Thomas Redcap appeared. "Rhiannon!" He dropped to his knees and gathered my corpse in his arms, burying his face in my hair and not caring that Excalibur sliced into his chest. "What have you done? What have you done, mo leanabh?" Holding me, he raised my bloody wrist to his lips—capturing me in the strange and unique way of his kind—and the pale rope fell away.

I could take care of the rest.

"I'm not a child," I whispered, back in my body.

Redcap's eyes widened and flame engulfed the amber. "Rhiannon?"

I tried to smile. "I didn't know any other way to call you."

Excalibur flared to life between us, awakened by my blood sacrifice, but it was no longer just the gold of good earth and wheat sheaves. It was also the shimmering, changing blue of a sun-lit sea and the translucent white of racing clouds. Encompassing them all was crimson and scarlet, alizarin and flame.

Earth, water, air, and the spark of life: fire. The blade seared its brand on my flesh and then healed all my wounds as it claimed me with the elements of the earth power.

Redcap kissed me and I fell unresisting into the fire at the heart of the world.

CHAPTER FORTY SIX

Peter was sitting at the end of my bed. It was his anger humming through our bond that woke me up.

"Good. You're awake. Now what the hell were you thinking? Do you know what it was like to feel you slit your wrists and to know I was too far away to get to you in time? Do you? Do you even care? Do you *get* that you *actually* died? That I *felt* it? And then to see you covered in blood . . ."

"And Thomas Redcap?" I joked weakly.

Peter's mouth opened and closed for a moment before he found his voice again. "If you hadn't already died once tonight, I think I'd kill you. I was almost out of my mind and poor Seolan was so freaked that I had to put him in your mom's room."

I pushed myself upright with shaking arms. "Excalibur?"

He snorted. "Alive and practically purring like a kitten. I can feel it through my bond with you. You wouldn't let it go until we got you back here, but then it let me take it. I'm guessing all this was for its benefit?"

I nodded. "Redcap told you about Viviane?" That's what she was to me now. She would never be Mom again.

"Yup." Leaning forward, he turned my arms over and exposed the pink scars on my wrists. The round bisected one almost looked like the hilt of a sword. "How did you know it would work?"

"I remembered something important my birth mother told me. She hid it in my mind until the time was right. The rest was intuition, but I knew Thomas Redcap would come at my death and capture my spirit before it went too far."

Peter's eyebrows shot up. "What?"

I shook my head. "It's a redcap thing. Excalibur is mine now and I was pretty sure it would heal me, just like it sent Arthur into an enchanted sleep instead of letting him die."

Peter snorted again. "Pretty sure?"

"Mostly sure," I amended with a grin that Peter couldn't resist returning, even though I could still feel his anger. He had a right to it. It had all seemed so logical at the time. Maybe the fact I was still alive was proof I knew what I was doing. As I got out of bed, the dried blood on my t-shirt crackled and reddish flakes fell to the floor.

Or maybe I'm just lucky.

"Excalibur showed me how it was made. An asteroid fell into a lake. Viviane found it and the metal from it was forged in fire and quenched in earth. My birth mother awakened the sword with her blood. When I was little, she told me what I would need to do, but I didn't remember. She told me that blood magic is the most powerful magic of all." I also knew she'd only had to give a small amount of her blood to bring the sword to life. Healing the terrible damage done to it had taken a lot more of mine. Almost too much.

"You remember her?"

"A little." I took a deep breath. "Could you grab me a clean top?"

Peter dug a clean t-shirt out of my closet and turned his back as I changed. Throwing the ruined one across the room at the small mountain of dirty clothes surrounding the hamper, I realized I'd probably end up burning them and going on a shopping spree before I ever managed to wash all of them. The movement pulled on my sore wrists, but otherwise, I felt great.

"Where is he?" I asked, even though I already knew the answer.

"Redcap? I don't know. You were out of it for hours. I wanted to take you to the hospital, but he showed me your wrists healing so there didn't seem to be much point. He wouldn't leave your side at first, but once it seemed like you were going to be OK, he left."

"Oh." I forced myself to push any thoughts of Thomas Redcap and that hot, confusing kiss aside.

As I pulled the new shirt over my head, I looked down at myself in dismay. It was truly desperate if the only clean thing Peter could find was a t-shirt with a flavor of the month boy band on it from when I was twelve. At least I hadn't gone up too many sizes in the bra department since then.

Let's hope anyone who sees me in this thinks I'm being ironic.

"You can turn around, but don't laugh."

I expected him to make a joke, but he just stared at me blankly. Concentrating on our bond, I finally caught the undercurrent of an anger running through it that had nothing to do with me.

"What is it?" I asked.

"You've got a couple of visitors. I've been holding them off until you woke up, but they're getting pretty impatient."

"Who?"

"Nope. You gave me the shock of my life. Think of this as payback."

I looked at myself in the mirror over the dresser and the face staring back at me from the mirror was now definitely a Rhiannon, not just a Rhi. Redcap's scratch down my cheek and the marks on my wrists couldn't be helped, so I gave up on the idea of making myself presentable and went into the living room.

I was expecting Daley and Tynan, or even Taliesin waiting to tell me off for taking such a stupid risk. I didn't expect my father sitting on the couch twirling Goodfellow's sprig of holly in his fingers. Boudica stood at attention by his side.

Holding my gaze, the Lord of the Grey Lands held the holly up. I watched in horror as the power and life in it was drained until it was a blackened husk.

Just like I did with the Dobhar-chú.

Crumbling what was left of the holly in his fist and tossing the fragments on the coffee table, he rose to greet me. "Daughter," he said, inclining his head.

"*Dad,*" I replied, hoping my voice wouldn't betray my fear.

I was rewarded with a wintry smile. "I suppose you know that I have been searching for you for a very long time."

"Yes. How did you find me now?"

Cernunnos wandered around the room, inspecting my belongings with interest and picking up an item here and there to examine more closely. I half expected him to put on some white gloves and check for dust. "I knew that when Viviane died, I would eventually be able to break through the spell she used to shield you, but then you revealed yourself to Boudica and saved me the trouble. Sending the Dobhar-chú was a little test to make sure. But since then, you've been a busy girl—raising the dead, killing yourself—I could have found you blindfolded after that."

Was it wrong that my heart lifted at the thought that he wanted me? Was it so strange that I responded to the unfamiliar and yet somehow familiar sound of his voice? His pattern of speech was more natural than his sisters'. In fact, I couldn't see any similarity between him and Viviane or Morgan at all. I crossed my arms to hide my shaking hands and the idiotic smiling boys printed across my chest.

Peter moved to my side and Cernunnos laughed softly. "Relax, Protector. Viviane stole Rhiannon from me for her own purposes; I only wish to claim what is mine."

A flash of crimson cut through me. I'd claimed myself when I quickened Excalibur. "I don't belong to you."

"Do you not?" His smile was wider now. "And if I tried to take you, do you think you could stop me?"

I was reminded of Daley saying almost the same thing to Goodfellow and grey doubt clouded my vision. I forced myself to smile back. "Maybe not, but Excalibur could."

His face didn't change, but I could feel the menace in him. "So you have the earth totem? I had assumed that when Arthur was awakened, it was by Excalibur's power."

"No. Morgan murdering her own son is what woke Arthur up."

His eyebrows arched. "Ah, I see. How fitting. And this was the same boy you resurrected, I gather." Cernunnos pursed his lips. "Mordred is mad, but of the four of us, only

Morgan and I have produced children." I tried not to flinch as he stepped towards me and lifted cold fingers to trace the scratch on my cheek. "You have no idea how important you are." His eyes were black with flecks of pure white.

"And yet Morgan stuck a knife in her son's heart. I don't suppose you would do any different."

Dropping his hand, Cernunnos turned to Boudica and laughed. "Did I not tell you, my queen? Is she not my daughter to the very core?"

"Yes, my lord," she murmured.

Through our bond, I could feel Peter's fury grow. He was poised to attack, but we were outmatched and I needed to deflect his attention quickly. "So are you two an item then? I wouldn't put a ring on it if I were you, Daddy. Bo has a habit of killing off her husbands."

Cernunnos' raised eyebrows were curiously fine and dark, as if they were drawn on. "And what does it matter to me that she dispatched the mewling druid?"

Closing my eyes, I concentrated on the woman. It had only been a guess sparked by quick flashes of the warm brown of good earth and the emerald green of leaves at the height of summer surrounding her, but I was shocked to discover I was right. Remembering the deep cuts that had almost severed Rowan's head from his body, I struggled against a surge of nausea.

Opening my eyes and forcing a smile, I drawled, "Because your girlfriend is haunted by her past, Daddy. Literally."

Cernunnos examined Boudica closely and then shuddered delicately. "Nasty creatures, ghosts. You know how much I despise the parasites, my dear."

"Yes, my lord," Boudica said meekly, but she glared at me. "I'll take care of it."

"Do not return to my presence until you do." With the barest flick of his wrist, the woman was banished into nothingness.

I let out my breath in a startled whoosh. "Where did she go?"

Cernunnos sat back down on the couch and crossed his legs elegantly. "Somewhere she can deal with her little problem. The woman has her uses, but I like my concubines clean and free of disease." His smile was the definition of wicked.

I was appalled, even for Boudica. "She thinks you're going to make her a queen again. She betrayed everyone for you."

He shrugged. "And I may keep that promise if it suits me. Now, enough about the Icenian, what are we going to do about our little problem?" He motioned for me to sit, but I remained standing. His mouth twitched as if he found my stubbornness amusing.

"What problem?"

He picked off an imaginary piece of dust from his knife-pleated pants. "Don't pretend to be a half-wit—Arthur, of course. Neither of us wants him to ascend to his power and we certainly don't want him to get his hands on that pig-sticker your young man is trying to hide." Peter flushed but didn't move from his position blocking the chest of drawers in the corner.

Cernunnos laughed again. "Really, my dear, is this the best you can do for a Protector? Once I knew you had Excalibur, it was a matter of moments to find it in the room." He paused.

"How did you quicken it, by the way? I had thought it was dead and useless."

I didn't answer and when he stood, I took a step backward in response. "Good," he said, surveying me with satisfaction. "Don't underestimate my power or my lack of patience for stupid children. Because of the Wall, my time here is short, so listen well. We share the same goal: to stop Arthur before he takes action against either of our worlds."

I decided to play along. "What do you want from me?"

Cernunnos' smile was a thin line. "Nothing more than what you were already intending. Our purpose at this moment is the same."

"And what's that?"

"Finding your mother, of course."

My heart lurched. It hadn't occurred to me until that moment that of course my father would know the identity of the woman he'd impregnated.

"My mother?" I asked, pretending not to care.

But the Lord of the Grey Lands wasn't fooled and his smile widened. "Yes, your mother—the earth witch Guinevere."

I couldn't speak. Not in a million years would I have guessed my birth mother was Arthur's spurned wife.

Merlin and Guinevere—boy did the storybooks get that one wrong.

Cernunnos was becoming transparent and I could sense the power of the Wall as it drew him back to the grey lands of Avalon.

And I recognized the familiar handiwork.

I smiled. "You didn't make the Wall Between Worlds to protect yourself from Arthur. Viviane made it to protect us from you. Don't bother denying it. I've seen her walls up close. And now that she's back, yours is as strong as ever."

I felt a rush of satisfaction as his eyes widened—he hadn't known Viviane had returned—but my father would not be bested so easily. "Then you had better find Guinevere quickly. She's the only one who can undo Viviane's spell and bring down the Wall. Without my help, you can never hope to defeat Arthur." He made a motion with his hand and a raging tidal wave of color obliterated the barrier in my mind. Screaming in pain, I could feel Peter catch me as I fell, but I was blinded by the color searing my retinas and the feeling of knives plunging into my skull.

There was a terrible pounding noise. Cernunnos turned in surprise as Seolan broke Viviane's door off its hinges and burst into the room. The hound looked at me with eyes that loved and forgave me and then leapt at Cernunnos.

Cernunnos caught him by the throat mid-air and the hound made a pitiful, strangled sound. Making sure I was watching, he smiled as he crushed Seolan's neck.

"NO!" I screamed as he tossed the lifeless body at my feet.

As quickly as it began, the pain was gone. Gasping for air, I searched through the new colors that filled me for that red I'd once seen that would sear the flesh off bones. Fire tipped with acid appeared in my hands, but Cernunnos made another small motion and the color was forced back inside me. For a moment I thought I might burst into flames myself, but then I contained it.

Cernunnos grimaced as he delicately wiped hair and blood from his fingers onto my couch. "Don't make a spectacle of yourself. I created you. Fulfill the purpose of that creation and I may let you live. Deny me and I will make your every moment a living agony until color eats through your brain and leaks out of your skull." A shock went through me as I realized that my father saw power as color too. "Good. I can see you understand me. You're going to be an obedient little girl and do what I say. You're first task is to find Arthur's abandoned queen." He took something out of his pocket and threw it on top of Seolan's broken body. "Use this to contact me when you're successful."

"I don't belong to you, Cernunnos," I hissed.

He ignored my bravado. "One last thing: I've decided I no longer wish to be known as Cernunnos. The Celts who gave me that name are all rotting in their graves. You may call me father, but tell the others I want to be known by a name as famous as Arthur's." He faded from view, but his voice rang through the room, rattling the cupboards and shaking the windows.

"Tell them my name is Merlin!"

Trembling, I pushed away from Peter and fell to my knees beside Seolan. Throwing my arms around him, I buried my face in his silky hair, but my tears had been burned away in flame.

I sat up. "Get me Excalibur." Peter retrieved the sword from behind the chest of drawers and handed it to me. I pulled just enough out of the scabbard to expose the sharp edge and make a long cut in my palm. Passing my hand over Seolan's face, I closed his dark, trusting eyes and stained the white fur with my blood.

"I will avenge you. I swear it." The scars on my wrists and the burn on my chest flared hot and I knew Excalibur witnessed my blood vow to the creature whose life I had taken twice. I would be held to that vow by the earth magic.

A small object rolled off Seloan's broad chest and I picked it up.

It was a pink apple from the orchards of Avalon.

CHAPTER FORTY SEVEN

I stared at the little pink sphere sitting on my coffee table. Was I supposed to eat it when I found Guinevere? Would I fall asleep like Snow White and wake up in Avalon? It didn't matter. I doubted Guinevere would be easy to find. I still had time to figure out how to free myself from Merlin's clutches.

I jumped at the knock on my door and when I opened it, I was surprised to find Miko standing outside. Taliesin's Jag was parked on the road.

We stared at each other for a moment. No one could see them when they were retracted, but the dark wings she'd schemed to get still hovered between us. "What are you doing here?" My encounter with my father had stripped me of politeness. "If you're looking for Peter, he's not here."

Peter was burying Seolan under the trees near the back paddock. I couldn't bear to do it.

She shifted uneasily and I saw she had her leather bag on one shoulder. "He called me earlier to tell me you re-made Excalibur somehow. That's amazing." She didn't sound amazed. She didn't sound like she cared at all.

346 · HEATHER HAMILTON-SENTER

Confused, I opened the door wider. "Do you want to come in?"

She shook her head. "It's OK. I need to ask you something, but maybe now's not the best time."

She was right—it wasn't—but I forced myself to care a little. "What's wrong?"

Miko took the bag off her shoulder and shoved it into my hands as if she couldn't bear to touch it anymore. I knew from the weight of it what was inside.

The fairy's eyes filled with tears and I saw that her irises were now large and black. "Binnorie doesn't belong to me anymore. She rejected me."

I could guess how much that hurt her, but she wasn't dumping the harp on me. I held out the bag. "Well I certainly don't want it."

She backed away. "I know, but I don't know who else to give her to. She won't go to any of the guys. I don't know who else to trust her with until she picks another keeper. You'll keep her safe until she does. I owe her that much."

I thought of Seolan and how I'd failed to keep him safe. "Binnorie hates me."

"Binnorie fears you. She'll obey you."

I shuddered. "I don't want anything to do with her. I'm only keeping her until she chooses someone else." I hated that I was now calling the harp 'she', but not as much as I hated being the guardian of a magical object made from the hair, bone, and spirit of a drowned girl.

"Thank you," Miko said as she turned and walked back to the Jag. I put the bag down on the porch and followed her. As she opened the door, she paused but didn't look at me. "I know I was stupid. I know Peter will never forgive me. I've never belonged anywhere—not with my father's people, not with my mother's. Taliesin tolerates me out of pity."

"That's not true . . ."

"I knew if I had wings, things would be different. I would be different." Her lips trembled and obsidian tears ran down her cheeks. "And now I am. Just not the way I hoped I'd be."

I didn't want to, but I felt sorry for her. "Maybe they're not the wings you wanted, but they're still good, right? And you don't give Peter enough credit. He'll forgive you. Things could go back to the way they used to be."

Miko shook her head. "More things have changed than my wings. I'm something new, and new isn't always good." I had to step away quickly as she pulled the car door closed and sped down the laneway.

CHAPTER FORTY EIGHT

The thing about growing up is you start to realize that nothing about life is simple and clear.

Arthur was my enemy, but he loved the world in his own blind way. I needed Merlin to stop Arthur, but he was a devil I'd been forced into a bargain with. Taliesin had vowed to stop them both, but he loved the woman who had killed the son of his heart.

I couldn't trust any of them.

There were no good sides. No wrong and right. No black and white.

Only all the colors of the world in between.

CHAPTER FORTY NINE

A few days before Christmas, Peter and I were on a plane headed for Las Vegas. He pretended to read while I stared out the window, thinking about the events of the past two months.

The others had arranged for Robin Goodfellow to take them home to the ranch in Nevada and Peter and I had promised to join them once the semester was over. The goodbyes were awkward. Daley was distant. Miko was sad and listless. Peter hugged her but stepped back quickly when she tried to return it.

Taliesin was still in mourning for Rowan and Morgan. When I presented Excalibur to him in its renewed glory, the bard turned away, overcome. Once he collected himself and began to ask questions, I was purposefully vague about how I'd quickened the sword and also how I'd discovered my birth mother was Guinevere. He was deeply shocked at that revelation. When he assumed Viviane told me, I didn't correct him. I didn't mention my visit from Merlin either, though I informed him of my father's name change. I could tell Taliesin's sharp eyes had noted the faint scars on my wrists, but if he guessed what had happened, he didn't say. It was a good thing he couldn't see Excalibur's outline branded into the skin between my breasts. He did let me know that the scabbard could make itself and the sword invisible if I commanded it to.

I didn't want to talk about Seolan and was glad when no one asked.

When Tynan pulled me aside and asked if he could speak with me, the others wandered away to give us some privacy. "So, about you and Daley . . ." I tensed and Tynan smiled sadly. "I just wanted to clear the air. I think you know how much I care about you. I realize we're half cousins through Cernunnos, I mean Merlin, but that doesn't mean the same thing to Greylanders as it does to humans. And though I don't really understand it, Dad told me that you saved my life. I wish I could repay you somehow. I wish . . ." He didn't finish saying what he wished. "But I know you have feelings for Daley."

There was no point denying it. "Yes."

He bowed his head and his dark hair covered his face. "He still loves Melusine, you know."

There was no point denying that either. "Yes," I said again.

Tynan stiffened and looked up, eyes blazing. "I get it, but it's a mistake, Rhiannon. And what about the redcap? What's your relationship with him?"

I was caught off guard. "Nothing. We're friends. That's it," I stammered.

"The redcap is dangerous and more powerful than he knows." Tynan's voice was darker and more mature. A shiver ran through me. It was Mordred's voice—the voice of a boy who at twelve, in that time period, was a man.

The voice of a man who had tried to kill his own father.

"I felt it, you know." He clutched his chest. "You did something and I felt my own heart stop."

Tynan was illuminated by the white of my own horror. I hadn't stopped to think that I was risking his life as well as my own when I cut my wrists. For the first time, the true enormity of what I'd taken on when I saved his life threatened to crush me.

He hunched his shoulders and seemed to deflate. "Anyway, you should be careful around both of them. I don't want to see you get hurt." His voice was hesitant and soft, the way it normally was.

"I'll be careful," I promised, but I didn't mean about Tynan and Redcap. I made a silent vow that I would be more careful about the life I held in the palm of my hand.

Tynan smiled shyly and the echo of Mordred was completely gone. "C'mon, you've got to see this. Goodfellow must feel really bad about everything because he's gone all out."

When I followed him through the patio doors, I wondered if I'd finally snapped. A massive wooden ship rested on the back lawn.

All it needs is the animals filing in it two by two.

"You've got to be kidding me," I said under my breath but Tynan heard me and chuckled. The sound was so normal that my heart lifted in hope. Maybe his darker half would eventually disappear.

Goodfellow emerged from a door onto the deck, his red hair blowing in the wind. "I told you, Miss Lynne," he called down to me, "I can make a Path look like anything I want." His laughter echoed across the sky and I couldn't help smiling back. I guessed that Taliesin had forgiven him for his deception and there was something about him that made me want to as well. It would be easier to stay mad at a forest than it would be to stay mad at the Green Man.

He gestured and fabric on the deck that I'd thought was a sail now filled with air and became a giant hot air balloon. When Peter joined me, I could feel my best friend's delight at the steampunk marvel in front of us.

Geek, I thought affectionately. When he laughed and stuck his tongue out at me, I knew he'd somehow heard me through our bond.

His joy faded as Miko brushed past him and then turned and gave him one last sad look. Despite the closeness I'd developed with the fairy, I hated her for dimming Peter's light.

The strange individuals who had entered our lives walked up the plank and into the hatch on the side of the airship. Daley was the last. He hesitated at my side as if he wanted to say something, but then walked away without a word. It amazed me that he couldn't feel the magenta bond that stretched between us and threatened to pull my heart out of my chest. He stopped again at the top of the plank, silhouetted against the opening into the airship, and I remembered the first day I met him. I thought of how I'd compared the two brothers as they stood side by side and found something missing in Tynan. I thought of Morgan and what she'd said about wishing she'd met and loved Taliesin before Arthur. Maybe I would have loved Tynan if Daley hadn't been there to outshine him. I thought of how that might have changed everything.

Daley looked back at me before he disappeared, and even at that distance, I could see the flash of lightning in his eyes.

I abandoned any regret. I'd chosen the storm. I wouldn't complain about the weather.

The hatch closed and the airship vanished.

Peter and I returned to our lives. He threw himself into sports, but I knew he thought about Miko all the time. He stopped going to church and that worried me almost as much as I knew it worried his parents. Sometimes I felt flashes of rage through our bond that frightened me.

We're all changing so much.

Without Viviane's hiding spell, I experienced normal school life fully. It wasn't all pleasant. I tried to repair my grades, but it was a hopeless cause. I even went on a couple of dates that left me longing for eyes pierced with lightning and the touch of sparks on my skin.

On the last day of November, Lacey returned to school and reclaimed her title as Queen of the Bumblebees. A bad case of mono was the explanation for her strange behavior and she was treated with all the sympathy due a tragic heroine. Given that he had used the same illness as an excuse, Peter got the blame for getting her sick. The Bumblebees gave him angry looks he was completely oblivious to. Lacey didn't acknowledge him or me as she walked into Mr. Porter's class on her first day back.

As I sat behind her and watched her pop back up the social ladder, I seethed with anger. She'd betrayed us so Cailleach could deliver a dragon to Merlin. I didn't know if Cailleach had forced her or if she'd gone along willingly and I didn't want to know. I didn't trust myself to not do something stupid if I didn't like the answer. Using my senses to search for any traces of power, I found her colorless.

But one swirling tattoo remained on her wrist.

It made what I had to do that much harder. Binnorie had been whispering to me for days until I wanted to smash the thing to bits. Now the harp lay quiet in the leather bag at my feet. When the bell rang, I picked it up and rushed after Lacey as she was leaving. I grabbed her by the arm. Hard.

I might have also used a little magic to make sure she really felt it.

As I guided—some might say forced—Lacey down the hall, through the stage door and onto the stage, I could feel her shaking. I released her and she stumbled away from me. Smiling, I channeled enough of the red of my anger into the air to surround the stage with a ring of flame.

When I gestured and Excalibur appeared in my hand, the would-be witch gasped and fell to her knees. I made sure she got a good look at it before I put it back in the scabbard belted at my waist. I gestured again and it disappeared. I just had to think of it disappearing for the thing to obey, but I was putting on a good show. We were on the stage after all.

"What do you want?" I could see Lacey's hands trembling, but her voice was calm and I had to admire her acting skills.

"What I want is for you to know that despite everything you did, Melusine is contained, the Lady of the Lake has returned, and Excalibur is mine." At least I hoped Melusine was still contained in her ghostly form.

Lacey got to her feet and straightened her shoulders. "I know. I also know who your birth mother is. Between her and Cernunnos, it's no surprise you were able to claim Excalibur."

I glanced at the tattoo on her wrist. I might not be able to sense any power in her, but the mark was proof that Lacey still had a few tricks up her sleeve. I remembered the fith-fath Rowan had made for her and wondered if she'd taken it from him after all and was using it now.

"I was bound to the crone," she said defiantly. "I didn't have a choice."

I didn't believe her, but it didn't matter. I slid the bag across the stage and she jumped back from it as if it might be filled with snakes.

"Pick it up." She approached it cautiously and obeyed. "Look inside."

Lacey opened the bag and gasped in shock. When she looked at me, her eyes were round and full of tears. "Why?"

I shrugged. "How should I know? She's claimed you and now you're her keeper. Binnorie's crazy, so that probably explains it."

"Thank you," she whispered.

"Don't thank me yet. I have three conditions."

"Anything."

"First, if the harp ever wants to go back to Miko, you won't stop it." Lacey hesitated and then nodded. "Second, if Taliesin asks you to find Potentials for him, you will." She nodded again, quicker this time. "And third, I don't want to see you in this school until after the semester ends." She started to protest but I stopped her. "I mean it, Lacey. I don't care if you call it a relapse, or exchange school, or a death in the family. Over the holidays, Peter and I are joining the others in Las Vegas, but until then, if I even *think* I can sense you anywhere near us, I'll take Binnorie and grind her to dust. Are we clear?"

Lacey rubbed her eyes and nodded. "I'll do what you ask, but you're right—I'm not sorry. Cailleach served Cernunnos, but he's no worse than the rest of them. There are no good sides, only a chance to gain enough power to be free of them all."

"That's exactly what I intend to do. Don't get in my way, Lacey." I waved my hand and the flames vanished. "I'll leave you two to get acquainted." As I felt my way in the dark for the exit, Binnorie began to sing.

Lacey was true to her word—a transfer to a Bible school in one of the southern states was the excuse. December passed quickly. Peter had already convinced the Larsens to let him spend Christmas with Miko in Las Vegas. He hadn't told them he and Miko had broken up. I wasn't even sure they actually had.

What's the protocol for breaking up with someone who only cheats on you to become a fairy/vampire hybrid?

And then there was the greatest surprise of all.

The night before our flight, the Larsens celebrated Christmas early and we feasted on turkey, chestnut stuffing, and cranberry-apple pie. I watched with excitement as the Larsens opened my gift—a white porcelain statue of a horse I found in a little shop downtown. I'd also paid the taxes on the property for the next year, but they wouldn't find out about that until after I was gone. Hopefully it would keep Windfield safe from developers a little while longer.

By midnight, we were sipping eggnog by the fire and Mr. Larsen was asleep on the couch snoring loudly. When Peter's mom motioned for us to put down our mugs and follow her, we grinned at each other. It was one of our traditions. Mrs. Larsen usually kept back a special treat just for us—Mr. Larsen was diabetic and she hated to tempt him too much. I hoped that this year it was her almond crescents—a family recipe handed down from her German ancestors for generations—but when we entered the kitchen, she was just standing there with tears rolling down her cheeks.

Peter rushed over and put his arm around her. "What's wrong?"

"I'm just going to miss you so much."

"It's only a couple of weeks. I'll be back in no time."

Mrs. Larsen tried to smile, but her lips trembled. "That's what they all say when they go to Taliesin. That's what my sister said, but she never did come back."

All the air seemed to have been sucked out of the room.

"The Protector curse comes from my side of the family," she explained quietly.

"Mom . . . ," Peter began, but she shushed him.

"I was eleven when my sister left and thirteen when my parents received the letter from Taliesin telling us she'd been lost. I knew exactly what you were the moment you were born. I knew you were Rhi's Protector the first time I saw you together. It didn't take too many late night football practices before I realized you weren't telling me the truth and that Taliesin had come for you both at last."

I could feel Peter's shock through our bond. Of all the changes in his world, this one was the worst and he could barely process it.

"Did you know what Viviane was?" I asked softly.

Mrs. Larsen shook her head emphatically. "No. And I don't want to know now. I was afraid of what it might do to Peter if I turned you away. That's the honest reason why I took you both in, but I let you stay because I grew to love you."

She put out her arms and the three of us huddled together in a teary embrace. I was taller than her now and it made me sad.

Pushing us away and wiping her eyes, Mrs. Larsen retrieved a photograph from the counter behind her. "This is Marie when she was seventeen. She was gone a few months later." The photo showed an attractive girl with blonde hair posing in front of a Christmas tree.

Peter took the photo from her. "Dad always said Aunt Marie died in a car crash."

"Your father never knew her. We told everyone she'd gone away to school. Taliesin had just relocated from Wales to Nevada—something about the opportunity of the 'New World' being a powerful attraction for monsters. When Marie disappeared, we made up the story of the accident to explain it."

"Disappeared?" I asked.

"We never found out what happened. Taliesin said there was no body." When Peter tried to give the photo back, she shook her head. "Take it with you. I always hoped Marie had changed her mind and run away when she got the chance. You never know, maybe you'll find her some day."

The photo was now the placeholder in the book Peter was pretending to read. He was running his thumbnail up and down the groove between his bottom teeth as he stared at it. I wondered if knowing about his aunt made him doubt his decision to join Taliesin, but I didn't intrude on his thoughts through our bond. I knew what I thought about it all. The bard had either deliberately concealed his knowledge of her, or worse, completely forgotten about the girl who had disappeared while fighting for him. Almost defiantly, Peter had promised his mother that he would be back, no matter what.

I didn't promise anything.

Resting my head against the window, I stared into the darkness beyond the plane. There wasn't anything left for me back home, only Seolan buried under the trees. I'd planted a holly bush over the spot to protect him in death the way I couldn't in life.

The seatbelt light went on and the pilot indicated over the loudspeaker that we were about to make our descent. As the plane approached the lights of Las Vegas, the emerald mystery of the city made me feel like Dorothy entering Oz. Candy apple red winked at me from out of the midst of the brilliant green, reminding me of Thomas Redcap, and I couldn't help smiling.

As I touched my fingers to the cold window, I thought of the day Viviane died and the feel of her skin and how I couldn't bear it. That moment began a journey that ended here. I pressed my hand flat against the glass. Las Vegas would be the beginning of a new one. Maybe Daley was out there right now, reaching for the sky, answered by thunder.

My heart beat faster and I could feel the slight echo of Tynan's after it.

"There's no place like home," I whispered as lightning flashed on the horizon.

EPILOGUE

Fear is white and thickly veined with sea-blue.
The specialist was talking, but I wasn't listening. Unlike the on-call doctor and his bright yellow concern, this one had no personal interest in me at all.

He was interested in my cancer though. He lit up all rosy pink whenever he was talking about the tumor in my brain.

He glanced down at the chart to make sure he had the name right. "Miss Lynne, do you understand what I'm telling you?" He probably thought my silence was a refusal to accept bad news, but I'd seen the corruption first hand and he wasn't telling me anything I didn't already know.

I nodded.

"Good. Then I'd like to have you admitted for surgery immediately. We're lucky the tumor isn't affecting any vital processes at the moment, but the scans show that its growth is steady and fast. The sooner we get in there and remove it . . ."

"I can't," I interrupted him. The doctor's eyes narrowed and I hurried to explain. "I leave tonight to visit family in Las Vegas."

"Your family will understand."

"But it's my grandma. She's really old and this might be the last time I get to see her. I want to be with family this Christmas and she's the only family I've got since Mom died."

Careful Rhi, don't lay it on too thick.

The doctor tapped his finger against my file and I decided to tip the scale in my favor. Closing my eyes briefly, I teased out a breath of indigo. I still found magic easier if I let it take physical shape and the doctor would have been able to see a faint misting of color if he'd bothered to look up from my file. Before he could, I bound him ever so gently to the persistent idea that I needed to go. I couldn't force him, but I could make him feel like he wanted to help me out.

"That sounds fine then." He put the file down on the desk. "Go visit your grandmother for the holidays and I'll tell Admissions to expect you on January third."

I didn't bother hiding the relief in my voice. "Thank you. I appreciate it."

"Family is important." Pulling a pen out of his lab coat pocket, the doctor scribbled something on a pad of paper. "Take this to the pharmacy downstairs. If the headaches get too severe, one of these will help." He handed me the prescription and then paused and frowned. Picking up the file again, he tapped it against the desk.

"Just make sure to check yourself in as soon as you get back. This is serious, Miss Lynne. Your tumor is aggressive. Left untreated, it will begin to press on your brain and you will experience seizures, blackouts, and a loss of motor and bodily functions. Eventually it will kill you." I promised I would return. For a moment I thought he was going to insist I stay, but then he said goodbye and left briskly.

A few minutes later, I was outside and tossing the prescription in a garbage can. I had my own way of dealing with the pain and no time for curious doctors—my time was running out. I needed to find my mother and a way to keep Merlin out of my head before Arthur made his move. I figured if Guinevere was powerful enough for Merlin to need her, then she might be able to help me stop her husband. Convincing Taliesin to take me to Viviane's sister Morgause, the Seer of New York, was the first step in that plan.

Settling myself into my beloved Celica—I would miss it when I abandoned it at the airport—I pulled out my passport and tickets to make sure they were in order. Goodfellow owed me big time for his part in the mess with Morgan and Tynan and a new name and fake passport were only the beginning of how hard I was going to squeeze him. I wasn't ready to let him put me on a Path again though, so I'd had him arrange flights for us.

I flipped open the passport. Lynne was the name Viviane chose to echo her title as the Lady of the Lake. I was on my way to find a new mother, so I needed a new name.

Rhiannon Caerleon.

I whispered the name, trying it out, and decided I was satisfied with Goodfellow's choice. Caerleon was the name of the city Arthur and Guinevere had ruled together before he spurned her for Morgan le Fay and made his home in Camelot. Placing everything neatly in my purse, I drove away with a lighter heart.

Las Vegas is as good a place as any to die.

Fear is white and thickly veined with sea-blue until it evaporates in crimson flame.

An exclusive excerpt from:
Caught In Crimson:
Book Two of the Sword of Elements
Coming September 2014

The sand was chilly under my bare feet. Even in the desert, a late December morning was pretty cold—maybe not Southern Ontario cold, but bad enough. I shivered in a swimsuit that was really only a few scraps of fabric and string.

I'd learned the hard way that clothing and fire don't mix.

Checking that my jeans, hoodie, and shoes were still stashed neatly a good distance away, I also did a quick mental scan to make sure no one else was around. The faint glow on the horizon was the only sign that dawn was coming, but serious hikers sometimes got an early jump on things. I'd learned that the hard way too.

In the week that I'd been in Las Vegas, I'd fallen in love with the color and light and artificial heat. They helped to drown out the increasing intensity of my ability to see emotion, magic, even personality as color. Without the barrier I'd placed in my mind, I somehow pulled that color into myself without meaning to. That made me a *leannan sidhe*—a kind of spirit succubus or vampire. Even with the barrier, sometimes colors leaked through. Every time they did, I wondered who I'd taken power from, who I'd hurt.

Thankfully, there were no colors for at least a mile around. It bothered me again that I had no identifying colors for myself. Most people had at least one or two that predominated. I changed with whatever was inside me at the moment.

And at that moment, I was every possible shade of red.

Each felt like a distinct emotion. Cherry, crimson, scarlet, berry, flame—anger and rage, yes, but also passion, desire, excitement, and even intense hope.

But I have to admit that right now I'm mostly just crimson mad.

My anger had driven me into the desert. Taliesin had forbidden me to use blood magic. Again.

It wasn't like I was tempted. Nearly draining myself dry to quicken Excalibur wasn't an experience I wanted to repeat.

But it's the way he just makes a proclamation and expects me to obey that burns me.

When Taliesin called me into his office, I was actually surprised he even remembered I was there. Mourning the death of the druid Rowan—and the loss of Morgan Le Fay to King Arthur—he'd ignored me since the day after Peter and I arrived. My best friend fell easily into training with the other Protectors, but I'd crossed borders to learn about my abilities and the bard acted like I didn't exist.

It's not like I have unlimited time to figure things out.

The thought increased the pressure of the pain struggling to break through the binding I'd placed on it. Stretching to release some of the tension in my neck and shoulders, I pushed the pain back. Whether it was a natural consequence of my human side, or the result of my body not being able to take the strain of my inhuman abilities, I had a ticking time bomb of a tumor in my brain.

That discovery hadn't helped with the whole flooded with red rage thing either.

Glancing around one last time to make sure I was alone, I unhooked my bathing suit top and let it fall to the ground. Stepping out of my bottoms, I shuffled a few feet across the frigid sand, but I couldn't feel the cold anymore. As I raised my face to the rising sun, my body was already warm.

Closing my eyes, I focused on the color swirling through me. I needed to remain in control—to float on top and not be consumed—but I couldn't hold on. Taliesin might be one of the good guys—maybe *the* good guy—but he could make me furious with one quiet word. It was just like my first night in Las Vegas. I'd told the bard everything about how I'd awakened the sword. Taliesin wasn't happy. He didn't approve. We argued.

That was the first time I burst into flames.

ABOUT THE AUTHOR

Heather grew up in a family where books of myth and legend were used to teach the ABCs and Irish uncles still believed in fairies. Raised with tall tales, she has always told stories too- first as an actor and singer, then as a photographer, and now as a writer.

Heather lives in rural Ontario, Canada raising Summer, Holly, and little Stephen to tell their own stories, cheered on by her biggest fan, her husband Steve.

If you enjoyed BOUND IN BLUE, please leave a review at: http://tinyurl.com/mk2wo77

Or you can join the mailing list to receive exclusive offers and be notified when CAUGHT IN CRIMSON is published: http://heatherhamiltonsenter.com

31853177R00226

Made in the USA
Charleston, SC
30 July 2014